SIGMET ACTIVE

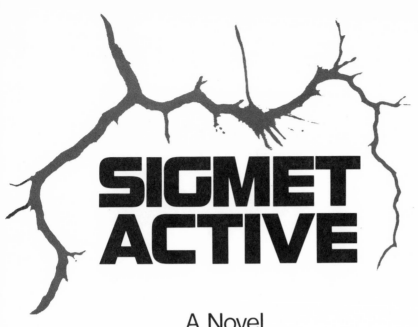

SIGMET ACTIVE

A Novel
by Thomas Page

Times
BOOKS

To Monika

Library of Congress Cataloging in Publication Data

Page, Thomas, 1942-
  Sigmet active.

  I. Title.
PZ4.P138Si [PS3566.A335] 813'.5'4 78-53307
ISBN 0-8129-0774-4

SIGMET: A weather advisory issued concerning weather significant to the safety of all aircraft. SIGMET advisories cover tornadoes, lines of thunderstorms, imbedded thunderstorms, large hail, severe and extreme turbulence, severe icing and widespread dust or sand storms that reduce visibility to less than three miles.

—Federal Aviation Administration

PROJECT
WINDOWPANE

X MINUS 45 HOURS

THE OLD man saw the lights first.

Seated in his accustomed place on the net pile at the stern of the crescent-shaped fishing boat, he stabbed at a bass fillet with his chopsticks. It was a clear hot night and the waters of the Pacific had an oily gleam. The swells were slow but powerful, concealing sea fury under the soporific regularity of motion.

The old man lowered his plate with trembling hands to watch the lights. There were only two and at first he thought them stars, but they were bright green and moved over the waters close to the horizon, sharp pinpricks undimmed by moonlight.

The old man looked away and tried to think of something else. He checked the net his son-in-law had repaired and realized the stitches were loose and sloppy. He tightened the sweatband about his head for the night was hot and windless. He rearranged the netting into a neater pile and pulled the bad stitches loose, planning to scold his son-in-law in the morning. He scraped the dinner from his plate over the side and emptied a pebble from his sandal. Little tasks that would keep him from looking at the horizon again.

He watched his nephew in the wheelhouse tuning the radio in an attempt to find a frequency without static. The other five men slept belowdecks. As captain, navigator, and owner of the small boat, the old man was their esteemed uncle, father-in-law, and cousin.

He finished cleaning up his small space, then ran out of excuses. Heart pounding, he looked out to sea. There were no green lights, nothing but the white, wavering path of moonlight. Obviously he was imagining things. It was a profound relief to be able to handle his age so well, to recognize a delusion from the truth.

The old man walked into the wheelhouse. His nephew in denim pants

3

and a tie-dyed shirt sat at the chart table wearing earphones and playing with the radio dial. He bowed respectfully to his uncle. The old man sat on a bunk bed under the porthole. It was warm in the wheelhouse, it was warm outside. There was no place to get comfortable.

His nephew removed his earphones. "You did not eat much."

The old man waved away the remark. "Old men lose their appetites, Heiko."

"You're not old, sir," the nephew said for what must have been the thousandth time.

The old man was pleased even though he knew it was a lie. His eyes strayed to the porthole. "What are the Americans doing?"

"I can't hear anything through this static. Aside from that destroyer, I don't think there are any more ships down here."

"There are many," the old man said. "The fleet must be farther back." His tongue unconsciously worried at the gold cap on his front tooth. It was loosening a bit, sending pain into his jaw. "A destroyer does not steam south at full speed alone." The old man looked out the porthole, patiently waiting for his nephew to notice he was in a philosophical mood.

"You do not sleep much, sir."

"Old men do not sleep much *or* eat much, Heiko."

"Are you worried about something?"

"I am thinking of the war again." The old man stared fixedly at the sea.

The nephew laid aside his earphones, then clasped his hands on the chart table. "That must have been a terrible time. You have such memories."

The old man settled himself more comfortably on the bunk. "One night we flew from Kwajalein to Guam. I had never been to Guam before and this was my first airplane flight. Normally the trip took about six and a half hours. I was afraid of airplanes. I'd lived my life on the sea. I was very alert to what was happening. Something happened."

His uncle was full of blood and thunder stories about World War II, tales of heroism, tragedy, and terror. Heiko expected a story of being shot down by American hellcats and flaming aerial dogfights. Instead, what the old man told him came as a complete surprise.

"There are small islands west of Kwajalein you use for fixing your position. We flew on a clear night, the navigator reported us on schedule, and then suddenly we were three hundred miles down course. We landed ahead of schedule."

4

The nephew tried to extract a point from the tale. "I see," he said politely, but did not.

"Our ground speed had increased by fully a third. This on a clear night much like tonight."

The nephew found the story intensely disappointing. No action, no suspense. "You have never told me that one before."

"No? I remember it better than the others. Seamen remember the unexplainable tales better than the adventurous ones. It seemed as though we had passed into the future by one hour, Heiko. In the 1950s, the Americans reported the same thing happened to their own planes. These waters, Heiko . . ." The old man nodded at the porthole. "Stay alert."

"For what?"

"For anything. For static on the headphones and for winds. Especially the winds, Heiko."

"There is no wind tonight."

"A storm is coming. We must plan to leave here as soon as we've made our catch."

There was no sign of a storm in this perfect night. Heiko thought the old man was contemplating death again and all the myriad oddities he could expect to view after he was buried.

The old man breathed deeply and to the nephew's surprise fell asleep. The nephew walked to the porthole hoping to find a breath of coolness in the heavy night.

Far out on the waters, four green lights were visible. The nephew watched them for several seconds, then said, "Sir?"

The old man awoke immediately, crossed to the porthole to look past his nephew's shoulder.

"It must be the Americans."

"Of course," agreed the old man, his eyes narrowed to slits. "Go south."

"Who else could it be but the Americans? It's a ship, isn't it?"

The old man put in the clutch and a puff of oily diesel smoke coughed into the air. The engine vibrated the small boat's shaky frame and phosphorescent bubbles gurgled up from the propeller wake. Below-decks the rest of the family awoke with mumbled curses as the boat jarred over the waves.

The boy remained close to the porthole, trying to hear above the clatter of their own craft some sound from across the water, but only the rush of water was audible. He watched the lights. The lights watched them.

5

X MINUS 26 HOURS

THE MONKEY shrank against the back of the cage as Edward Croft's bearded face peered benevolently through the wires. In one hand was a hypodermic needle. The other fumbled open the cage door. "Easy, Lancelot, this won't hurt. It'll keep away the pain entirely."

The monkey allowed the hand to lift him out of the cage into the fierce sunlight. The sunlight was of such brutal intensity that the other animals on the ship's deck cowered in their own cages. The goat, the calf, and the hog were in the open, tethered to iron clamps set in the deck. All of them had shaved areas on their bodies to which were taped long metal wires that snaked to a large device with an antenna set on top.

Doug Tregaskis held his breath as Croft lifted the monkey up. A squirt of fluid cleared the bubbles from the needle, then Croft gingerly aimed it at the monkey's arm, murmuring softly to him.

The monkey screeched and tore off Croft's glasses, sending the needle smashing on deck. Furred paws grabbed a handful of Croft's shirt, then the monkey spidered over his shoulders to land on the deck, screeching in surprise at the hot iron. Tregaskis made a blundering attempt to catch him, but the monkey bounded over a hatch cover and scrambled up a crane hoist high in the azure sky until it found a handhold. From there, it chattered furiously and hurled a handful of excrement down at them.

Croft combed his fingers through his white scraggly beard. *He knows*, he thought. *He knows we brought him here to kill him.* "That fellow knows treachery when he sees it, Tregaskis. I raised him myself and he was a perfect gentleman until I put him on the plane."

"What do we do? You have to wire him." Tregaskis's soft voice matched his feminine mannerisms, his hesitant phrases, his tightly curled, perfectly combed hair, and the aftershave he slathered on his face in such amounts, the animals recoiled from him.

"We'll have to do without him, that's all. He could stay up there forever. We'll make do, we have other specimens."

Croft leaned against the rail and waved to the seaplane below. The engines wheezed and roared, whipping spray from under the wings, then the ungainly plane forged like a beetle over the hot glassy sea and lifted into the air. When Croft turned back to Tregaskis, the botanist was patting down the soil around a baby spruce tree embedded in an earthen tub.

Croft wiped the sweat cascading from his face. The *Knoxville* was an old liberty ship whose hull was little more than painted rust. They had been warned not to go belowdecks for fear stairs and floors would crash through from their weight. There would be huge rats down there, Croft decided, which even to a biologist were unpleasant creatures. The old iron ship retained heat from the sunlight and sent it shimmering up through the deck.

In the heat haze, Croft looked at his animal cages littering the forward deck to the bow. They contained insects, birds, white mice, guinea pigs, even earthworms. The larger animals had been drugged and wired with electrodes to record vital functions, heartbeat, perspiration, respiration, and brain waves. The electrodes in turn were attached to a transmitter set on the deck.

Croft's animals shared the *Knoxville* with Tregaskis's plants. Some of the plants were trees, some were mere grass and seedlings buried in soil, but most were plants that provided food—corn and wheat, potatoes and turnips, lettuce and tomatoes and even a sprig of parsley. Croft placed his hands against the small of his back and rotated his torso, feeling every second of his fifty-two years. His eye fell on the metal containers lined up along the stern. "What, pray, is that, Tregaskis?"

"Weather balloons," Tregaskis answered. "Holden said they will inflate automatically just before Windowpane."

Croft pulled his hat over his forehead to protect his eyes. "You realize this makes no sense at all, don't you, Tregaskis?"

"Why not?"

"It is close to ninety-four degrees here and the Soviet Union is an arctic country. They do not die of sunstroke in Russia the way that goat is about to do. The atmosphere is thicker at the equator than in Russia and the ozone layer is lower here. Wouldn't it make more sense to do this in Antarctica?"

Tregaskis rubbed his nicked, dirty hands, the only disheveled part of him, with a handkerchief. The violent sun, the roasting skillet of the *Knoxville*, the intense headaches caused by light reflecting off the sea—none of these seemed to faze him. "Mason said the Russians can monitor weapons tests in the arctic and antarctic easier than here." Tregaskis felt the enraged simian eyes of the monkey staring down at him. "Why do you raise your own animals?"

Doug Tregaskis, Croft decided, was an inordinately sensitive man. "It's cheaper than dealing with a biological supply house. The hog, goat, and cow I bought from a farmer." Croft shaded his eyes to look up at Lancelot, uneasy under the beast's stare. "He fathered about a dozen offspring, I guess, and they're all bad-tempered. It needed another

7

generation to bring it out.'' Croft smothered an impulse to say something to the monkey. A benediction perhaps. ''Well, the study of life is the study of death when you get right down to it.''

Tregaskis looked around at his plants. Everything was in order and he was eager to get off this floating coffin. He watched Croft slip a food cup into the guinea pig's cage. ''Can I hold him?''

Croft studied Tregaskis for a moment, then withdrew the animal from its cage and handed it to Tregaskis, who cradled its sleepy, drugged warmth in his arms.

Tregaskis said, ''It's awful to think about. How can you kill animals for a living?''

''Young man, it's been my experience that animal lovers are people haters. Your sympathy will be more appropriate when we experiment with live humans.'' He snatched away the guinea pig and locked it back in the cage. After a final check of the telemetry wires, both men picked up red, loose-leafed binders stamped PROJECT WINDOWPANE and made notations in them.

Croft looked up at the sun. The source of life on earth, he thought. The source of death for the creatures on board the ship if Windowpane worked. He shrugged. The end of them, too, if any calculations were off by so much as a hair.

''I'm ready,'' Tregaskis said. Croft nodded. Tregaskis walked to the port railing and waved at the gray destroyer two miles distant, lying in the calm sea like an open knife.

The U.S.S. *Adair* rode at anchor on the gentle oily swells which the waters of the Pacific exhibit on clear, calm days. The *Adair* was a missile destroyer and naval architects were fond of describing the destroyer as the closest that any twentieth century warship would ever get to beautiful. The *Adair* was light and narrow as a blade. Her raked, racing profile surged at the bow and sloped toward the stern, and her silver gray hue blended with the shifting shades of sea and sky.

Recent modifications had broken the grace of the *Adair*'s lines. Aft of the stack and forward of the plug-shaped fire director a rotating parabolic mirror had been erected. The forward gun mount had been replaced by a tangle of heat shields, capacitors, and other machinery which culminated in a device resembling the nozzle of a garden hose.

Chief Petty Officer Samuel Mason studied the device from his vantage point on the bridge. It was certainly impressive, yes, sir, the end result of millions of dollars of brainpower and time spent by gnomic academics in sequestered colleges figuring out new ways to deal out death. But Mason shook his head sadly. One good wave would wash the whole goddamned erector set overboard. Personally he would feel safer with a gun up there. Guns were dependable. They were mechanical and understandable. Guns had barrels from which shells came out, breeches and buttons which fired them. Yes, sir, this goddamned machine could only be worked by a goddamned university, and half the time they probably would not know what it would do.

Mason swung the binoculars to the *Knoxville* and watched Croft and Tregaskis set up their experiments. He had laughed out loud when the monkey ran up the crane hoist. Smart little monkey. Mason would have bet his pension the animal was running from that flit Tregaskis. Tregaskis smelled like a garden.

Mason climbed down narrow stairs toward the electronic room, his short, square body with its wide flat feet stabilizing him against each wash of the waves. The *Adair* was a lonely place to be these days. Its normal complement was two hundred fifty men. Only a hundred were aboard now.

Mitch Farnsworth sat on a swivel chair before sonar controls, earphones clamped to his head, his eyes dazed with concentration. Years before, an oil burner explosion had seared Farnsworth's face into a waxy, tight mask of pink scar tissue. His nose was shaped like a hog's snout, his eyes slanted and permanently red, his mouth enlarged to a toothy, goofy smile. It did not take much imagination to understand why Farnsworth was unmarried. It was some moments before he realized Mason was in the room with him.

"I have to do everything around here," Farnsworth complained, removing his earphones. "Even the Captain's out polishing the mirror."

Mason stuck a cigar in his mouth and lit it. "Did you see Tregaskis? Did you *see* him?"

"I saw him get off the plane. Why?"

"You know what he is? He's a flit. He likes *boys*! Can you believe that? He's going to jump in bed with us if we don't watch out." Mason sat in a chair and chewed savagely at the cigar stub. "Maybe you have to be nuts to be a bachelor, but Tregaskis! He's perverted!"

Farnsworth turned his face as he took a bite of his sandwich. He had learned that the sight of his scarred mouth and crooked teeth caused others to avert their eyes. "It wouldn't be the Navy if they didn't overdo everything. They must have checked out twenty, thirty thousand single men for this job and came up with us. They pulled me off the *Skate* in Subic Bay."

9

"I was on the *Oriskany* in Japan," Mason said.

"What's the difference if a married man or a bachelor goes up in smoke?"

"They have a point," Mason rasped. "No widows, no orphans, no pensions, nobody to ask questions. Remember the crap the CIA took over LSD tests? They don't want it repeated. They don't want lawsuits from families."

"Oh. I thought they figured single men were useless."

"Well, I think flits is carrying things a bit goddamned far. You can blackmail them, can't you? Seems to me I read that somewhere."

"Are you kidding? They advertise it these days."

Mason leaned past the thicket of switches and controls protruding from the wall and spat into a trashcan. "Anything interesting on the sonar?"

Farnsworth handed him the earphones. The Petty Officer listened to the creak of an anchor chain, the crackle of fish, and a rhythmic bubbly sound which he could not place.

"That's Axton's diving lung. He's about three miles away, and there's not a Russian in sight."

"Suppose you hear a sub? How do you know if it's one of ours or one of theirs?"

Farnsworth took back the earphones. "For one thing, theirs are noisy. We have ships that record the sound of each new sub as it leaves its pen. Each one has its own sound signature. We tape it and put it on a computer and match them when we pick them up. If they ever put mufflers on them . . ." Farnsworth shrugged.

Mason's face was a crumple of wrinkles, carved by wind and sun. Compared to Farnsworth's pink-scarred visage, he looked bearish. The wrinkles exaggerated his expression, and for the past several days he had been expressing irritability, a trait normally prized in Petty Officers. "Who's kidding who? Half the Pacific Fleet's running loose down here. You'd have to be a cretin not to get suspicious."

Farnsworth said, with deliberation, "Mason, they were not Russians."

Mason grunted. Restlessly he walked to the porthole and looked out at the distant *Knoxville*. "I saw them, Farnsworth. Twelve degrees off the port bow."

"Yes, sir." Farnsworth opened a red Windowpane binder and checked his notation. "Round lights, three of them green, one of which changed to orange. I didn't pick up anything here and the *McClusky* pilot didn't either. It's weird, sir." *And so was Mason*, Farnsworth thought.

"The whole goddamned Pacific Ocean is."

There was little to argue with Mason about. Last night he had seen strange lights and no one else had. The scare had scrambled a fighter plane off the aircraft carrier *McClusky*, which covered the hundred miles to the *Adair* in nine minutes. Mason's alarm raised everybody on the ship and sent a coded scare back to the states, which had probably made the Pentagon quake. Axton, the oceanographer, had blamed the lights on phosphorescent sea life and plankton. They were all terrified of Russian reconnaissance. Farnsworth was about to speak when the radio beeped.

It was Croft on the *Knoxville*, asking Mason to pick them up in the launch. By the time Mason got underway, Croft and Tregaskis were descending the rope netting slung over the side.

Tregaskis settled himself on the launch, noticeably distant from Mason. Croft closed his loose-leaf binder, then as a thought struck him looked up at Mason. "Mason? I do believe I've caught a flaw in this business."

"Yeah? What."

"How are we supposed to get back on the *Knoxville* if the whole ship is radioactive?"

"Axton tells me that sea water is the best protection against radiation because it's constantly circulating," Tregaskis answered.

"It doesn't circulate on deck," Croft replied petulantly. "Really, there's so many holes in this . . ."

"We won't be on deck that long," Tregaskis interrupted. "Didn't you read the schedule?"

Tregaskis's chronic clumsiness nearly capsized the launch as they hauled in Stephen Axton. The oceanographer's face reminded Mason of a lemon. He was laconic to the point of total muteness. He sat on a seat, stowed away his diving lung, and peeled off his face mask.

"See any sea serpents?" Croft joked.

Axton thought the question over seriously, then answered simply, "No."

"I was just kidding. Seeing as we're going to be living together for a couple of days, it helps to joke a little."

"Oh." Axton removed a flipper. His mournful presence tended to dampen conversation.

11

Mason wheeled the launch toward the island, its presence discernible only by the ghostly mass of clouds rising above it. He decided it was time to play Petty Officer, directing himself at Axton. "Axton, I happened to look at your Red Book this morning."

Axton glared at him, face turning pink under its tan.

"That's what petty officers do, remember? I'm supposed to make sure we're all doing our job. Anyway, among all those chicken tracks, which I being a dumb sailor will never understand, are a lot of blank spaces. You were supposed to carry out salinity tests this morning and last night."

"I did."

"But you didn't log them. Log them, Axton. That goes for all of you."

Tregaskis curled up in his seat, avoiding Mason's glare, instead watching the waves as the boat bounced over them. Only Croft seemed untouched by Mason's temper. Axton removed his other flipper and dropped it on deck. "There's a warm current flowing south of here. Most of the sea life is in it. I think it splits in two around Itrek and continues south."

"Log it, Axton."

"I will."

Mason considered trying to gouge a "sir" out of him and decided it was not worth the effort. *Know thy crew.* He watched the *Knoxville* fade behind them in the sunlight, a hulk dissolving in fire. It may be the world's biggest navy, he mused, but it was still the Pacific Ocean. He remembered planes passing through time, ships vanishing at sea, all the half-formed fears professional seamen feel in their bones. Despite the massive heat of the day, he shuddered.

The monkey waited until the launch was out of sight before climbing from its perch to the hot deck. Cautiously it made its way among the sleepy animals, its apprehension not so different from Mason's. It sniffed at the various foods set out for the other animals, picking up the drug taint, then paused by one of Tregaskis's earthen tubs and plucked at a spruce shoot.

By now wariness was changing into persistent rage at its predicament. Finding some shade cast by a deck hatch, it huddled in the feeble shadow, chattering angrily at the drowsy animals and squinting from time to time at the cobalt blue sky.

X MINUS 25 HOURS

THE ISLAND was named Itrek. None of the engineers who had slashed away the ferns, trees, and viny vegetation on its north shore knew what the name meant or who had bestowed it. Itrek had been a mountain but a volcanic blast millions of years before had left only part of a crater wall long since eroded to flatness. Insects lived in the jungle in such abundance, the men were swollen with multiple bites. Large red-legged spiders infested their shoes. The thick strips of rain forest were filled with birds which were consumed within hours after death by drillworms and millipedes. There was no reason for humans to visit Itrek; the fishing was poor and the heat in midafternoon indescribable.

Within the slashed vegetation, naval engineers had erected a Communications and Data Acquisition station, the machinery employed for tracking satellites. A sea wall protected spidery towers festooned with radar shields and weather-monitoring equipment along the shore. The towers looked to Jeffrey Holden like an army of spindly legged robots threatening to march over the squat plug-shaped CDA station.

The interior of the station was lined with computer banks and television consoles. It was air-conditioned to keep the computer happy. Beside the radar screen loomed a pair of large television screens in front of which Harold Kilgallen sat eating a candy bar and making notations in a red leather binder. When he saw Holden striding down the beach shaking his head, Kilgallen knew what was about to happen.

"Get out your screwdriver, Kilgallen, there's a gremlin in the works."

Kilgallen pouted, "There's nothing wrong with my satellite."

His satellite. At Kilgallen's elbow was a set of specifications as thick as an encyclopedia for the ESSA satellite which had been launched solely to observe Operation Windowpane. Kilgallen, an Electronics Officer, could not have looked less like a sailor. Grossly overweight at twenty-five, he had been educated by the Navy at a cost of thousands of dollars in computer programming, astrophysics, and engineering. He could repair faulty satellites by designing esoteric microwave signals that nudged malfunctioning parts back into place. In return for its investment the Navy was guaranteed a few years of Kilgallen's service, after which, everyone believed, he would go into industry and make a fortune.

Holden sat in a swivel chair and flipped through several pages of his

13

red binder. He wore a neckerchief to protect his skin from Itrek's virulent sunlight. Like Kilgallen, suntan cream coated his face. "Well, either something is wrong with your satellite or Mason is right. The Pacific Ocean is screwed up. There's a big seventy-mile block of ocean where my equipment shows more infrared reflecting off the earth than your satellite does."

"How much more?"

"Two hundredths of a micron."

"That's not serious, Holden."

"Did I say it was serious? I am saying it's peculiar. I even checked the sea reflection this morning. You don't have to be a meteorologist to smell a rat about this island."

"Suppose something is blocking the infrared, Holden? What could it be?"

"Let's ask it."

Kilgallen wiped a dab of cream from his nose and punched the ESSA satellite to life. On the twin television screen there appeared a sight which, although he had seen it hundreds of times, never failed to chill Holden.

The ESSA satellite sat motionless in space some twenty-two thousand miles above the Pacific Ocean. Yet there on the left TV screen was Itrek, colored, detailed, magnified to a view that a bird passing overhead might see. Perpetual clouds hung over the island, tatters of pure white against the dark green of the foliage.

Kilgallen punched another button and the picture blurred into an even more marvelous sight. A turquoise earth, her seas gleaming under the sunlight, lay before them. Kilgallen's microwave order had switched lenses on the satellite, changing the image from a bird's-eye view of the island to a God's-eye view of the planet itself.

The right TV screen retained the picture of Itrek but with a major difference. The picture was ghostlier, less defined, a negative image, the whites rendered to blacks and the colors exchanged, red for blue, green for orange. This image originated in a device called an infrared radiometer, the key instrument in weather analysis. The radiometer measured infrared heat. Holden recalled that during the Vietnam war, infrared systems could detect the fading heat from a single soldier's footprint in a jungle. Atmospheric gases absorbed differing amounts of infrared and these absorption levels were measured in microns. By tuning a dial and watching the colors change, Holden and Kilgallen could determine what gases were in abundance by how much infrared they absorbed.

The screen faded to a blur of snow, shaped roughly by Itrek. "That's carbon dioxide," Kilgallen explained. Carbon dioxide was heaviest around Itrek itself with its abundant plant life. Holden made notations in the Red Book as Kilgallen spun the dial past the various gases, water vapor, nitrogen, oxygen, and ozone, which barely comprised a hundredth of one percent of the air. At thirty-nine hundredths microns, the picture of Itrek looked as the human eye would see it.

Holden recounted the percentages as the screen had given them in digits and shook his head. The satellite percentages still read lower than his equipment. "I'm still missing two hundredths somewhere. Maybe the satellite isn't calibrated right. Is that possible?"

"These things don't make mistakes, Holden. They used this system during the Yom Kippur war and we sent the Israelis exact information on the location of every bloody soldier and tank there."

"As I recall, the Israelis nearly lost the Yom Kippur war. They were kicked out of Suez."

In the CDA station there were two thick reinforced windows, one facing south onto the beach where Holden's weather towers were mounted, the other facing north past cliffs to the sea. Through the north window, Holden saw the white sliver of the *Adair*'s launch forging toward them. Sea, sand, and thick, perspiring vegetation made Holden grateful to be in the air-conditioned CDA.

Kilgallen looked sideways at Holden. "Can I ask you a personal question?"

They had known each other only thirty-six hours, they would know each other only forty more, after which they would probably never see each other again. Holden asked warily, "How personal?"

Kilgallen scraped at a pimple on his cheek. "I don't figure why someone like you is involved with this. What are you doing here?"

It was a personal reference indeed, even, Holden smiled, a compliment. Unlike the many physical or emotional misfits involved with Windowpane, Holden appeared normal. He was six feet one, in excellent physical shape, something of a cheerful, slop-jawed, southern jock.

Kilgallen knew only that until a year ago, Holden had been a flight instructor in the Air Force and that he had resigned his commission to go to college.

"I'm here for the same reason you are, Kilgallen. Get a few brownie points with the government and this could be a career."

"Can't imagine you sitting in a weather office with a slide rule all day. You don't look the type."

"That's not the idea. Did you ever hear of the Jasons?" Kilgallen

15

obviously had not. "I don't know who gave them that nickname but basically they're a core group of scientists who work as consultants for the Defense Department. Some are well known, some not. That's pretty much what I'm aiming for in about ten years, assuming I get the degree and a reputation as a weatherman."

"You weren't even in the Navy and this is a Navy project." As he shifted position in his chair, Kilgallen scratched his crotch.

"My father was. And his father and his father. I'm a Navy brat right back to the Civil War, Kilgallen. I broke the mold with the Air Force but I guess somebody figured I was a good security risk." Holden stretched out in his chair as comfortably as his size would allow.

Kilgallen shook his head. "How can you just jump out of the Air Force and go back to school? I'd be scared stiff."

"I must be crazy," Holden agreed.

"I mean it. You get spoiled, you know? I wouldn't even know how to look for a job. Have to get my clothes cleaned myself, pay rent and all that. I'm scared just thinking about it."

Holden took a can of orange juice from a small refrigerator and debated whether or not to loosen up with the ensign. Since they would never see each other again, he decided to risk it. "I've had this idea in my head since I was a kid. The older I got, the bigger it got, and I figured since I wasn't outgrowing it, I ought to work it out."

"What is it?"

"I like air. Air is haunted. That's why I went into the Air Force instead of the Navy."

Kilgallen had been raising a candy bar to his mouth. "Beg pardon?"

"Everything in creation is a fluid of some kind, right?"

"Right."

"Air, water, fire, even the earth because continents float around on basalt. I live in a fluid called air, fish live in a fluid called water. Everything alive walks, swims, flies, or burrows through a fluid. My daddy spent his life on top of a fluid called water and breathing a fluid called air. Since fluids are all different versions of the same thing, I figured that by joining the Air Force instead of the Navy, basically I was doing the same thing he did. You with me?"

"Um."

"I like flying more than floating but after awhile I figured I ought to leave the Air Force and figure out what air actually is. Air to me is what the sea is to Mason. He's scared of the sea, sometimes I'm scared of air. It's invisible, yet you can set three or four tons of cargo plane on it. So I decided to go back to college."

16

"Did you just decide to quit suddenly?"

Holden chewed a fingernail. A quick flash of memory made him wince. "I never told anybody this, not even Security. I first started seriously thinking of quitting one morning after I committed incest."

Moist chocolate dribbled down Kilgallen's chin to his lap. Without any immediate family, he wondered how incest was possible, let alone imaginable. "What? Who with?"

"A sister, I think. I picked up this girl in Hong Kong a couple of years ago. Now, Daddy was stationed in Hong Kong right after the war. You know what they say about sailors on leave. He might have made a lot of Holdens and never knew about it. They'd be about my age now. So I was with this girl, it was a dark bar, dark night, dark apartment, and we had us one grand old time that night. Except in the morning I looked at her and she looked at me and we looked just like each other only she was half Chinese. It was like looking in a mirror."

Kilgallen breathed, "Jesus Christ, Holden."

Holden crumpled the orange juice can and lobbed it into a trash can. "Yup. Somebody was telling me, Jeff, old boy, get out of the Air Force, you're screwing yourself." He smiled at Kilgallen, who wiped the chocolate from his chin, stared at Holden, and nibbled without enthusiasm, feeling a little sick to his stomach.

X MINUS 11 HOURS

ITREK WAS located eighteen degrees latitude north in a section of ocean seemingly designed to drive Holden crazy. They were too far off the shipping lanes and flight paths for commercial travel so the normal inflow of information on weather conditions to the global Weather Network did not exist. Although he had use of all manner of sensitive equipment, a satellite, weather balloons, potentiometers and reconnaissance planes from *McClusky*, he felt he had been required to paint a Mona Lisa in less than fifty hours with a stubby pencil. Itrek was one of dozens of useless swatches of land scattered across the ocean in the zone of trade winds. The closest civilization was the Philippines hundreds of miles west of them. Because of the trade winds, the sea currents mishmashing into each other, and the year-round heat which boils air upward as the earth's spin deflects it, Holden knew that he was the weak link in Windowpane. The climate around Itrek was a hopeless stew of wind and heat. His first government contract had turned up an ace of spades.

He kneeled beside a galvanometer on the beach and dug his bare toes into the warm talcum-powdery sand. The night was filled with legions of mosquitoes. The island hooted, buzzed, and rustled with living things. The men had just completed dinner in uncomfortable silence, then broken up to attend to the schedules in their Red Books. Holden's tests required him to make readings of the equipment mounted on the beach.

In the two days the six of them had lived on Itrek with each other, little lines of personality had sprung like faults among them. Kilgallen rarely left the CDA to expose himself to the sun. Axton spent nearly all of his time by himself, away from the CDA. Tregaskis took cuttings of the flora around the island, and Croft slept a lot, probably because the climate played havoc with his age. Mason was the source of tension. His palpable hatred of Tregaskis seemed to ignite the air, making them await an explosion. The Petty Officer was a garrulous sort, nervous as a cat who had attached himself to Holden. To Holden's annoyance, the Petty Officer was hurrying down the beach toward him, cigar jammed in a corner of his mouth.

Mason expectorated a stream of brown juice into the white sand. Some vague sanitation impulse made him kick it under. "Well, son of a bitch," he said cordially enough, by way of greeting. "Ain't we a beautiful Navy?"

"You sure are, Mason. You're the king of the sea."

Mason chortled. "Not me, sonny. I won't miss the crapping sea when I retire. People wind up sailors because they're no good at anything else. You don't do what you want in life, I decided. You do what you're good at. Am I right?"

"I'm a weatherman and there's no such thing as a good weatherman."

"Give me a forecast anyhow."

Holden checked the galvanometer. "According to all my stuff, it's raining cats and dogs right now. The humidity's seventy-two percent and the air's so full of electricity, you could light your cigar by waving it."

Holden checked the thermometers encased in their wooden shelters and made notations in his Red Book. Mason sat on the sand, resting his elbows on his knees. "So how come it ain't raining?"

"I don't know. To be perfectly honest, Mason, I cannot make head nor tail out of the weather here. I've just checked how much salt there is in the air and it should be raining like hell. Ask me something simpler."

"How come you ain't married like normal people?"

Holden stubbed his toe on a brace holding the anemometer. "How come you aren't?" he shot back.

"I was married once."

"You're kidding!" Holden hoped he did not sound insulting. If he did, Mason chose to let it pass.

"For two weeks back in 1952. She run off on account I gave her the clap. Or vice versa, she might have given it to me. She got around a lot." Mason sent his cigar spinning against the sea wall where it burst into a kaleidoscope of sparks. "Women!" he said.

So Mason did not like women any more than he liked Tregaskis. Probably he did not like anybody much which, Holden decided, is a good reason for making a career in the military. Instead of feelings, the Petty Officer had superstitions. He had told everyone about his green lights the previous night, embellishing the story each time until it became a marauding fleet of UFOs, shock-trooping a massive Russian attack. Such incidents as green lights over the sea touched Mason in depths normally reserved for feelings of lust, greed, and ecstasy.

"You like women, Holden?"

"Sure, I like women fine."

"Then answer my question."

Holden sighed and sat beside Mason to gaze over the sea wall at the white lines of the incoming waves. A dreamy Pacific island choked with frangipani vines, terns cracking open seashells, fruit bats milling about in the tree foliage, and six bachelors who were about to help spend millions of dollars to kill a handful of worms, mice, guinea pigs, and farm animals. "Why are you asking me this? Is it official or something?"

"No. Should it be?" Mason looked at him suspiciously.

Holden began, "There I was, going to school, when my faculty advisor tells me this strange little man with no face wants to speak to me. He was some guy from the FBI or the Defense Department or the KGB . . ."

"That's not funny," Mason said.

"I don't know where he was from. He's the guy that sprung Windowpane on me. Some computer in Washington must have landed on my service record, found out I was going to get a doctorate in two years, and figured I was a good risk. In fact the only reason I'm here is because somebody figured it might be nice to have a pilot on Itrek. Did they check out your sex life before bringing you here?"

19

Mason ruminated, "They went over every fitness report for twenty-five years."

"Well, they told me I nearly lost out to a Japanese-American named Matsuko Kayama, who's an expert on electrical weather properties. He teaches at the University of Colorado. That agent or whatever he was could tell me who I voted for, practically. At the time I didn't have any girlfriends. At the time."

"What do you mean by that?"

Holden scratched his scalp with both hands, digging sand out of his hair. "You know what they say about coincidences. Not one week after I was cleared for Windowpane, this old girlfriend I haven't seen for three years just pops up. She's staying at my place in Pensacola."

Some seconds passed before the implication exploded into Mason. "You're living together!"

"Yes. I'm wondering if the contract excludes that, too. It just said that I should be single."

"I hope you trust her and all that. How well do you know her?"

Holden lighted a cigarette with the end of Mason's cigar. "We almost got married in school. Except I went into the Air Force and she wound up with a painter. Her name's Gina Lambert. She's got a two-year-old kid named Dennis."

"She's not married now, for Christ's sake, is she?"

"No, her husband died about a month ago and she came looking for me."

They smoked in silence, feeling the wind, listening to the surf, sensing the jungle behind them. Holden wondered if tropical nights inspired philosophical thoughts.

Mason said, "Why didn't you get married in school? Not that I give a crap about your private life."

"She didn't want to be an Air Force wife. That was ten years ago, though, and people change. Look at me, I'm not in the Air Force anymore. I did run into her again three years ago, in Pensacola. She was busy running out on her husband. We spent a weekend together."

Mason snarled, "Shit!" and hugged his knees. Holden had apparently struck a raw nerve by mentioning the idea of running around with a married woman. It must have reminded the Petty Officer of his own brief fling. "Did she go back to her husband?"

"Yes. They even had a kid."

"Know what I would have done? I'd have thrown her out on her ass if she'd stepped out on me. In fact that's exactly what I did." Mason's bitterness, Holden decided, was too ingrained for any argument to have any effect. "You wake up one morning, she's run off with your cash and some salesman and she leaves you a note telling you, you're a snake. You never know."

"I'm only telling you this because you're the boss on Itrek, Mason. I don't want anybody to think I concealed anything."

Mason spat at a bougainvillea vine, sending a lizard scrambling for safety. "I'd shut up about it, Holden. If she can be trusted, which I can't imagine, everything's all right. If she's a radical or a damned Red Chinese or something, it's too late to do anything. She'll dig it out of you . . ."

Holden pointed out to sea. "Mason? What is going on out there?"

Several miles out, Itrek's cloud cover gave way to clear skies through which moonlight shone. Like the running lights of a ship, four green lights were grouped together, moving softly over the horizon of the sea.

"Nothing," Kilgallen said, bending close to the plan-position radar. His spine was shaped into a curve, perfectly designed for slumping before screens. "Doppler is negative, fog and vapor negative. Hold on." He tuned the screen. "I might be getting some static here. Do you confirm, *Adair*?"

Static electricity in the air would appear on the radar as small wavy lines called sferics. Kilgallen undoubtedly had sharper vision than Holden, who could not see anything on the screen at all. Axton, Croft, Tregaskis, and Mason with binoculars crowded the west window of the CDA watching the distant lights.

Farnsworth's disembodied Olympian voice came from a speaker mounted in a ceiling corner. "Negative, Itrek. I can't see a blinking thing on my stuff. They're eyeballing it on the bridge, though, so I guess Mason wasn't drunk after all."

Mason lowered the binoculars and called out, "Choppers, Kilgallen, I'm sure of it. They're airborne."

Plaintively, Farnsworth repeated, "Negative, damn it. I repeat there's no hard contact here. Can anybody make out the distance?"

Kilgallen protested, "How can we tell the distance if we don't know how big they are! Come on!"

Holden nudged Mason and took the binoculars from him. Through the lenses, sky and sea merged into a single impenetrable velvet in which the green lights moved. They were separating from each other like beads unstringing from a necklace. The more he studied the lights, the more puzzled Holden became. He could see no craft at all, no reflection from metal, but then the craft could be covered in a nonreflecting dull coat. There was no method to the lights' motion. Sometimes they dipped over the sea in graceful sweeps, then became jerky and unsteady. "It doesn't make any sense how they're flying," he said to Mason. "Maybe they're drunk or something."

Tregaskis asked, "What about drones or robot camera planes?"

Mason snarled, "You stupid scumbag, we'd pick up a drone on the radar and there ain't no such thing as a goddamned robot camera plane."

"How do you know?" Tregaskis asked defiantly.

Farnsworth's voice interrupted Mason before he could fry the botanist. "Itrek, our sonar is negative too. We've informed Flag and they're scrambling a tomcat from the *McClusky*. Any suggestions?"

"One." Holden answered. "I can get there faster in our own helicopter. How about it, Mason?"

"I'll come with you," the Petty Officer answered. "If it's World War III, I want to fire the first shot."

Kilgallen shook his head slowly as he peeled a candy wrapper. "Static. There's static out there. I'm sure of it."

Holden swept the helicopter on a stomach-dropping loop around the CDA and flew due west. Two of the lights were rising skyward, one orbiting in a circle, the other hanging motionless over the sea. The Bell Long Ranger helicopter was equipped with a target acquisition radar for hunting surface ships. Holden examined the screen. Nothing. Either they were all hallucinating or the lights were devoid of substance.

"Kilgallen, do some guesswork. How far are we from the lights?"

"One mile and closing. What do you see?"

The lights were intensely bright. One of them was changing color to a deep orange. Then, as they watched through the windshield, two of the green ones winked out. "They've seen us," Mason decided.

Holden had mastered the ability to stretch his senses to a wide thinness that felt the most minute vibrations of wind and peripheral motion. He half-expected a burst of shrapnel or the streak of a missile, "Did they shut off their lights, or what, Mason?"

Mason raised binoculars to the rising light and hissed sharply as it blinked out. He continued watching the sky where it had been. "It went out at about two thousand feet, didn't it?"

"Yes."

"Well, I can't see anything at all, Holden."

Holden hovered warily above the last light shining a green reflection off the sea. Easing his airspeed, he began a cautious descent.

The light was about three feet in diameter. Holden got the distinct impression of a floating balloon as it lowered to the sea. The light met its own reflection on a wave, then vanished. Holden switched on the Long Ranger's landing lights and cast a bright glow over the white foaming swells.

There was no wreckage, no oil slick, nothing. The sea breathed with infinite calmness. Freed of the Itrek clouds, the moon shone down on a pristine, clear night.

"Holden?" Kilgallen's voice crackled in his headphones. "I've lost my static."

Overhead a silver Tomcat fighter from *McClusky* came streaking in, dipping its wings at them as Holden weaved over the water searching for some trace of the light. "They're gone from here too, Kilgallen."

Mason cut in on his own mike. "They didn't go out till we went after them."

Holden began, "We don't know that, Mason . . ."

The Petty Officer barked, "You have eyes, don't you? They moved away from us. Kilgallen, tell *McClusky* we *chased* them away."

Kilgallen said, "I'll tell them anything you want. But if the Russians have planes that don't show up on radar we ought to surrender Window-pane to them because they're a long way ahead of us."

"They weren't Russians," Mason said. "They weren't choppers; they weren't planes."

"Wilco, Mason," Kilgallen responded. "In that case, I guess they weren't there."

Within the hour, the sky swarmed with helicopters from *McClusky* ranging from weather reconnaissance craft to sub killers that probed the sea with sonar fingers. The craft crisscrossed the sea in a hundred-mile radius and discovered something of particular interest to Holden, who sketched it out on a millibar chart, as Croft bent over his shoulder.

The millibar chart was a mass of swirling lines depicting levels of air pressure at sea level and upward. The design which Holden marked out with swirling wind arrows as data came in over the speaker was of an oval-shaped low-pressure center.

Croft blinked at the chart through his eyeglasses. "It looks exactly like an egg. With us and the *Adair* inside of it."

To Kilgallen, Holden said, "Remember that gremlin this morning?"

"Yes."

"Look at this."

Kilgallen peered at the outline. At the narrow end of the egg-shaped center were the positions of Itrek and *Adair*. "What about it?"

"It's the size and shape of the gremlin. All it is is a mass of warm air, but that's kind of surprising, isn't it? It's so weak I never noticed it."

"I told you there wasn't anything wrong with my satellite. We're in a warm air-pressure center that's soaking up about two hundredths micron of infrared."

Holden played with the swivel lamp and tapped at the paper with his pen. "I still don't know what's doing the soaking, though. Water vapor, sulphur particles. I accounted for every atmospheric gas I could think of."

They listened to the pilots' reports of clear skies and peaceful seas for the next hour and a half. Holden doodled at the millibar chart, then with a considerable gathering of fortitude called the *Adair*'s Weather Officer, a man named Arnold Jameson, whom he had met only once. Jealousy had emanated from Jameson, the kind of hostility that showed he resented the fact that a kid was on Itrek and he was stuck on the ship. Jameson alone had worn his uniform on the destroyer. The rest of the crew had worn shorts and T-shirts.

"What's your problem, Holden?"

"No problem. I'm just wondering what you think of this low-pressure center. I think it's been here for a couple of days."

"Why?" Jameson replied.

"It's shaped like an infrared blotch on my satellite stuff. Now I checked out every gas I could think of and it's absorbing more radiation than it should."

"How much more?"

"Two hundredths of a micron."

"Mr. Holden," Jameson said tightly. "There's such a thing as getting carried away. You realize that?"

Often it had occurred to Holden that bitchiness was not a mannerism confined to women. The most lethal examples he had encountered were in the military with infighting officers clawing for promotions and characters like Jameson playing all sides at once. "Well, I know two hundredths doesn't sound like a lot but it's been consistent for two days now. I thought you'd like to know."

"Put it in the Red Book and forget about it. It's comforting to know you're taking precise measurements, Holden."

After their intense search, the *McClusky* crews were unable to find any trace of the green lights, and returned to the carrier. Farnsworth called again, "Hi, boys and girls! They'll make another run in the morning. By the way, Holden, we got flashed from California. The

24

Naval Weapons Center wanted to tell you they called in some guy named Kayama.''

That goddamned Jameson! Kayama was Matsuko Kayama, the man who had nearly ended up on Itrek instead of Holden. Jameson had probably called California and told them Holden was an incompetent, so they had brought Kayama in to help. Jameson would wind up looking like a steady head who had restrained Holden from some kind of hysterical overreaction to a low-pressure center.

Croft looked over his animal telemetry. ''No Russians anywhere,'' he said. ''The guinea pig is relieved.''

''I bet the Russians know all about it anyhow,'' Kilgallen commented, toying with an unopened candy bar, unable to decide whether to eat it or not. ''It's just a game.'' He put away the candy, opened a leather case and withdrew a camera and tripod. He mounted it at the west window facing the sea, then after adjusting for time exposures, sat down before it. ''If they come back, I'm going to get some shots of them.''

''What if they come back at four in the morning?'' asked Tregaskis.

''I'll be ready. I wasn't very tired anyway.''

None of them were tired. Windowpane was set to go in less than ten hours. Their individual tension, unspoken but shared, was evident on all their faces.

Outside, the night was a living darkness. As Holden walked toward the hut where the bunks were, Itrek's insects swarmed around the floodlights and windows, drawn by the siren call of the lights. Jungle moths, flying roaches, mosquitoes, gnats, dragonflies, assorted beetles, all slapped and buzzed past him.

''Hey, Holden. I got to talk to you a minute.'' Mason was running toward him.

''What's the matter?'' Holden hoped he would have no more complaints about women to endure.

''Instincts. Instincts are what's the matter, Holden. I'm not educated but I got instincts.'' Mason spoke as if he were about to impart a heavy secret.

''You've got more instincts than you know what to do with, Mason.''

They were alone but Mason pushed Holden toward the foliage, out of hearing of both the CDA and the hut. ''You ever hear of the *Ourang Medan*?''

''Nope. That a ship?''

''It was a freighter. Back in 1947 or '48, I think it was, the *Ourang Medan* was running through the Moluccan Straits down in Indonesia

25

when it sent out a distress call in Morse code. Two ships, one British, one Dutch, picked up the signal. It was a panic call, you know, dots and dashes all over the place—but they made out that everybody on the ship was dead. Officers, crew, everybody, cat too for all I know. Then the radio operator tapped out two words in perfect English.'' Like a small boy telling a dirty story, Mason paused for effect.

"I give up. What were they?"

"I die. End of transmission."

Holden gazed at the face of the Petty Officer, lit by the yellow light of the CDA. Mason was scared, no doubt about it. His cigar was unlit and his eyes moved around the jungle at each sound. "I'm listening," Holden told him.

"Yeah. So the British and the Dutch hauled anchor and sighted the *Ourang Medan* two hours later. It was dead in the water, floating like a barge. They sent over a boarding party and, by Christ, everyone of them *was* dead, including the radioman."

"Dead of what?"

Mason hissed, "There wasn't a mark on them, Holden! At least if there was it wasn't on the report and you can bet they tried to find out. They figured they'd take the ship under tow and try to claim the cargo. They weren't on board that tub twenty minutes when a fire started in the hold and blew up the boilers. The ship turned turtle and went straight to the bottom."

"We're a good ways from Indonesia, Mason. The Moluccan Straits are on the equator."

Mason bit his lip and looked down the beach at Holden's weather equipment. "Yeah, I know, I know. The world's full of sea stories that'd make your hair fall out. Bermuda triangle and all that. There's stories about places in the ocean where gravity is so strong it makes holes in the water and boats can't get out of them. But I got instincts, Holden. I think a lot of that stuff has something to do with the weather."

"You're worried about the pressure center," Holden stated.

"I was listening to you tonight. You don't like it either. Neither did Jameson but he's standard shit, he won't step on any toes."

Holden lowered his voice. "What toes, Mason? Whose toes?"

"Let's just say I wouldn't mind getting off this island right now," the Petty Officer said fervently. "That thing's set to go at oh nine hundred hours. Tomorrow morning!"

"I know that. Whose toes, Mason?"

"You get something like Windowpane going and it just sort of steamrollers along. Takes a lot of guts to stop a steamroller . . ."

"Mason. The weather's fine. I'm not worried; you're off your gourd." Holden tried to push past him.

Mason grabbed his sleeve, stopping him again. "I just want to say this, Holden, just listen a minute. If you think something's not right, you do what you think is right, and I'll back you up."

Mason refused to let go of his sleeve. Holden said, "Mason, will you calm down? I've got to get some sleep."

"Pleasant dreams, sonny. Listen, did I tell you how they found the bodies?"

"No."

"They were all lying on their backs, eyes wide open, looking at the sky." Mason released his sleeve and gave him a comradely punch on the shoulder. He slouched back toward the CDA in the eerie yellow light, his crumpled form resembling some unlikely sea creature dredged out of the surf and trying out his legs for the first time.

Holden jumped, scratched a sand flea from the hairs of his leg, then started back toward the bunk, determined to dream about something pleasant, something that would push Jameson, Mason's hysteria, and his own tension from his mind, and forget the possibility of his own imminent death in the morning. Gina. He would think about Gina.

It was a Tuesday evening, nine o'clock. Holden was seated at his desk in his Pensacola apartment, the Red Book and specifications on Project Windowpane before him, making copious notes on a yellow lined pad. He was in a state of euphoria, bordering on ecstasy, for the faceless man had placed a glittering future before him. Get his doctorate and be a Jason. Leaving the Air Force had been the right step after all, for now he had a career that satisfied both his own interests and the Holden military destiny. He was *of* the military but not *in* the military, about to shoulder more responsibility than any Holden had ever dreamed of.

There came a faint, hesitant knock on the door. Since good things happen all at once, some sense warned Holden that another momentous event was about to occur. He slipped the Red Book and notes into his desk drawer then, smoothing his hair and tucking in his shirt, he opened the door. A tremendous emotional wallop sent his feelings flip-flopping from shock to tenderness.

"Gina?"

"Just no getting rid of me, is there?"

Gina Lambert was a slim woman with large almond-shaped eyes, crowned by thick chestnut hair. Her features were wide and emphatic: a graceful jaw, prominent cheekbones, and sensual lips. It would have been a pug face except there was nothing cute about her. Holden had never liked cute women. Gina Lambert was handsome, that was the word. Not hard or mannish but handsome.

This time she appeared frail and sad, the light gone out. Clinging to her fingers was a child, wearing faded denim overalls, who regarded Holden with his mother's large, grave eyes.

"His name is Dennis and he's dying for some orange juice. If you have some."

"For God's sake Gina, come in. Of course I've got orange juice . . . No, I don't have orange juice. Pineapple juice, how's that?"

"That's fine."

He watched dumbly as they entered, glanced around the apartment, then sat on the ratty lawn sofa pushed against the wall. To Holden she looked perfect on the sofa, very much in place somehow. He locked the door, feeling ferociously excited and almost short of breath. It was the child who seemed out of place, and apparently he felt the same, for he tried to hide from Holden behind her. "How are you?"

"Not too bad. And you, Jeff?"

"Great. Fine. You're a mother."

She did not respond to the obvious, merely ruffled the boy's hair.

"Would you like some coffee?"

"That would be marvelous."

Holden gushed water into a dented tin pot and shook instant coffee into two cups. "Cream but no sugar."

While waiting for the water to boil, he sat in his desk chair, arms resting on his knees, mouth slightly open as he stared at her. It was amazing, he thought, how the presence of the opposite sex, no matter how casual, could change radically the feel of a room. Something about Gina centered the scattered papers, debris, textbooks, and cheap furniture around herself. Holden said, "It's been three years."

"Yes. I had the devil of a time finding you, Jeff. I called half the Air Force before thinking to look in a phone book. That's really logical, isn't it?"

"I'm not in the Air Force anymore. I'm in school."

"Since when?"

"Since a year. I'm a thirty-four-year-old freshman. At this rate I'll be a thirty-six-year-old Ph.D. in climatology. If I make it."

He could tell she was surprised by the uncertain look that moved across her face. "Did you mention that before?"

"You know I was always interested in weather. Actually, I've got a

28

head start on everybody else in school because I was in the Air Force for so long. I'd been thinking about quitting for a while and finally I did."

"You're safe from the family curse, then. None of the Holden men making it to the age of forty."

"I will."

Her eyes rested on the group of photographs ranged around his desk, several of them tintypes, all set up the way a father would place family pictures. Her face softened in recognition. "When did you get those out?"

"Not long ago."

"You used to think they were Mickey Mouse stuff. Ancestor worship and all that sentimental crap."

"I hauled them out for courage. Every time I have an exam I salute old Oscar there and he tells me to damn the torpedoes."

The men in the pictures were the Holdens who had been in the U.S. Navy since the Civil War. Oscar Holden of the U.S.S. *Hartford* posed with hand in coat next to David "Damn the Torpedoes" Farragut. Emerick Holden in dress whites squinted under the Filipino sun next to Commodore Perry of the Great White Fleet. Holden's own father, hair tousled, grinned with a Kill-the-Japs smile on the carrier *Enterprise*. Killed in 1957 when the backwash of a Douglas Skyraider blew him off the deck into the ship's propeller wake.

"Christ, it's good to see you again, Gina. You look . . . well." Holden was about to say "great." She did not look great.

"You too. You haven't gained an ounce of weight, which makes me jealous."

As he took the water off the stove and poured it, Holden thought over ways to pose a question delicately. He decided bluntness was the best policy. "Are you just passing through or what?"

"I'm on my way to Miami." She sipped her coffee, her hair slightly covering her face. The dim apartment light erased the sensuality from her features, even her sex, rendering her hollow eyes and sharp cheeks into a carved statue.

"Are you still with Lambert?"

"No. James died."

Holden gripped his cup tightly, afraid to say anything that might unsluice a cataract of emotions, yet knowing he should respond somehow. "I'm sorry. When?"

"About a month ago. I buried him in Oregon."

Holden examined the child, attempting to assess what James Lambert had looked like, but all he saw was Gina in his features. Gina, he remembered, left her stamp on everything. "What happened?"

"We had a power failure and since we didn't have a cent to our names, James figured he'd fix the fusebox. Something went wrong, I don't know what. James's parents live in Miami and they want to see Dennis and that's where I'm headed."

"I'm glad you came by. If I can do anything at all . . ."

She set down her cup, then placed her hands flat on her knees studying them. "Did our weekend constitute adultery?"

"Well, we're not exactly strangers. Besides, I thought you were leaving him for good."

"So did I at the time. But I think a marriage is a kind of legalized friendship as well as legal consorting or whatever the phrase is. Think of it as friendship and not just fidelity and that's a more serious kind of commitment. I went back because he was a friend more than my husband."

"Did you ever tell him about running into me again?"

"He knew something had happened but didn't want to know any details. Anyhow, when I showed up at the Portland airport we both figured we were stuck with each other and we weren't getting any younger. That is the origin of my monster here." She patted her son.

Three years previously Holden had delivered a cargo plane to Pensacola's commercial airport, and finding himself with a weekend to kill before returning to base, he had wandered into a bar. Three stools down sat Gina Grossman, ex-girlfriend from schooldays, an almost wife, the girl to whom he had lost—or rather thrown away as unwanted baggage—his virginity. She had just walked out on her husband who had sold their house out from under her, quit his job as a graphics artist with an advertising agency, in short uprooted her whole life without warning in order to go to the wilds of Oregon and be Paul Gauguin. It was, she told him over a second old-fashioned, the last straw in a bumpy, nerve-wracking marriage and she was now planning to find a job somewhere.

"It was good seeing you again," she said, smiling. "I tell you I'm the worst argument against cheating on your husband. I figured it would be casual, something that just happened. You let off steam and then you forget about it."

"It's never that simple."

"It sure wasn't for me. For me it all ended up like a bad Victorian novel where the adulteress is punished for her sins. I wonder what would have happened if you and I had married after all."

"Exactly the same thing. You didn't want to be a military wife. I expect we'd have fought tooth and nail. I think a lot about that weekend."

The room light congealed into two sharp reflections in her eyes as she examined his face. "Is that the truth, Jeff?"

"It is. I'm glad I never met Lambert. Stay with me." Holden jumped to the point with an adroitness that surprised him.

"Really." The trace of another smile gentled her face. "I was hoping you'd say something like that. I guess that's obvious."

"What the hell! We're not going overboard, I'm not proposing or anything. Take a couple months off and stay here. There's not much room but you can stow stuff in the basement."

"I'm not very good company these days, Jeff."

"You're great company, you were always good company. I need company. You said you were on your way to Miami?"

"Yes."

"Well, that fits perfectly because in a few days I'm off to the Pacific for a week." Holden told her only that he had a government contract. The Jasons. A big, fat secret, possibly the groundwork for a career.

She was distinctly impressed. "You're James Bond."

"There you go. All told I'll be gone a week. That gives you plenty of time to see the grandparents in Miami and come back here. You can fix the place up any way you want." The spread of his arms overwhelmed the tiny four walls.

"It needs that."

"I *want* you to stay, Gina."

As he spoke he measured the good and bad of having her with him. The good was indefinable. Until she reappeared he had not realized the insidious subtlety of loneliness, how it confused his decisions and drove him so deeply into himself he could not deal with the world. And happiness was equally insidious. She seemed to draw light around her, she somehow made him more relaxed, things were not right without her. She was capable of placing control back into his hands; how, he could not begin to analyze. He felt that good things could happen with the same inexorable force as catastrophes which, he mused whimsically, might be a discovery for astrologers to ponder.

The bad list was small but precise. He was getting older and her presence was a constant reminder of that. As she sat on the sofa, Holden remembered how thin and lithe he had been in school and how his pilot's reflexes were slowing because of age. He wondered if he could get the same kind of head start in his career as he had when he was with her in school and about to enter the Air Force. That had been ten years ago; where would he be ten years hence?

Worst of all was the possibility that Operation Windowpane might kill him on Itrek. He might die in the service of his country, he thought bitterly. Better if the unseen James Lambert had waited another week before expiring so Gina would have missed Holden. Would her life, then, have become more stable, he wondered?

X MINUS 90 MINUTES

THE SUN rose over Itrek, resplendent in a flaming hot dawn that burned mist from the jungle by seven-thirty in the morning. Holden had thought about Gina all night, drifting in and out of a sweaty sleep, remembering how she had looked, moved, talked, made love.

Kilgallen still sat before his camera, two Mounds bars on his lap. He sneezed as Holden poured coffee from the percolator.

"Gesundheit," Holden said.

Kilgallen wiped his nose with his finger, then wiped his finger on his shirt. "Is there ragweed in the jungle?"

"No. Cheer up. It's probably just syphilis."

The satellite screen was on and Holden contemplated the Earth in its infinity of darkness. The morning twilight zone was passing over Itrek. "Any visitors?" he asked.

"A lot of bugs," Kilgallen retorted. "The planes will be back in half an hour for a weather check."

"Aren't you tired?"

"I couldn't sleep if you hit me with a sledgehammer. I keep thinking I ought to make out a will, but I don't have anybody to leave anything to."

By the launch dock, Holden watched Axton climb out of the water in his wet suit, carrying a net bag full of shells. He sat on the wood to peel off his flippers.

"I don't figure him," Kilgallen said. "Up at five in the morning for a swim. He's not worried. I don't think he's human. He lives in the water."

Farnsworth's voice crackled out of the speaker, startling them both. "Hello, Itrek. We've got a hard contact southwest of you moving this way. Can you see it?"

Kilgallen switched on the plan-position radar. A blip was visible, pulsing brightly with electronic fire. "Affirmative, *Adair*. Looks like a boat of some kind."

"It's headed for the test area. Get Holden to chase it away, will you?"

"How far is it?" Kilgallen asked.

"Looks like about forty miles. Don't get your bowels in an uproar, it's probably just a Russian suicide sub." Farnsworth's giggle rolled out of the speaker like broken teeth clattering over tin.

Mason sat by Holden in the Bell Long Ranger with an automatic pistol strapped to his waist, peering down at the boat through binoculars. It was a wooden fifty-foot craft trailing nets from the stern. A clot of black diesel smoke hung over the single stack. The boat carried seven men, several wearing bright sweatbands around their foreheads. Their faces were turned up to the copter as it circled them. One of the men grinned and waved.

"They look Japanese," said Mason. "Japanese or Okinawan. No radar, no heavy radio stuff. Maybe all their gear is underwater."

"Then again, maybe they're just looking for fish," Holden replied.

"Set it down on the port side. They're throwing a line for us."

"What if they don't speak English?"

"Don't be a jerk. Everybody speaks English. Even Hirohito speaks English."

A circle of water flattened into spray as Holden lowered the copter onto the sea. Mason slid open the cockpit door, caught the rope, and tied it to the fuselage ring as the crew pulled them almost alongside the hull.

Mason jumped lightly onto the deck, but Holden tripped and sprawled onto the wood. The boat stank of fish. Salmon scales and crab claws littered the deck. Two lean brown arms helped him to his feet. In the wheelhouse a teenager smiled and waved. They carried no firearms that Holden could see, just scaling knives tucked into their belts. Plastic plates and chopsticks scattered about indicated they had been eating when the copter arrived.

Mason doffed his cap. "Good morning. Does anyone speak English?"

A flood of Japanese answered him and arms pointed to an older man with gold teeth seated on the stern, one foot resting on a pile of rope. They all seemed to defer to him. He had a long melancholy face and hair secured in back with a knot.

Mason bowed to him. "Good morning. My name's Mason. *Mason.*"

The man pointed a thumb at himself and said, "Kanabe."

"And this is Holden." Mason swept an arm toward the pilot who had just lurched against the wheelhouse.

"Horder."

Like an actor proclaiming an introduction to the cast, Mason's arm took in the copter. "U.S. Navy. Navy! Understand?" He pointed to the braid on his cap.

Kanabe smiled, sunlight blasting off the gold teeth. "Navy. Guadalcanal. Tonga."

"No kidding! The war?"

Kanabe shook Mason's hand and pointed at him. "Guadalcanal?"

"No. Oh, no. I got in just after the war."

At that moment a breath of wind stirred the smoke column hanging over the boat. It was a light touch, barely discernible by the hum of the radio wire, but Kanabe's head jerked, nostrils flaring, and one hand touched his throat. East. Had the weather not been on his mind, Holden would not have noticed.

"Mr. Kanabe," Mason said, "This area's not safe. Not safe. Understand?"

"Bad," agreed Kanabe, nodding his head. "Very bad."

"Navy test. Understand?" Mason made slashing motions with his hands. "Rata-tat-tat. Boom! Maneuvers."

One of the crew asked Kanabe something and Kanabe asked it of Mason. "Bomb? Boom?"

"He means atom bomb, Mason," Holden said aware of the fear on their faces. They hung on Mason's every word and gesture.

"No, no, not atom bomb," he shook his head vigorously. "Rata-tat-tat." He pointed eastward and made three fingers. "You must go east. Okay? Go east."

As Kanabe spoke in rapid Japanese to the crew, Holden felt the start of a headache and slightly sick to his stomach. Son of a bitch, he was actually getting seasick.

"When?" the old man asked.

Mason pointed to the numeral nine on his watch. "Nine o'clock." Again he pointed east and held up ten fingers. "Ten miles. Twenty miles. Go away. Sayonara. Understand?"

"Yesss," Kanabe hissed through his teeth.

A hand tapped Holden's shoulder, as the boy in the wheelhouse motioned to him to come inside. Holden wondered fleetingly how much he would be worth as a hostage.

In the cramped wheelhouse both portholes were open but the breeze only moved the humidity around. The boy pointed to the compass, indicating the instrument did not work. It was an old device, set in a brass gimbal, the needle stuck to the indicator ring.

"Mason! Get in here and look at this."

Mason was followed by two of the crewmen as the rest hovered in the doorway.

Holden said, "Damned if it isn't magnetized. How did this happen? How?"

The boy cocked his head and spoke to the others, and they in turn spoke to Kanabe. Finally Holden said, "Never mind, I'll get you another one."

He opened the survival gear in the helicopter and took out a waterproof Navy compass which he carried back to the boat and presented to Kanabe.

"You're awfully goddamned generous, Holden," Mason muttered.

"They're a dime a dozen." Holden pointed at the wheelhouse. "When did it happen? When?"

Kanabe tapped a finger against his lips, studied the men, then pointed northward with thumb and forefinger forming a circle, and moved his arm slowly back and forth. "Rights. Rights?"

"Lights! You saw the lights!" Holden burst out. "Last night? Green lights?"

Kanabe nodded solemnly, then looked eastward as another puff of wind laved the boat. "Bad. Very bad."

"What were they? Do you know?"

Kanabe shrugged and muttered.

"What was that? What did you say?" Holden kneeled before him.

"Ku." Kanabe shrank back. Holden had the flushed, hairy complexion that many Asians believed smelled like warm, raw steak. The Japanese watched him through narrow eyes, trying to determine if the word meant anything to Holden.

"Ku? What does that mean? The lights fouled up your compass?"

Kanabe rubbed his lips. Mason noticed one crew member smiling and shaking his head at the old man. Kanabe shook his head and dismissed Holden with a wave of his hand.

"Holden, let's go. We haven't got all day."

Regretfully, Holden stood and bowed. He and Mason dipped and smiled back to the helicopter. Still smiling, they waved while rising into the air, sending spray over the boat, and headed for Itrek.

"Hello, good buddies. Flag wants to know if they were little green

35

men." Farnsworth's voice on the radio with its nasal cheerfulness was becoming irritating.

Holden answered, "Mason says they're Martians, I say they were Japanese fishermen. Take your pick. We didn't see any radar or sonar gear. Just a lot of fish scales."

"Thank you for your very concise helpful report. The clock is running. Stay tuned for an enlistment commercial."

Holden swept Itrek's south end, then hovered over a pitted beach of black volcanic rock all but buried by foliage. "Ku. Is that what he said? What did he mean when he said that, Mason?"

Mason pursed his lips. "Maybe it's Jap for 'Get lost.' Did you think about what I said last night?"

"Damn it, Mason!"

Mason stared out the window. "I won't mention it again. Right up to zero hour I won't mention it. Even when things go haywire, I'll shut up. You're smarter than me, Holden."

"Nothing can go wrong." Holden feared Mason's glumness would spread to him like some kind of skin disease. "Lay off."

"Just make sure I'm not buried in the Pacific. Okay? I know I won't get a minute's peace if I'm buried anywhere around here."

X MINUS 30 MINUTES

CROFT, TREGASKIS, and Axton returned from the *Knoxville* after a final check of the plants and animals. Croft mopped his forehead with a handkerchief. "That monkey knows. He ran up the pole the minute he saw us coming. Isn't that right, Tregaskis?"

"He ate half of my seedlings," Tregaskis grumbled.

Kilgallen ran a final check of the satellite system, filling the screen with the magnificent turquoise globe of the earth. The weather was clear over Itrek and a large chunk of the Pacific. Except for the stubborn low-pressure center, it was a normal day. Kilgallen examined a candy bar and after a struggle put it away, popping gum into his mouth instead.

The sky was filled with the rush of F-4 Phantom jets launched from the *McClusky*, loaded with cameras and radiation equipment which would fly over the island at various heights taking atmosphere measurements. In these final moments, Farnsworth's voice was cold and devoid of levity, calling off the minutes. The *Adair* had moved west to a station more than fifteen miles from the *Knoxville*. "Itrek, we read thirty minutes and counting."

"Affirmative," Kilgallen answered, his voice higher than usual.

"Better seal off the CDA."

From a metal case Mason doled out five rubberized bundles with attached oxygen tanks. They were heavy radiation suits, floppy overalls with hoods and mittens which made it difficult for them to work their controls. Because of the suits' weight, the heat was stifling.

Mason and Holden drew heavy lead shutters across the windows and a steel panel over the door, plunging the CDA into a steel and plastic gloom, dancing with the skittery colored computer lights and the glow from the televisions. Now they were completely enclosed in a block of steel and lead supplied by recirculated air and auxiliary power. Holden listened to his own thunderous breathing and Farnsworth's voice on the speaker.

Like pollen seeds rising on the wind, radiosonde balloons on the *Knoxville* inflated and leaped from their boxes. Holden touched a button and watched the telemetry. The temperature was a fat ninety-six, humidity sixty-eight. Several minutes later the balloons were followed by a second set and then a third, all of them spacing themselves at different altitudes.

Croft watched his telemetry of the animal functions, noting that the heartbeat and respiration of the goat and hog were climbing. A reaction to all that sedative? Or did they also know what the monkey did?

The only one with nothing to do was Tregaskis, who sat at the chart table nervously tapping a pen on the paper. "Stop that!" Mason roared at him. Tregaskis jumped violently, his pen clattering to the floor.

"Farnsworth?" Kilgallen's voice was muffled by his hood.

"Yes, Itrek."

"You're my witness. If anything goes wrong I'd like to will my electric train set to the United States Naval Weapons Center." The remark was followed by a sneeze. Kilgallen cursed, unable to wipe his nose in the radiation suit.

"Gesundheit," Farnsworth said laconically. "One minute to firing."

X MINUS 1 MINUTE

MASON WAS watching him, his face invisible behind the mask, but Holden felt fierce attention emanating like a beam of light from the Petty

37

Officer. Holden's hands were clasped before an Abort button which if depressed would stop the test.

He read over the telemetry. It was a beautiful, balmy, sunny tropical day. The balloons were at height, instrumentation in order, and all the myriad systems moving perfectly. He would need a good explanation for stopping Windowpane and he did not have one.

Holden felt a surge of contemptuous anger for the Petty Officer. Mason was a stupid primitive, a superstitious fool, haunted by nameless dreads and demons. No doubt other Holdens had been like that, too, fearful men, too fearful to examine their lives or change their destiny. Holden would not be like his fathers or Mason. God forbid that he go through life like Samuel Mason, scared of the sea, scared of the air.

Even their own fears were exaggerated. All this lead shielding and radiation garb, all these unattached, lonely, familyless men were mere ornament, excessive caution. Windowpane had been calculated to the last micron. It would work.

The seconds wound down. Holden moved his hand from the Abort button and sat on it. Mason rocked in his swivel chair, which emitted faint creaking noises.

Holden found himself thinking of Gina Lambert. In Florida, it would be three o'clock in the afternoon. She would be romping with Dennis at a playground in Miami as the child's grandparents looked on. Or maybe she was settling into the apartment, busily redecorating it while Dennis napped on his sofa cushions. Perhaps Dennis whimpered in his sleep, dreaming strange dreams, his psyche fractured by the inexplicable loss and burial of half his world. In school, Gina had been heavy on sweaters and cotton pants and that was probably what she would be wearing while moving her stuff in . . .

Christ!

They were not married.

Not only that, they had not even established residency. If Holden died she would be penniless. There would not even be any insurance.

Holden's hand clenched. Mason stopped rocking.

No, you gave your word. Not for her, not even for her.

Holden's hand moved slightly.

The digital clock hit oh nine hundred hours. Farnsworth's voice sounded disembodied, faraway, "Firing is commenced."

X PLUS 1 SECOND

THERE WAS no explosion to shake the earth. No cloud of smoke, blaze of fire or concussion to indicate that a tremendous event had taken place in the atmosphere. What occurred over the next ten seconds occurred unseen by the human eye, unheard by the ear, producing no sensory impact.

At precisely oh nine hundred hours, power surged from the capacitors under the *Adair*'s parabolic mirror into the apparatus on the forward gun mount. There was a microsecond hesitation as sunlight was converted into voltage, then from the nozzle pointed skyward seared a pale, blue-green shaft of laser light.

The heat generated by this light was incomprehensible by normal terminology of degrees or temperature. It tunneled through the gases of the troposphere, past the barrier of the tropopause, dividing the earthbound air in which all life survives from the ionosphere. Twenty-five miles above the earth, where the skies are dark blue, the light struck the ozone layer, the thin shield of ionized oxygen in the atmosphere which protects the Earth from the naked radiation of the sun, and burned a "window" in it.

The heat of the laser light created a thermal blossom, a superhot tube of air comparable at its focused point to the center of the sun. Through this vaporized hole in the ozone poured gamma rays, ultraviolet rays, X rays, the sheer withering fission of raw sunlight onto an area of sea two miles in diameter, the *Knoxville* in the center.

This radiation was not in the range of human eyesight, but still equivalent to the detonation of dozens of hydrogen bombs directly over the ship. It was silent death which damages no structure, blew away no city. The *Adair*'s laser was a rudimentary prototype, achievable only through advances in laser technology. The next generation, however, if the test were successful, would be able to cut a hole in the sky large enough to cook a continent and every living organism thereon—foliage, bacteria, animals, and humans—with a rain of unfiltered sunlight.

X PLUS 2 SECONDS

THE TELEMETRY tapes hissed into their bins in the CDA station. Croft watched the animal reactions but saw nothing, realizing it would take several seconds for them to react. Holden noted a jump in radiation from the uppermost balloons.

On the *Knoxville*, Lancelot had just stolen seeds from Tregaskis's tubs and was eating them in the hatch shadow. Then he looked around wildly, cocked his ears, sniffed, and scrambled for the open hatch.

X PLUS 3 SECONDS

ONE OF the Phantom pilots thought he saw the ghostly, transparent laser light silhouetted against Itrek but he was not sure. Against the bright day, the light was invisible. A burst of wind struck his plane.

The uppermost of Holden's balloons registered radiation so high the needle moved to the edge of the meter and remained there. By now all the balloons were picking up the sunlight.

On the infrared screen, they saw a fiery spot of light swell over the sea. Farnsworth said, "We have a window, Itrek." Forty miles south of Itrek, Holden was startled to see clouds appear. He rubbed the screen but they remained there, forming a crescent line.

X PLUS 4 SECONDS

ALL OF them heard a low wind spring up from the north and whisper past the CDA in a steadily growing motion. Holden's anemometer read out a five-knot breeze which was still growing. Clouds were now appearing north of the island and the galvanometer which measured the electrical potential of the air began to twitch. Holden hit the screen again. The clouds were forming with impossible speed. The astonished voice of a pilot came through. "We're getting shear up here. Do you confirm? Something's happening to the weather." Vertical winds were ripsawing the planes.

X PLUS 5 SECONDS

ON BOARD the *Knoxville*, hell broke loose. Croft watched the respiration, heartbeat, and skin temperature of the animals rise on the telemetry. Sheer terror had broken out among them. The goat's telemetry suddenly went dead, indicating the beast had torn the electrodes from its body. The old freighter had become a frying pan of gamma rays. Beneath the *Knoxville* Axton had suspended cages full of fish in the waters. If his readings were accurate, the radiation poured down with such intensity it speared over fifty feet into the sea.

Lancelot was burning to death, yet no fire or smoke was apparent on his fur. As he scrambled down hatchways, chattering in terror, his skin swelled until his entire body became one huge burn blister. He pawed at his fur, pulling it out in handfuls, then plunged into a cargo hold full of brackish water as the other animals thrashed around in their cages.

X PLUS 6 SECONDS

THE WING leader of the Phantoms screamed: "Break off, break off. Get back to the carrier. *Adair*, we're aborting this flight."

"Affirmative, *McClusky*," Farnsworth answered in a shaky voice.

From one end of the horizon to the other, giant clouds sprouted like mushrooms from clear air, plunging the sunlight into a dusky gloom. Sudden winds sent planes spinning. Beneath the squadron leader an enormous cumulonimbus thunderhead blossomed like a huge bubble, blowing his aircraft into the air like a cinder fired from a cannon.

X PLUS 7 SECONDS

THE MEN in the CDA looked fearfully at Holden as a gust of wind slammed into the building. Holden turned away from his telemetry to stare in stupefaction at the mantle of gray clouds obscuring the test area. A storm had built up in eight seconds.

X PLUS 8 SECONDS

CROFT WATCHED on tape as the hog had a heart attack. The heartbeat jerked and flickered, then stopped, and except for fading brain waves, the telemetry ceased. The skin temperature of the guinea pigs soared past one hundred eighty degrees.

Kilgallen stared at the radiation counter for the CDA. So far, thank God, none of the stuff had touched them.

Holden's anemometer jolted to a reading of a twelve-knot wind. On the infrared screen, the low-pressure center was changing color. The rain would come down in a cataract.

X PLUS 9 SECONDS

THE BAROMETER fell like a stone. One pilot reported a thirty-knot wind at thirty-five hundred feet heading south. Outside the CDA, the wind was still rising. "Stop it," Mason murmured to the television screen. "Turn it off."

X PLUS 10 SECONDS

FARNSWORTH REPORTED, "Firing completed." On the *Adair* the laser shut down, the mounting glowing red with heat.

On the infrared screen, Holden watched the angry red sore of the window begin to fade as sunlight converted the oxygen in the air to ozone. The ozone layer, it appeared, was healing itself.

The balloon counters began a slow drop to normal levels. The highest balloon indicated the electrical charge in the ionosphere where the laser had penetrated was still high.

Mason spoke between clenched teeth. "Holden? What's that wind? What's going on?"

"There's a negative charge in the ionosphere," Holden explained, trying to be as precise as possible. "This section of ground is losing its charge trying to balance it. That's why those clouds are forming . . ."

"Holden, try plain English."

"Its like a storage battery. The earth I mean. It's constantly losing its charge into the ionosphere. The charge is returned in the form of thunderstorms. We're going to have a thunderstorm."

They could hear the wind shaking the foliage, moaning through the microwave antennas on the roof.

"Blew up kind of fast, didn't it?" Mason wanted to know.

"They predicted something like this in the Red Book. They knew the window heat would convect air upward but nobody predicted anything this big."

Farnsworth's voice crackled around the CDA. "Itrek, what's your radiation reading?"

The remark reminded them that they were all still alive. Their fear had been that the window would cook all of them in gamma rays. Holden thought again of Gina. The danger was past and they were still functioning. Kilgallen laughed into the microphone. "Zero. My wristwatch is hotter than this."

"Keep your stupid electric trains, then."

They stripped off their coveralls and tossed them in a heap onto the floor. Sweat plastered their hair to their heads; their clothes clung to their bodies.

Mason slid open the shuttered window. The sight that greeted them stunned each of the men into frozen positions, Kilgallen with his hand on the microphone, Croft with the coveralls around his knees, Tregaskis combing his hair, and Holden marking wind arrows on the chart. Only Axton seemed unmoved as he folded his coveralls into a neat square, then opened the other window.

Eastward past the wind-bent trees, skudding towers of iron, black clouds flowed across the sky like a gigantic river. The blue sea was rippled with whitecaps tossing spray into the air. It looked to Holden as if the trees were weeping. Seconds before, the sun had shown from a hot burnished sky. Now night was rushing over them. Holden noted the time in his Red Book.

Mason looked at him as if he were to blame. "I said it would rain," Holden said. "I didn't say when."

Something hit the station wall with a thump, then thudded to the ground. It was followed by other thumps that splashed into the sea or tumbled through the moaning brush.

X PLUS 30 MINUTES

As HOLDEN stepped outdoors, wind-blown sand stung his skin. The air had chilled, drying the sweat against his body. Lying on the ground was the small feathered body of a dead bird, some kind of tern.

"Don't touch it, Mr. Holden," Croft warned, the wind wisping his thin hair. "It may be radioactive. Killed in flight by the laser. Get the geiger counter, would you please, Kilgallen?"

In the distance the grim, churning clouds were split from the sea by a gap of dirty, orange sunlight. Holden struggled to put this fury into some kind of rational perspective, to connect heat with convection, convection with rain, and electricity and rising cloud masses to wind. The connections were too fragile. A more accurate impression was that Windowpane had angered some gigantic, wrathful animal sleeping in the sky.

Kilgallen spoke softly. "Gang, I think we're going to win the next war with that laser." The wind whipped away his words.

Croft looked thoughtfully at the clouds. "Something is not right. Don't you feel it?"

"Yes," Axton said. "There isn't any lightning or thunder."

Axton had nailed it. The weather was silent but for the mournful, ominous rush of wind. Such skies, in their experience, were accompanied by dramatic flashes of lightning and rolls of thunder, catalysts of theater. To the men it felt as though the lightning in its total fury was being withheld for a more appropriate moment.

Through the door, Holden could see the galvanometer face. The needle had moved well off mark, meaning that ions were rushing from the ground into jagged discharge points—treetops, blades of grass, metal corners—to await the cataclysmic overbalancing of charge that precedes a thunderbolt.

"Kilgallen, we'd better make sure everything in the CDA is grounded."

"Don't worry about that, Holden."

"It might not be a bad idea to cut off the big cables altogether and stay on auxiliary power." Holden never finished the sentence. Much later his memory reconstructed the details leading up to that moment. He distinctly recalled his irritation at Farnsworth's voice. "Itrek, the pressure center is rising. We're launching balloons from here *tout suite . . .*"

The galvanometer needle leaped across the meter face. Holden's foot kicked at a dead bird as the CDA station was miraculously transformed into a big-bellied spider glaring at him with eight eyes, its spindly legs crouched in pouncing position. Instead of fear he felt anger as Farnsworth's voice choked and stammered, ". . . sandwich, sandwich . . ."

Their hair stood out from their bodies, ballooning around their heads, tickling their arms and chests. Sparks spat from the metal trim on their clothing, belt buckles, Croft's steel glasses, Tregaskis's high school ring, and the metal lace holes on Holden's shoes. From the aerials and gutters of the CDA roof to the towers on the beach, the rotating radar dishes, the microwave receivers, and the suspension wires, shimmering blue coronas of electricity sizzled against the brown sky.

Holden screamed, "Get down! Lightning!" but did not remember hearing his own voice as an agonizing convulsion pitched him to the sand. The muscles of his back, shoulders, legs, and abdomen cramped into twitching clumps of pain while through his mind a parade of vivid memories ran together like a picture collage. The mental horror was as profound as the physical pain—thoughts, feelings, images fishhooked out of his head. He saw his mother sitting in an overstuffed tattered chair, pineapples blossoming from the ground, and a MIG 21 streaking in toward his port wing as he turned back toward Norway. Gina sat in the taxicab next to him, lay in the bed beside him, her soft hands touching the hairs of his chest.

He writhed on the sand, choking in pain and confusion for what seemed forever but, as they later found out, was barely thirty seconds.

For several minutes they lay in contorted positions, gasping for breath and staring up at the tormented clouds. Mason crawled to Croft and loosened the biologist's shirt. Croft seemed to have aged twenty years in sixty seconds.

Holden climbed to his feet, uncrimping the knots in his muscles, and staggered into the CDA. "*Adair! Adair!* Farnsworth! Is anybody there?"

Other voices squawked from the speaker. Farnsworth apparently had company. His voice was ragged and weak. "Affirmative, Itrek. Did you feel that?"

"We sure did. What happened?"

"I don't know. Hold on, I think we took some casualties."

Mason helped Croft into the CDA, bracing him with his arms as the biologist protested, "I'm all right, really." Axton, his face pale, sat in a chair, hand pressed to his forehead, his lips muttering as though he were trying to remember something. Kilgallen pawed over power meters at each console, tuning a knob, raising a switch, and once tapping a meter glass. Then he rudely pushed Holden away from the microphone. "*Adair.*"

"Yes."

"Some kind of charge passed through the CDA. If I didn't know better, I'd say we were hit by lightning. What's your power situation?''

"It's getting back to normal. I think you're right, a hell of a current ran through here. Do you realize I thought I was eating a grilled cheese sandwich?''

"That's nothing. I came in my pants,'' Kilgallen answered with brutal self-revelation.

"I saw a spider,'' Holden contributed absently.

They all spoke at once in a confessional rush. Mason was back in the Atlantic after falling off a launch in 1962. Tregaskis had shown a flower to his father who slapped him in the face. Croft was on a honeymoon in Niagara Falls with his deceased wife. Axton maintained his customary remoteness but his moving eyes revealed that he was listening and pondering some equally sharp memory behind a blank face.

Farnsworth said, "Man, this whole boat went totally crackers. We were just standing down from action stations when it happened. Do you realize we're carrying missiles here? Some bozo could have hit a switch just like that. What was it?''

"Mass hallucination,'' Axton answered, calmly waving a hand.

"Thank you,'' said Croft wiping his glasses. "Would you kindly explain how?''

"The same thing that caused the power surge, obviously. The two events were concurrent with each other.'' His narrow head faced Kilgallen. "We *were* hit by lightning, Mr. Kilgallen, weren't we?''

"We wouldn't be here if we were. We'd be barbecued.''

"Then I guess it was most unusual lightning.''

Mason said, "Somebody log the time, damn it. I make it nine thirty-eight.''

"And how long it lasted,'' Kilgallen added. "Not that we'll ever get it precise. I figure about thirty seconds . . .''

"Twenty-four point seven seconds,'' Croft corrected. "And it occurred at exactly nine thirty-seven and nineteen seconds.'' The biologist was examining telemetry tape ticking into the bins. He yanked a section out and spread it on the table. With a pen, he circled encephalographic waves of the animals on the *Knoxville*.

Croft gazed benignly at their faces. "That enlarges the scale of it somewhat, does it not?''

Kilgallen snatched a handful of tape and screwed up his face, his lips working. "He's right. Here it is right next to the time marks. Brain waves! Alpha waves, beta waves . . . Everything was charged! The *Adair*, the power station, the animals on the *Knoxville* . . .''

Axton nodded, "All right, if it happened to those animals as well as

46

the humans, it's not unreasonable to suppose it happened to every living thing on the island. Birds? Beetles? Mice? How about that, Croft?''

"Yes," Croft agreed, letting the tapes slip back into their bins. "I wonder what guinea pigs see when they hallucinate."

"Electrical fields!" breathed Kilgallen, tapping his nose with his forefinger. "Wait a minute, gang. Croft, did you know that you can cause hallucinations in people by sending an electrical current from electrodes through certain parts of the brain? Memories, visions . . . By God, that's all it was."

Everyone but Mason comprehended that. "I don't get it. You think we got a needle stuck in our heads or something?"

"Well, yes. Basically, it's very simple. Thoughts are electrical waves, memories are an arrangement of neural paths, an arrangement of electricity. The whole human body is an electrical field. Holden's spiders, Croft's honeymoon, my . . . well never the hell mind what mine is." The Ensign turned scarlet. "Anyway. Humans, animals, and machines are all electrical fields. Some kind of current passed through all the electrical circuitry."

Tregaskis clasped his arms around his chest and regarded the windy beach. "It was a rotten experience, whatever it was. It's like being . . . burglarized or something."

Holden remembered his helpless disgust. Some part of his soul had been profoundly outraged by having memories forced upon his consciousness. "I felt the same."

Croft smoothed the hair on his pate and breathed deeply. Holden asked, "Are you all right, Croft?"

"What? Yes. I'm a senile old man but aside from that I'm in perfect physical health." Croft's face had grown heavier, his expression sagging like a basset hound's, his eyes dim and sad. "I saw my wife just as she was forty-one years ago. I recall every detail. She wore a rose tulle hat and we were standing on a lookout above Niagara Falls."

Holden said, "It sure beats spiders."

"We all have our own thoughts, don't we? They're as individual as fingerprints." Croft looked as though he were about to say more, then shook his head. "Well. Back to work. We must board the *Knoxville* and take samples." He looked at the telemetry tapes of his animals as they ticked out of the console. "They're all dying. That's the point, isn't it?"

Axton murmured, "Is there some way we can figure how large the scale of this thing really is? The *Adair* was fifteen miles away when it hit them."

Holden looked up at the infrared screen. Forty miles south of them the clouds were piling up into an enormous anvil-shaped thunderhead. To Holden, the sliced tops of the clouds indicated high altitude winds, and unless he missed his guess, the flickers indicated lightning over sixty thousand feet above ground level. The anvil cumulonimbus was directly under a section of sky where the laser had penetrated. "I can make a guess," he said. "I think it happened to everything inside the low-pressure center. But the real question is why."

X PLUS 4 HOURS

LANCELOT OPENED pain-wracked eyes and recognized the face of Croft behind the face plate of the radiation suit. Huge blisters ran copious fluids through the blackened, suppurating bald patches on his body. He watched Croft squirt the needle into the air, summoning just enough strength to sink his teeth into the rubberized glove. When Croft pulled his hand away, Lancelot's teeth came with it. By the time he reached for the monkey again, Lancelot was dead.

Croft had found the beast huddled in a puddle of brackish water belowdecks. Topside, *Knoxville* was a charnal house of death and pain. Those animals still alive were scorched bald, in some cases to the bone. The goat lay panting under a mast shadow and did not even react to Croft and his needle. Croft was an angel of death, a messenger of tranquility with his poison. The calf had been unable to get to his feet; the guinea pigs lay still in their cages; the earthworms were dead under three feet of soil.

Belowdecks, Croft listened intently. From bow to stern, *Knoxville* was cleaned of even the most elemental vermin. Rat carcasses lay on the floors. No slime moss slopped in the dank waters of unused compartments, no spider webs or cockroaches hid in corners. Until today Croft had thought there would never in history be a ship in which not even a beetle could be found. A ship without life was a contradiction in terms, yet now a doctor could perform surgery on the *Knoxville* without fear of a single microbe causing an infection. *Knoxville* was completely sterile.

The radiation count was still high. They worked quickly, Croft excising skin, blood, and fur samples from Lancelot; Tregaskis poking for seedlings through soil, scooping up bark and leaves from the tubs. They roped their samples together and lowered the lead bottles in a net down to Mason standing by in the launch, then descended the rope netting. Axton heaved out of the water with his sealed bottles of sea water and dripped all over the launch. "No barnacles," he reported to Mason. "They all died and fell off. The hull is smooth as glass down there."

The seas were choppy, the skies grim and Wagnerian, but still rain did not fall. "I sure wish this storm would go away," Tregaskis complained.

Mason spoke into the microphone. "*Adair*, we're away. You can fire when ready and all that crap."

While the others stowed their samples in the CDA, Mason stood on the sea wall watching *Knoxville* through binoculars. By now the *Adair* was miles away preparing to give the missile crews some practice.

The missile was a fire streak skimming over the angry, windy waves guided by the Fire Control Center on the destroyer. A mushroom cloud of dirty gray smoke boiling with licks of fire enclosed the ship. Mason watched falling debris dapple the water for hundreds of yards around. He continued watching as the smoke was blown away, leaving an empty sea. No matter how worthless, decrepit or old the ship, he always felt sad when one went to the bottom.

X PLUS 5 HOURS

THERE ARE certain cataclysmic events in life which although rapid in occurrence seem in retrospect to be separated by years. The catastrophic events which took place during the remainder of that day occurred within a few short hours, yet in Holden's memory some protective reflex separated them from each other lest they overwhelm him.

In the space of three hours, Holden watched as the southern storm cell pushed itself to a height of almost twenty miles. On the infrared it was a glowing red wound of heat and lightning yet no rain was reported by any of the pilots who skimmed the edges of it.

Farnsworth chortled over the speaker, "Hey, Holden, you should see Jameson sweat. He doesn't know this storm from nothing but he just sort of walks around looking like he's got everything under control."

"That cumulonimbus is rising, Farnsworth. It's going straight up. There's no cold front or land nearby to push it up. Axton, hand me that chart."

Axton had mapped out sea currents in the vicinity of Itrek and farther south. Holden looked at the swirly lines indicating temperature and direction and said, "Farnsworth? Lay this on Jameson."

"I'm ready."

"It's not one storm, it's really two close together connected by high altitude winds. I can just make it out on the infrared. The smaller storm is right over a place where Axton said he recorded the warmest sea temperatures."

"I'll tell him, but I don't get it."

"One storm is feeding moisture to the other from the only warm water in the area. It's a real smart storm, Farnsworth. It knows where the hot water is."

He switched the infrared to show up the disposition of the water vapor. The storm changed appearance dramatically, from a huge gray growth to a pair of flaming towers connected by an umbilical of water vapor. The winds connecting the systems must be around a hundred knots, Holden figured.

Croft overheard him from his chair, "How clever of it, Mr. Holden. Is that the word?"

"I've run out of words for ridiculous so I guess it'll do. It's working backwards, you see? Normally the major winds are at the base of a cell. These are high altitude." Holden could have reeled off all kinds of arcane oddities about the storm but the basic pattern was clear. He had never seen anything like it and could not even begin to understand what it was doing.

"You're doing admirably, Mr. Holden." Croft gave him an avuncular pat on the shoulder. "You have clearly stated that nothing makes sense. Isaac Newton never quantified bewilderment with greater precision than you."

"Kilgallen?"

The ensign had been mooning over his console. "Yeah. What? I'm here."

"Feel like playing a few games with the radiometer?"

"Check the composition of the atmosphere. Right." He fumbled through his Red Book.

"No, not that. Games. Why don't we go ghost hunting? Since everything's going in overdrive, maybe we can find that little gremlin that's eating up my two hundredths of a micron of infrared."

Kilgallen played the ESSA satellite like a concert pianist preparing for a detailed concerto which only he has mastered. He cracked his knuckles. He rolled his sleeves. Then after flexing his round, stubby fingers, he began playing delicate music on the infrared screen.

Water vapor. The screens showed the storm as two red blots connected by a thinner one, like a blood vessel feeding pulsing organs. Carbon dioxide. The white gas around Itrek was now a fuzz sucking toward the storm because of the winds. He passed through the ranges of absorption of the regular gases. Then he turned the dial into a dark area of low absorptivity well below the lowest level of carbon dioxide.

The colors disappeared and the screen sank into blackness. Kilgallen's fingers explored a world of ethereal phantoms so insubstantial their forms were invisible to the infrared eye. Then in the region of twenty-five microns, far below the level of any known substance, they all saw it at once.

An oval of darkness against the deeper darkness, crisscrossed by lines, a skeleton of the low-pressure center which was so bedeviling to Holden. They could only guess at what was absorbing infrared this weakly, some trace element, some gas so rare it had not even been plotted. The shape flickered on the screen for barely two seconds—just long enough for them to note that the lines formed patterned swirls at each end. Then, like a ghost, the web thing was gone and Kilgallen's most skillful efforts to find it again proved futile.

"Everybody saw it, right?"

They nodded. Mason said, "It was big. It was seventy miles long at least."

Croft said, "I liked your word 'gremlin,' Mr. Holden."

Kilgallen said, "Those lines coming out of the end. Did you ever sprinkle iron filings on paper and put a magnet under them? That's what it looked like. Some kind of magnetic field . . ."

"Itrek? Itrek?" Farnsworth's voice was urgent. "Stand by please. We're taping a distress signal."

Kilgallen shoved his way over to the receiver but only picked up static from the storm. They waited for Farnsworth to come back on. Mason looked out at the overcast; Tregaskis smoothed a crease in his pants; Croft twirled his glasses in his fingers.

Farnsworth sounded subdued when he spoke again. "Kilgallen, there's an island called Loa south of here. That's where the signal came from."

"Any idea who it is?"

"I think it's that fishing boat you chased away. Listen to the tape. He turned the radio off himself."

It was a high voice that babbled in Japanese and fractured English, interspersed with blasts of static and cries of panic in the background.

Farnsworth's voice was calm, almost melodious. "Acknowledge, please. Do you read me?"

"Hello, hello. Dead . . . dead . . ."

"Please acknowledge. We have your position, we are sending help."

"Heiko! Heiko! Yohah, yohah . . ."

The voice sounded like that of Kanabe, the patriarch of the fisher. Heiko must have been one of the crew members. Yohah sounded like Loa.

"We are an American ship. Help is coming. Are you sinking? Sinking?"

After a shattering roar of static, Kanabe's voice returned, miraculously transformed to a placid calm as though the imminence of death had stilled his terror. His words were clear and in perfect English. "It is finished. They are dead. My family is dead."

Mason slid down in a swivel chair, his head nodding with the voice as though agreeing with a profound truth.

"Listen, hang on whoever you are. We're sending a helicopter. We've got you on radar, help is coming . . ."

"No. Ku. You will die."

The message ended with a click. Farnsworth tried for a response. "Damn it! Answer me. Hello? Hello?" Then the tape ended and Farnsworth was back on. "Holden?"

"Yes."

"Can you get out to Loa?"

"I think so. The wind's pretty reasonable right now. It doesn't sound very encouraging, though."

"You're the closest one. There's a couple of local squalls down there but they're moving away. You shouldn't have any trouble landing in the water."

Holden glanced at the chart which showed Loa as a coral crescent barely the size of a football field. The boat must have sheltered there during the test.

On the way to the hangar, Mason shouted at Holden. "Am I right, Holden? What's the saying about history repeating itself?"

"I don't know, Mason. Was it raining on the *Ourang Medan*?"

X PLUS 6 HOURS

WHEN THEY reached Loa's lagoon, the wind was rocking the copter in the air and the sea was brushed by gusts of rain. In the south, the main storm was a mountain range of jagged cloud peaks and valleys. Holden circled the boat. The anchor was down, the nets out, and the deck was littered with bodies. One was near the bow, the others piled around the wheelhouse door in a tangle of arms and legs. They had been trying to get in when the disaster struck. One of the men lay on his back, his arms shielding his face.

"Let's make it quick," Mason grumbled as they settled in the choppy waters. He tied the copter to the boat. Holden hoisted himself over the gunwale to find himself looking into the puffy eyes of a swollen, blackened face. The man's right hand clawed the air with frozen talon fingers. For formality's sake, Holden grasped the pulse, unsurprised to find it still.

Mason slipped off his shirt and opened the engine hatch. Black, fuel-oil smoke bellied up. Mason slid belowdecks and Holden heard him slapping his shirt against the machinery. "Real sweet," he coughed. "This raft hasn't seen an electrician since chopsticks were invented."

"What was the *Ourang Medan* carrying? Anything explosive?"

"Maybe, maybe." Mason heaved himself out of the hatch and put his shirt on again. "There's scorch marks everywhere down there, especially around the wiring. Let's get out of here, they're all dead. The *Adair* can pick it up."

"In a minute. I want to look at the radio operator."

In the wheelhouse the boy was lying on the floor by the chart table. His clothes were tattered and disheveled as though a tremendous blast of wind had hit him. The starboard porthole was open, the brass edge of it scorched. The radio was in operating condition and papers from the chart table wafted over the floor each time water slapped the hull.

The old man, Kanabe, was slumped over a chair on the floor, his arms folded stoically. His mouth was open and a fused lump of gold protruded. His gold bridgework had melted.

Holden tore open Kanabe's shirt. Across the scarlet red skin of the old man's chest were streaks of black char. Holden touched a hand and a fingernail clicked onto the floor. Kanabe's hair crumpled to greasy dust under his touch. The old man, the boy, and the rest of the crew had been burnt. "Mason?"

"Yeah?"

"Lightning. It came through the porthole, nailed the kid and the old man. And it didn't hit anything else. Understand?" Holden raised his voice above the thunder roll. "It didn't touch the mast, the radio, or anything else. Just the people."

The sky would have been black and heavy over their heads, Holden surmised. The approaching bolt would have tickled their bodies, making them panic. The man on the forward deck was probably hit first, then the others as they tried to cram into the wheelhouse. Heiko must have been the boy killed by the first bolt through the window and Kanabe would have known his situation was hopeless. He had turned off the radio and folded his arms to await his death.

The line of mountainous thunderheads blocked all but a yellow fan of sunlight that split through a crevasse in the hulking mass of cloud. Darkness was spreading over the Pacific like a great black boiling wing.

Holden waded back to the helicopter and raised the *Adair*. "Farnsworth? They're all dead. They were killed by lightning."

Mason climbed in beside him, squeezing water from the tail of his shirt. He slid the passenger window shut, and began strapping himself into the seat.

Farnsworth broke in, "We'll get a boat there and take it under tow after the storm blows away. Jameson says it should break any minute."

"Jameson doesn't know his ass from Mammoth Cave. The squall that killed them? There's no sign of it now. It came and went in half an hour."

"That's the tropics, isn't it?"

Holden rested his hands on the pitch stick. A decision had been growing in him for the past hour despite his best efforts to evade it. Now he knew he had no choice. He was the weatherman on Itrek and a question would be raised at the Naval Weapons Center where they had chosen him rather than Kayama because he was a pilot. "Are any planes from *McClusky* checking out the storm?"

"No, I don't think they'll go near it."

"Call *McClusky* and tell them to get a Harrier to Itrek immediately. It's the only plane that will land on the beach."

Mason scowled at him, hands poised on the seat-belt buckles. "Where do you think you're going?"

"I'm going for an airplane ride."

"You could have died more helpfully on the *Knoxville*, Holden," Mason snapped. "Croft could have used an extra monkey."

After a pause Farnsworth said, "Are you sure you want to do that?"

Holden interrupted, "If the storm breaks I'll head for *McClusky* and be home before anybody. I don't think it will break yet. We've been picking up lightning on the ESSA for two hours but the satellite looks straight down on it. I want to see the storm from the side. I have to see what that lightning's doing."

54

X PLUS 7 HOURS

HOLDEN ROUGHED out a flight plan as the stubby winged interceptor lowered over Itrek's beach, landing gear dangling like an insect's legs, and settled into an exhaust-blown sand crater. The Harrier was the only Vertical Take-Off fighter in NATO and could land like a helicopter.

As Holden carried his helmet to the plane, the pilot said, "I need forty-five minutes of fuel to make it to the *McClusky*, okay?"

"You'll have more than enough. I'll stay within forty miles of Itrek, Kilgallen. If you see any rain on the radar keep me away from it."

"Okay."

Holden climbed into the Harrier, strapped the parachute and seat belts and settled himself in the canted seat.

Mason called, "If you get lost, be sure to drop a little bottle with a note in it." Tregaskis giggled and Mason dragged him away by the shirt collar as the engines whined to life.

Holden closed the canopy and waved as the whine deepened to a throaty, bone-shaking roar and the downward pointing exhausts blew sand into a cloud. Eyes glued to the exhaust indicators, Holden lifted the plane into the air. For a few seconds it swayed dangerously in the wind, the sand blackening underneath the exhaust nozzles. Then it moved forward at increasing speed.

Holden turned out to sea and called the *Adair*. "Hello, Farnsworth. Are you tracking me?"

"Like a hound after the hare, good buddy. Have a nice trip and send lots of postcards."

Holden angled the plane west and studied the storm. From this altitude, he saw it as a huge heaped black mass with a sharpened edge like the blade of a wedge lying over the sea. He jotted each course change with grease pencil on his kneepad as the Harrier flew around the western side.

From the side, the storm looked vaguely like a saddle, two thick bulges of overcast bridged by winds, the southernmost one losing itself in the high level layer of clouds. That cloud deck went up to thirty thousand feet. Holden would have to get through it in order to take a look at the major storm cell.

Holden's breath hissed into his mask, the colored oxygen indicator showing each expiration. According to the satellite, that cloud layer was free of lightning. He had memorized the tracks of the wind, which had not varied in hours. The Harrier sailed into the clouds between the thunderheads and caught itself in the winds which lifted the plane into mist that darkened to pitch blackness.

At seven thousand feet, Holden switched on the cockpit lights. He felt himself suspended in a gray bumpy limbo with drum hammers of air slamming against his fuselage.

The Harrier clawed its way through snakes of changing wind to ten thousand feet where Holden leveled off. Kilgallen's voice was flattened by the headphones. "Come east a little, Holden, about two degrees. There's a rain cell ahead of you." This close to his ears, Kilgallen's voice was a comforting, intimate whisper.

At fifteen thousand feet, Holden figured he was dead center in the clouds. A streak of rain flayed across the canopy as he struggled up to the thin air of twenty thousand feet, and the Harrier, designed for ground level flight, began handling like a pig. Outside it was as dark as the blackest pits of hell.

At twenty-five thousand feet, the turbulence was so bad, Holden's straps scraped his shoulders raw under his nylon flight suit. He scratched out a new heading on his kneepad, figuring that one more push would get him out of the soup.

At thirty thousand feet, the Harrier surged out of the mush into a blazing, sunlit dreamscape of pillow clouds, rolling in oceanic waves to infinity. Howling tubes of wind tunneled the air, one of which tipped his wing and kicked him back into the overcast just as he was sliding on his sun visor. When he grappled the plane up again, he was pointed directly at the larger of the twin storm towers. The sight was a brain-numbing spectacle of color and fury of such magnitude, it defied rational contemplation and summoned forth dark, mythic legends of angry gods hurling thunderbolts at each other and rendering humans to dead stone by their mere presence.

This is what the world was like when life was created, he thought dazedly.

The clouds were all entwining into a titanic fireplug of black cumulonimbus that pulsed with gigantic rings of fulminating electricity. The lightning strokes went straight up in belching flaring majesty from the top of the tower to the sky and seemed to split the air apart with their detonations.

The dark blue sky above the tower shone with green, red, and thick limpid orange light—a fingerpainted mass of deep, rich primary colors that rainbowed the sun. Holden was looking at the aurora borealis in broad daylight. To Holden the sky looked like a crown of gorgeous colored jewels over the black finger of the cloud tower.

"Kilgallen? I'm looking at aurora borealis. The ionosphere is negatively charged because of Windowpane. Do you read me?"

Only static answered him. Holden warily kept his distance from the cloud tower. A ten-mile-high thundercloud was considered a giant. On rare occasions they had been known to climb as high as the tropopause, twelve miles up. The ozone layer was twenty-five miles high. This monster had massed its bulk almost twenty miles high.

Now he had all the answers he would need. He wheeled around for a last look at the tower. He knew why no rain had fallen yet. All of it was locked up in that thunderhead, every molecule of fuel it would need to power its push to the ozone layer. Once there, it would level out the negative charge with lightning and create a few billion cubic feet of ozone.

White spots streaked before Holden's eyes. The Harrier shuddered as a burst of wind hit it. From a deep canyon of cloud, four glowing green lights rose toward him. Holden rubbed his eyes under the sun visor but they kept coming. It was not his imagination, they were real.

One of the lights circled his plane then hung off the port wing, pacing his speed and course, its green glow piercing through the sea of white cloud like a piece of sun.

"Itrek, do you read me?"

Kilgallen's voice was barely audible. ". . . Yes . . ."

"Our lights are back. It's ball lightning, Kilgallen. That's what we saw last night. I'm looking at one now."

The globe was three feet in diameter, drawn out to a comet's streak by its passage through the air. The light bounced up and down over bits of turbulence, then swerved in and touched his wing. It vanished and the power meters jumped on the control board. Holden heard a rip of static on his headphones.

He tugged the plane toward the west. A dozen more lights blazed out of a misty shoulder of cloud and tumbled through the air in varied colors like diamonds, rubies, and emeralds. Holden leaned on the stick and shaded his eyes.

The Harrier stood on its nose and dived, the spheres streaking over him like tracer bullets. In the space of seconds, thousands of feet of altitude were lopped off from under him and he was back in darkness.

"Watch it . . . watch it . . . What are you doing, Holden!" G forces tided Holden's blood and body liquids into his head, flooding the cockpit into a bloodshot daze interspersed with the St. Elmo's fire caused by the friction of his passage through the charged air. He floated weightlessly in the restraining straps trying to sort out which of the two sinking altimeters was the real one. The blood crowded his eyes, confusing his vision, and he kept pawing at the oxygen feed.

His left hand caught the valve and turned it up. Oxygen gushed into his lungs, holding the daze at bay. His eyesight stabilized at thirteen thousand feet. He eased the plunging plane's nose toward the horizon. "Okay," he gasped. "Sorry. I lost a little altitude."

"You went down like a sinker. Come left or you'll wind up in South America."

Holden coasted out of the clouds. His thumb touched a camera button. Damn! He ground his teeth in frustration. One move two inches to the left and he would have caught everything on high speed film. That was the only chance he would ever have. He punched the camera button anyway and emptied the film with shots of Itrek lying in the sea ahead.

Kilgallen regarded Holden's reddened eyes with awe. "Ball lightning. I didn't think there was any such thing."

Holden sipped coffee as he shrugged out of the flight suit. "Neither did I. They say that when General Electric conducted lightning tests on the Empire State Building in the 1930s, the engineers saw four of them going down the tower after it had been hit by lightning. Since it didn't register on the oscilloscope, they didn't officially report it. That might explain a lot of UFO stories, too."

Axton asked, "When will it hit the ozone layer, then?"

"At its present rate, I'd say about an hour. That ought to be some show. It's going to blow out radio and reception over half the Pacific." He jammed his hands into his back pockets trying to read secrets from the swirl of colors on the infrared screen. "In a way, none of this has anything to do with Windowpane."

Mason had been gloomily watching the darkening sky and rising wind through the window. He turned to Holden. "Now ain't that funny. Ain't that a coincidence that a storm comes out of nowhere just when we drill a hole in the sky."

"The low-pressure center was here when we arrived. The laser caused it to do something, but *it*, Mason, *it* has been here for days. Blame the Navy for the laser but not for this storm." Holden noticed the blip of the *Adair* was a good forty miles away—still in the area from which it had sunk the *Knoxville*. "Why are they so far away?"

Kilgallen retorted, "Why do you think! They didn't want to get caught in the rain."

Holden yawned to ease the pressure headache in his skull. The coffee was making him feel worse rather than better. He longed for a beer.

"What happens after it touches the ozone layer?" Tregaskis asked in a small voice. "Will there be lightning?"

"Yes. And rain by the bucketful."

"The reason I ask," the botanist persisted, "is that I'm a little, well, nervous around lightning."

Mason looked him up and down, from his curly hair to his pressed pants, then spat into a trash can. "Don't worry, digger, you won't even feel it when it hits you. Unless you're just paralyzed maybe and suffocate and we don't realize you're still alive . . ."

"That's not funny," Tregaskis said. "I can't help it, it's a phobia. Besides, look what happened to the fishing boat."

Croft broke in, "He's made a painful point, hasn't he? What did happen to the fishing boat, Holden?"

"They were too close to the storm," Holden told them. "I don't think we'll get any lightning up here."

"Is that a U.S. weatherman prediction?"

"Look," Holden answered, "I'm sure the purpose of the storm is to balance out the ionosphere charge. I can't think of a reason for it to move up this way."

None of them looked very happy. Croft complained, "Electrical fields. Electrical charges. Ball lightning. Everything from my wife to the storm keeps coming down to electricity. Mr. Kilgallen, in engineering, why does one pass an electrical charge through an electrical field?"

Kilgallen rested his cheek on his hand. "To amplify it maybe. Pick it up. We goose signals from deep-space probes so high you can hear the molecules bumping together."

"Is that conceivably what happened to us? Is it possible we were amplified somehow?"

Kilgallen looked as if an odor had emanated from Croft. "No. But— for the hell of it—why?"

"Like your space signals. To be picked up. Recorded on something."

Axton shook his head at Croft's apparent daffiness. All of them appeared acutely embarrassed by the biologist's wandering thoughts. Tregaskis suddenly found his shirt buttons fascinating and Holden ran his fingers over the console buttons.

"Recorded on what, Dr. Croft?"

It occurred to Holden that Croft may not have entirely recovered from the effects of the hallucination. He had been preoccupied all day and now looked more frail than ever. It could have been some kind of physical fatigue, but Holden suspected Croft was still thinking about his wife. He recalled the banked emotion behind his voice when he spoke about her and that sad look, so different from his general liveliness, seemed permanently etched on his features.

"I am a biologist," Croft observed quietly. "Sometimes you get a feeling for when a causal force is natural or . . ." His voice petered out and he smiled self-consciously.

Holden said, "Or what, Dr. Croft?"

"Never mind. I will enter my mad thoughts in the Red Book and let posterity amuse itself over them. You said the storm will touch the ionosphere in an hour, Mr. Holden?"

"That's a guess. I plan to watch it from the roof."

To Mason, Croft said, "Customarily I collect fauna samples from the varied locations where the government sends me. I wonder if I might do some poking around for insects for awhile."

"You don't have to ask me, sir," Mason said.

They did not speak until Croft, a canvas bag full of screen-topped bottles on his shoulder, was safely out the door and poking down the beach with a walking stick. Kilgallen spread his hands and looked quizzically at them. "Can anybody tell me what he was getting at?"

"I don't think he's gotten over his wife," Axton mused. "Corny as it sounds."

Holden turned back to the satellite screens. He rubbed his eyes and barely stifled an exclamation. The tower was now only two or three miles short of the ozone layer, but it looked to his still-dazed eyes as though the smaller storm had separated itself and moved north. He glanced out the window at the anemometer, which revealed the wind moving directly south. It had to be his imagination. He swallowed two aspirin and yawned to relieve his headache.

X PLUS 7 HOURS 30 MINUTES

"Farnsworth?"

"Yes, Itrek."

"Get a prognosis on the storm from Jameson. You see what's happening." Holden spoke in a low, tight voice. "As soon as he comes up with something, call me back immediately." Holden grabbed a pair of binoculars and his windbreaker jacket. "Mason, we should be able to see it from the roof. Want to come up with me?"

The separation of the storms had not been Holden's imagination. On the infrared screen the wind bridge between them stretched taut as the smaller storm pushed northward straight for Itrek while the south tower made its final thousand foot push to the ozone layer. On the screen it resembled a microbe splitting in two. Radar showed it closing around Itrek from five miles away.

Unimpeded by trees or the sea wall, the wind on the roof tore against their clothes, forcing Holden to grip an antenna stanchion for balance. Mason leaned against the wind, feet braced on the concrete.

The CDA overlooked the trees, past the cliffs of Itrek's south shore, and they could see the storm approaching. It was a massive, flat yellowish gale, slightly concave with tendrils of rain dangling from its belly. So far there was no evidence of lightning.

Both studied it in silence through the binoculars. Then Holden looked at the antenna wires humming in the wind that blew against his back, his mind completely confused.

"Holden?"

"Yes."

"It's going directly against the wind. A twenty-nine knot wind."

"Yes. That's why it's flat like that."

"This is a new one on me, Holden."

"Me, too."

The storm moved with deceptive speed, its mass swallowing up the sea and the higher black clouds flowing south. Lacking lightning and thunder, it seemed placid enough but its behavior was imcomprehensible. Its stolid motion was slow but steady at ten miles an hour, but Holden knew a killer storm when he saw one.

"You better send somebody after Croft right now, Mason."

Mason was descending the ladder when the sky ignited in a pool of silent lightning that fired the smoky overcast. Holden dropped his binoculars and covered his dazzled eyes as more bolts concatenated across the heavens.

The lightning was continuous, of sunburst intensity, and it frosted the tossing foliage and heaving sea with turgid, rich color that converted Itrek into an unearthly landscape of mad hues from a Bosch painting.

"Bull's eye," Holden cried, hand shading his eyes. "It's hit the ozone layer."

The wind swept over the jungle wet and warm, smelling of rain as they clambered to the ground. In the CDA, Kilgallen was busily clicking color exposures of the fiery sky with his tripod mounted camera.

"Kilgallen, run out and bring back Croft," Mason ordered.

Kilgallen swallowed loudly and looked out the window. "You mean now?"

"Yes, now," Mason roared.

"There's a tidal pool at the other end of the island," Holden said. "He's probably down there collecting samples. *Now*, Kilgallen, before the storm gets here."

Kilgallen's jaw clenched but he kept his temper as he pulled on a waterproof poncho and dashed out the door. Holden banged on the radio and called the *Adair*. "Damn it, Farnsworth, what's Jameson doing?"

A babble of voices, then Jameson spoke with forced cheerfulness. *You dumb bastard, you're on the fence now*, Holden thought. "Holden, we think the island will break that storm of yours up. The front's already weakening."

"Who's we?"

"Me and *McClusky*'s weather officer. It'll all be over in about an hour."

A blizzard of static all but buried the words, but they could hear each other faintly. "Does anybody know why it's going against the wind?"

Jameson said, "No. We'll have to analyze our data back in the states."

That was the best Jameson could offer. The storm would break up in an hour or so after hitting the island and in truth Holden could not think up anything better. He joined the other men at the window.

Mason said, "I was watching you. You almost stopped Windowpane, didn't you?"

Holden remembered his hands hovering near the Abort button. "I thought about it, but I didn't have a good reason."

"If you'd had another minute could you have come up with one?"

"Yes. And another reason not to."

Rubbing his jaw, Mason studied the thick, dark clouds roiling among themselves. The sky crawled with movement and the wind blasted spume over the sea wall.

Then wisps of yellow cloud began to creep over Itrek's swaying trees, obscuring the high-altitude lightning. The storm was a swirling shroud of fog moving directly opposite the higher clouds and as it dimmed the lightning like a sliding hatch cover, the birds and mosquitoes grew quiet. The wisps became a wall, seamless, relentless in its forge against the winds. Slowly the storm settled heavily over the entire island.

They watched for a sign of Croft and Kilgallen. Axton leafed through a magazine with an exaggerated show of calm and Tregaskis occupied himself with placing an avocado pit in a glass of water. Holden switched on the interior lights and watched the infrared screen. Itrek was completely buried under the blanket of clouds.

The CDA was a refuge, a fortress island within an island, squat and hunched in the sand, built to withstand intense solar radiation. Holden tried to feel safe with this realization. On the *Adair*, Jameson would be watching the radars, riffling through charts and mumbling meaningless words about squall lines and occluded fronts.

What had Croft been trying to say?

Static screeched in a long wail from the speaker. Holden heard a muffled exclamation from Axton and glass break as Tregaskis dropped the avocado and rushed to the window.

Across the length of Itrek, thousands of spinning lights trailing gossamer threads of smoke appeared in the air like swarms of fireflies that dappled the foliage, the tormented sea, and the thick, yellow clouds. Some flopped over the ground, some rose struggling from the jungle but most streaked about in the eddies of wind.

Axton activated Kilgallen's camera as one of the lights bumped into the reinforced glass window. It was a burning moth, electrical fire haloing its body. It glowed for a few seconds, then disintegrated to ash scattered on the wind.

Mason, Axton, and Tregaskis watched the dark miracle in silence. Holden's eyes went to the galvanometer which measured the electrical content of the air. The needle was climbing upward in small charged jerks.

Tregaskis spoke. "Mr. Holden, what's happening?"

"The same thing that happened to the fishermen. Only moths and other insects have the simplest nervous systems. They're the easiest to find."

Axton said icily, "You're talking as if the storm were alive."

"Yes. That's what Croft would say if he were here."

When the lights appeared, Edward Croft was on Itrek's south end bent over the body of a shark that had washed ashore. The dorsal fin was notched as though a bite had been taken from it. Spreading across its body were burn streaks. It had been killed with a single bolt of electricity.

Croft's feet were tired and his legs ached. Only five years ago, he could walk beaches for hours and feel deliciously tired when he returned to his house for tea. The body he had always taken for granted was giving up on him. Climbing over the black volcanic rocks had wiped out his frail reserves of energy. Puffing for breath, he sat by a tidal pool and lowered his sack to the ground to watch the storm move in over the island.

He was not frightened, indeed he was mildly content, for the sight of his wife on the Niagara Falls lookout kept wafting into his thoughts. He did not want to push the memory out—it was too pleasant and his loneliness had been so painful since her death. He contemplated his life and found it on the whole successful. In the sample bottles were several species of moth and a red unidentifiable spider digging at the glass wall. He had led a placid, rather circumscribed life examining creatures such as these.

He tried to push himself out of his reverie and consider the problem of the fishing boat. It was quite simple, really, no more complex than taking a photograph. Instead of light the gremlin, as Holden termed it, saw electrical fields. Instead of printing on photographic paper, it printed them on . . . on . . .

He looked up at the yellow clouds overhead. Suddenly he had the strange sensation that the world had turned upside down and he was suspended in the air looking down at a bubbling cauldron.

Croft's life had been spent studying life. He knew by instinct when life was present.

Eyes still fixed on the sky, Croft climbed to his feet as Itrek erupted with glowing sparks, *quite beautiful really*, describing eddies of motion that hopped over the ground. Sand fleas formed little arches of light as they flopped on the sands and the gnats and flies were pinprick stars beside the sullen glow of the dragonflies.

A bird flapped out of the trees, its wings fighting the currents of air. It soared in clumsy bumps over the sea, then circled in again.

A crooked strand of clear, white, blindingly intense light seared into Croft's eyes, one end anchored to a fat bulge of cloud, the other delicately touching the bird. Trailed by blasted feathers, the bird's steaming body plummeted into the surf and a whipcrack of thunder trembled the ground.

Croft felt his body tingle as though a net were tightening around him. His beard spread into a frizz, the hairs on his body tickled from his skin and stood erect.

Croft splashed through the tidal pool for the trees, dragging his sack behind him. Then everything disappeared, the seas, the jungle, the sky itself and Windowpane became something that would take place forty years in the future. He was back on his honeymoon standing by his bride looking into the misted depths of Niagara Falls.

Kilgallen had been puffing through the trees to the beach, preparing to shout at Croft when the bird was killed. When Croft began running, he realized there was absolutely nothing he could do, save flatten himself out on the ground.

Croft was almost to the trees when the bolt struck him, a sinuous vein of cold distilled fire, thousands of feet long. The superheated air separated by the lightning slammed together in a pointed thunderclap that whirled sand into his face. Croft fell to the ground, stiff as a board. More bolts crackled into his canvas bag killing the creatures in the bottles, blasting canvas and glass over the sand.

On his belly Kilgallen backed into the trees. He could feel that thundercloud pressing down on him. Lightning occurred when ions swarmed out of the ground into pointed, jagged objects—a treetop, a steeple, a house, a person—called discharge points as the insulation of the air dispersed and an imbalance built up into a thundercloud overhead. Humans could feel themselves turning into discharge points by the tingle of the skin.

Kilgallen lay motionless as rain scoured in from the sea, pounding craters into the sand, and tearing the jungle fronds and leaves to shreds. It was warm rain, smelling of ozone. Kilgallen looked at his fingers. No tingle. He jumped to his feet and, regretting his lapse from Catholicism, pawed through real and imagined sins as he raced through the drizzling foliage back to the CDA.

X PLUS 8 HOURS 30 MINUTES

THE LIGHTNING flared across the island and the roll of thunder rattled the windows. As if a drain had been opened, rain came booming up from the south.

Mason asked, "Where did that hit, Axton?"

Axton pointed south. "Over there. A tree, I guess."

The ionospheric lightning was dwindling and the burning insects had all died. Holden realized he would never have to worry about spiders on Itrek again. Bitterly he watched the storms on radar. The main tower was shrinking, the lightning cooling off, which meant the ozone layer had been sealed up again. "Farnsworth?" he said into the microphone. ":What are you picking up on radar?"

"A lot of static. What's going on?"

"The storm has just killed all the insects on the island."

"Huh?"

"Huh!" Holden mimicked him. "They were electrocuted just like the fishing boat."

"Stay inside, good buddy, that's all I can say. Jameson still says it will break up in an hour."

"If you call me good buddy again, Farnsworth, I'll punch you out."

They heard the shouting above the rush of rain. Mason yanked open the door. Down the beach they could see through the gloom the white form of Kilgallen running toward them. As he passed the equipment towers, Holden saw the galvanometer needle tick to the side and click against the screws. The towers were surging with ions.

"Get on the ground!" Holden screamed out the door. "Lightning!"

As Kilgallen stumbled to a confused stop and looked for shelter, the wind paused as though a deep breath were being drawn prior to a burst of activity. Holden cried, "Get *down*!"

Kilgallen pancaked into the sand as serpents of fire split out of the air and touched the towers. They flew to pieces in a pinwheeling hail of glass, wiring, metal casings, and crossbraces. The bolts sent a tidal wave of current surging through the ground cables into the CDA where bedlam broke loose.

Sparks of blue flame popped connector plugs from consoles and hurled plastic bits over the floor. The radar and TV screens exploded simultaneously like grenades as the circuits within the walls and machinery were savaged by heat into lumps of plastic fused with metal. The fluorescent lights flared, then extinguished with a sizzle, plunging the CDA into a choking gloom. Holden threw the auxiliary power switch before it could automatically come on, fearing the current would attract more lightning.

On the beach Kilgallen peeped over his arms at the smoking holes where the tower foundations had been sunk and which now held blackened concrete blocks. He climbed to his feet and started running again. Holden thought the expression on his face was that of someone who had seen a dead man. Maybe Croft. Maybe himself.

The heavy ensign managed one last look at the yellow sky as the first stroke blew him clean off the beach in a vicious stab of light and thunder. He hit a tree, then was forked back into the air by two more bolts before falling into the brush.

All but Mason were paralyzed with horror. He grabbed Axton's shoulders, pulled him from the door and closed it tight, then rolled the steel shutters across the window. Pushing Axton across the room he booted him in the rear. "Close the shutters on that window!"

Tregaskis cowered under the chart table. Mason grabbed his ankles and dragged him out. "It's metal, you dumb flit." He kicked at the debris littering the floor, then hauled Tregaskis to his feet. "Close the shutter and then clean this mess up or we'll be falling all over the place." Tregaskis stumbled across the room and helped Axton fasten the latches.

Again the wind paused, then light flared through the interstices of the metal shutters and the tiny crack under the door. Instead of thunder there was a subsonic grunt and the crash of the microwave towers and ladder toppling from the roof. A second soft, engulfing *whump* spilled in more white light and curled the metal trim around the door. Millions of volts pumped through the finery of the microcircuits, crumpling and over-powering them. The CDA equipment was totaled. Even if they turned on the emergency power, there were no circuits left for it to flow through. They were sealed off from the world.

"Isn't there . . ." Axton cleared the squeak from his voice. "Isn't there a small radio downstairs? I believe I stacked my bottles next to it."

Holden pulled wires from the broken light. "The walls are two feet thick in here. Who's going outdoors to call the *Adair*?"

"Now wait a minute," Mason said. "Farnsworth told me all about his equipment. If they can pick up a sub through fifty miles of ocean and thermal layers, they can hear a radio. They could sniff out Tregaskis's hair spray."

Tregaskis stood up clutching a piece of fluorescent tubing. "Mason, lay *off*!"

"Go down and get the radio before you have a heart attack."

Tregaskis ran a trembling hand over his face. "We should try to find Kilgallen . . ."

"Go ahead. Right out the door. Feel his pulse. And after *you're* fried, I'll send someone out after you."

Tregaskis dropped the tubing and slouched through the low door leading to the storage room downstairs. As soon as it closed behind him, Axton said, "Not that I understand the loneliness of command, Mason, but I fail to see why you treat him like that."

"He's a freak, that's why. He shouldn't even be here. Holden, where's the lightning now?"

"I expect it's trying to figure out how to get at us. It knows where we are but it can't come in. The antenna cables must still be intact. They're our ground."

Holden chewed a fingernail, listening to the whispering rain. "A couple of things could happen," he admitted. "If the air gets too damp, it could lose its insulation quality. And a few more strokes might melt the antenna wires like Kanabe's teeth and we won't be grounded after that. We have to keep the CDA as tight as a drum even if we suffocate. We can't let it in."

Axton regarded Holden coldly. "It's sort of like a bloodhound, isn't it?"

"That's right. Only it sniffs out electrical fields. I think Croft was saying it imprinted our nervous systems with that charge this morning so it could find us again."

"I don't see why it didn't kill us when it had the chance then."

"I don't think it had the strength. Imprinting all those bugs and birds and the gear in here and the destroyer used up a lot of power. It takes ten minutes for a cloud to recharge after expending a bolt. Besides, it wanted to conserve its energy to get up to the ozone layer." He kicked away a fused circuit board from the television. "It's got the strength now. It could probably blow Itrek out of the water if it wanted."

Axton looked at Mason for confirmation of what he was hearing but Mason was watching the door as though a tiger were caged behind it. "Holden, is there any precedent for this thing?"

"What can I tell you? Lightning's always been capricious. It can kill a baby in its mother's arms and never touch the mother. Sometimes it hits the same tree year after year and ignores the radio tower next to it. Maybe there's something about certain people or objects that gets imprinted on storms and draws electricity, something about discharge points we never knew."

Tregaskis backed into the room dragging a box with U.S. NAVY stamped on it. The radio was packed in waterproof, shockproof stuffing and to Holden it looked too small to signal anything. Mason set it on the floor and tuned it to *Adair*'s frequency.

To Holden's amazement, in less than a minute the destroyer's gear had reached across the seas, through the storm, and into the room to snatch the signal. Farnsworth's voice came in clearly. "Itrek . . . Hello, Itrek . . . What's going on there, Holden?"

"The power's out. Croft and Kilgallen were killed by lightning. Get Jameson again."

The forced cheerfulness was replaced by a deep calm, as though

Jameson had decided to subdue panic. The son of a bitch should be a radio announcer, Holden thought.

Holden ground his teeth together before speaking through them. "Jameson, it's killed two men, all the insects and birds, and wiped out the CDA. What else is it doing?"

"According to our radar, there's scattered lightning all over Itrek. Not even lightning, actually, just bits of static."

Birds. Snakes. Bats. Reptiles. The storm was picking out everything alive on the island. For an instant, Holden hoped wildly, the storm would forget about the humans, become so occupied with the vermin that its charge would abate or move away.

"What does *McClusky* say?"

Jameson sighed. "Holden, try to relax. The forecast is the same. Computer data clearly states the storm will be gone in an hour. Just sit tight and stay cool. Okay?"

Fearful that the tiny battery current would somehow attract the fury that had destroyed Kilgallen, Holden shut off the radio. The four men looked at each other. Two days before they had been total strangers, now their kindred spirits might soon be orbiting each other for eternity.

If they survived, he would laugh about this with Gina in a few years. He knew he should be thinking more about Gina. People were supposed to remember friends, loved ones, and good times when their lives were in peril.

The wind rose again and Holden knew their respite was over. The flashes were so hot, they steamed the water leaking under the door and made the sweep hand of his stopwatch as visible as if he were standing in sunlight.

Like artillery shells coming in with spaced regularity, the bolts smashed into the CDA an average of four times a minute. Each bolt, Holden explained, was not a single flash but a series of "steps" inching down from a cloud at a speed of a fifty millionth of a second behind a leader that twists its way past nonconductive air, thus giving lightning its crooked appearance. Three quarters of the way to the ground, streamers of electrons rise up to meet the leader like a lover greeting a returning mate. The kiss lasts no longer than a hundredth of a second, but it releases an average of thirty-seven hundred million kilowatts of power, more than the combined capacity of every electrical power plant in America.

The CDA air grew so hot and sticky they removed their shirts. The bolts raised the hairs on their bodies until the constant itch had them scratching welts in their skin. Tregaskis reached for a glassine envelope full of seeds. As his arms went above his head, ten blue coronas spat from his fingertips. The botanist screamed, then collapsed to the floor. Mason picked him up and put him in a swivel chair, curled up against the flaming, lurid blasts with his head in his hands. His body had become a ground conductor.

The glass on the east window burst under the heat in a spray of superheated droplets that sizzled against the steel shutters. The current passing through the wires in the walls pumped heat into the air. "It's turning into an oven," Mason whispered to Holden. "But the walls are holding. So I guess we'll just cook."

More than these physical anomalies, Holden felt a creeping invasion of his mind. He saw spiders everywhere, crouching in the blown-out television, hiding in the light fixtures. He confused his memories of Gina with those of his mother and saw faces he had not remembered in years.

Tregaskis fainted twice. The second time he could not remember where he was. Axton kept confusing the west window with the east and Mason muttered about a Manila prostitute. Those whom the Gods destroy, Holden reasoned, they first drive mad.

Holden anchored his hopes on the passage of Jameson's hour, but after thirty-five minutes hairline cracks had appeared in the ceiling of the CDA. He struggled between memories of Gina and fear of spiders to comprehend this latest development when he became aware the lightning had stopped.

They listened to the rain. Axton said, "Maybe Jameson was right."

"It's not letting up," Holden replied. "The rain's too heavy. Something else is happening."

"Son of a gun," Mason breathed. "Somebody's walking around with a light out there."

A glow shone through the shutters facing west, slatting into bars of light that spilled across the floor. Tregaskis walked to the window.

"It's a searchlight," Axton mused. "It's too bright for a spotlight. The ship must be here."

"Tregaskis, stay put," Holden warned. "I don't like this."

The light moved sideways from the window toward the back of the CDA, circled the blockhouse and, with an ugly, audible hiss, appeared behind the other shutters. Ripples of rain flowing down the glass caused wavering patterns on the wall from the illumination.

The light brightened; then, as soft dough squeezes through a collander's holes, a three-foot globe of light seethed through the shutter slats into the CDA, it's fiery surface writhing with swirls of energy.

"It's ball lightning," Holden said calmly. "Stay away from it."

The globe, a hovering, disembodied eye that wafted over the chart table toward the metal ceiling fixtures, smelled of ozone.

Holden picked up the console microphone and cord, wound the metal plug of the cord around a table leg and knotted it. Then he swung the metal microphone around his head like a bolero and loosed it at the lightning. The microphone struck it dead center, force-grounding it like a burst balloon. The cord writhed and sparks spat from the knotted end. Holden drew back the microphone and awaited another one.

The glass sprayed out of the west window shutters in fiery drops as a second ball slid in. Smaller and faster than the first, it soared to the ceiling where Holden failed to hit it with the microphone. The ball dropped to the floor, and rebounded toward Axton, who was hiding behind the chart table. The microphone touched the edge, the ball burst with a nervous pop, and again sparks shot out of the cord.

The third ball, the size of an orange, whizzed merrily around Mason's head before sucking itself into oblivion on the television screen rim. Holden passed the cord to Mason and switched on the radio. "*Adair. Farnsworth?*"

"Yeah, Holden. The Captain's here with Jameson."

"The air in here is conducting electricity. We've had it."

The Captain had a thin, taut voice. "Holden? Jameson still insists the storm will break soon."

"Captain, this storm won't break until we're dead. We can't get out the door."

The Captain said, "We cannot mount a rescue or anything like that, Holden. We couldn't get a boat close enough."

"I think I've got an idea. What's your position?"

"We're about forty-two miles west of you, just outside the storm."

"Are there any clear skies near you?"

"Yes. It's pretty calm west of us. The big storm is breaking up south of here. In fact you've got the worst weather around at this point."

"My idea is to run Windowpane again. I don't mean at full strength. Just to get the light up to the ionosphere and tickle it a little. I think the storm will go after it." He was amused to hear Jameson's feeble protests.

The Captain said, "Stand by, Itrek. We're going to talk this over."

Tregaskis was seated in a chair, hands clenched together, his nerves

71

obviously pulled to the breaking point. Although Holden felt sorry for people unable to fit themselves in anywhere, he saw that Naval Weapons Center had chosen him shrewdly. Tregaskis needed to prove himself in the worst way. "Won't be long now until you're back at your crabgrass," Holden said consolingly.

Tregaskis unclenched his hands and sat on them. "I can't get those balls out of my mind. They hung there like they were watching us. I *know* they were watching us."

"We were watching them, too. It goes both ways in the jungle, Tregaskis."

The Captain's voice came over the radio. "Okay, Itrek. We're targeting the ionosphere northwest of our position about twelve miles away. No window, just a lot of heat. Hang on."

They pulled their wet shirts back on and gathered their Red Books. Tregaskis stuffed seedlings into his pocket.

Holden said, "What we do is we run for the copter as soon as we're sure there's no more lightning. Then fly straight to the *Adair*. That is if I'm right. If I'm not right, I'll go around to each and every one of you and offer a sincere apology which I hope you'll accept as we go to heaven. If that's where we're going. I'm not sure about Mason."

As Holden tucked in his shirt, Farnsworth called, "Thirty seconds to firing." He smiled. The destroyer crew must be setting a record for cranking up the laser. They were probably still running to action stations.

Mason stood before the door, hands on hips as if challenging it to a duel. This time their feeling was one of anticipation, rather than fear.

"Firing is commenced."

Holden clicked off the seconds on his stopwatch.

"Firing is completed."

The wind shifted direction toward the west and blew rain through the shutters from the broken window. For several minutes the storm howled the length of Itrek, musical thrums singing from the fallen aerials, rain gurgling down the walls. Then the air in the CDA cooled and sweetened. The rain faded to a drizzle. Still they waited, until, through the slats of the shutters, Holden saw faint orange bars of sunlight.

X PLUS 9 HOURS 30 MINUTES

Mason pushed the door against the tangle of fallen equipment and stepped outside. Around the building, a thicket of clawed, twisted branches had sprouted from the sand. Holden touched one, feeling it crumble to crusty grains of sand. "Fulgurites. The lightning petrified the sand into the shape of the bolt. I bet they go down four or five feet."

The gnarled bushes coiling around their feet seemed the only things alive on Itrek. Nothing moved and no sound came to them save the dripping rainwater. False life, Holden thought kicking at the fulgurites. Sand turned into imitation brush.

Kilgallen's remains were buried in brush, his scorched poncho covering his head. The bolts had burned most of his clothes and the Ensign looked fat, vulnerable, and pitiful lying in the mud. They looked silently at him for a few seconds, then at the clouds moving west of them. The squat plug-ugly CDA was silhouetted against the clouds, its bulk subtly reduced into powdery corners, cratered walls, and cracked plaster.

Tregaskis covered his face and turned away. For once Mason did not taunt him. The Petty Officer jammed a stick into the mud as a marker. "The *Adair* can pick him up. They'll find Croft, too. It's still a twelve-knot wind, Holden. Can you lift off in this?"

"I could fly underwater to get out of here."

The copter and hangar were untouched by lightning. On the beach they faced the copter into the wind. Axton and Tregaskis clambered into the cargo area, Mason strapped himself in beside Holden. In the air Holden circled the CDA once, then roared out to sea. "So far, so good, Farnsworth. Where should we rendezvous?"

"We're headed northeast now. Holden?" There was an undercurrent in Farnsworth's voice. "Do you think you can make the *McClusky*?"

The gas tank was half full, but that would get them to the carrier, barring another disaster. "I think so. What's up?"

"It looks like your storm is coming straight for us. The wind's up. I don't think you can land."

"I don't get it. I thought you'd be north of it."

"Oh, nothing to worry about. The Captain says it's just passing us on its way to the window. Try us again in ten minutes or so." Farnsworth gave Holden a rendezvous point which he marked on his kneepad.

Their last view of Itrek was of the island lying wet and green in the sea, lonely and rather fragile. The storm formed a curved boomerang in the sky, the north horn spreading between the copter and the *Adair*.

The destroyer would be moving fast at flank speed. It would have got underway the second the laser was shut down. Nevertheless Holden tried to shake off the coldness creeping up his back.

*   *   *

Half an hour later, the Long Ranger was hovering in the winds, helplessly witnessing a disaster in the making. They were at the rendezvous point, but the *Adair* had hit heavy seas and was forced to reduce speed.

Mason chewed a knuckle and peered at the haze through binoculars. "I don't get it," he said over and over. "The storm is fast but it ain't that fast. That ship can do forty knots."

"It's the fault of whoever targeted the laser. They should have fired south. The storm has to pass the ship to get to the window. Don't worry, they'll make it."

Holden climbed another thousand feet, fearful of getting too close to the storm. All they could do was stay within radio range so the *Adair* would not feel alone.

"Itrek, this is Flag. Do you read us?" It was an unfamiliar voice. Flag was the carrier *McClusky*, probably tracking what appeared to be a goofy helicopter.

"This is Itrek, *McClusky*."

"Can you give us anything on this storm? It was supposed to break up over Itrek. Now it's growing again."

"They fired the laser in the wrong direction. The storm's cut the *Adair* off."

"What? Laser? Say again."

Holden felt the foolish vertigo resulting from putting one's foot in one's mouth. *Adair* had never cleared the laser with Flag. "*McClusky*, did you talk to Jameson about the storm?"

"He said it was just a squall. What's this about the laser, Itrek? Say again." The voice was impatient, demanding, scenting a secret.

"Oh, shitfire," Holden breathed. Static blossomed around the *Adair*'s blip. Lightning was assaulting the ship. Holden pushed the copter higher as rain rushed over them. "Farnsworth?"

Farnsworth's words were fractured by interference. ". . . all over the damned place. This is really unbeliev . . ."

"Can you run the laser a third time, Farnsworth? Shoot it back to Itrek?"

". . . can't get on deck. Ho ho . . . a ro . . . coaster."

Holden drove straight into the winds until the thermals swirled the copter about with sledgehammer blows. Mason braced his arms on the dash and Tregaskis, with a choked apology, threw up in the cargo area. Holden corkscrewed another five hundred feet of altitude until the windscreen was a spray-blasted blank. The small gain brought Farnsworth's last words to him.

"Everything's battened down like a drum here. Itrek? Now I know why they call these boats tin cans. Isn't this fun? Isn't this a barrel full of . . ."

Static screamed out of Holden's headphones, a rampaging banshee racing through his skull. The *Adair*'s blip vanished on the radar, replaced by a glitter of flying metal. Outside the windows the blasts combined into a pulsing sun trying to break through the murk as thousands of tons of high explosives, ASROC sub torpedoes, surface-to-air missiles, and packed ammunition ignited in the rain. The ship continued exploding even after the debris had fallen back into the sea, until absolutely nothing was left and shock waves catapulted the copter backwards.

"Flag, Flag! It's blown up, the *Adair*'s blown up!" But Holden's cry was lost in the babble of Fleet Communications crowding the airwaves, all reporting the explosions simultaneously. Where the *Adair* had been, waves of lightning continued to hit, sending thunder grunting through the winds. They were picking off electrical components, modular housings, batteries, capacitors, and survivors, anything with an electrical field.

"Itrek, can you effect a rescue?"

"Negative, Flag. Stay out. Keep all air and sea traffic out of there. Nobody's alive. We're coming in."

Sick to his stomach, Holden faced the copter toward the sunlight, homing in on the carrier's beam. *McClusky*'s voice came at him again, loud and deliberately alarming. "Itrek, you are being tracked by a missile, range five thousand yards and closing bearing . . ."

Holden clawed the copter upward with such violence, Axton and Tregaskis went tumbling down the floor in a confused mass of seed containers and bottles.

"Range three thousand yards and closing, continue evasive action."

It would be a Hawk missile with a heat-seeking nose, sucking in from low on their left toward the Long Ranger's exhaust. The exploding destroyer had triggered it. The altimeter agonized past two thousand feet, three thousand three hundred, four hundred . . . Mason half stood in his seat watching the clouds.

"Range one thousand yards and closing." Then Flag counted off the distance with metronomic regularity. "Nine hundred yards, eight hundred yards, seven hundred . . ."

At five hundred yards, Holden plunged the copter toward the sea, flinging Axton, Tregaskis, and the gear onto the roof. The waves rushed up to the windscreen as a lance of fire flashed by them, its backwash slapping the copter rotors. Fifty feet above the sea, Holden laid the copter on its right side and peeled off as a fighter pilot banks in for the kill.

The missile looped around and came at them again, flicking between main and tail rotors too close to the water to rise again. The explosion was a steamy concussion whose shock wave hit the copter just as Holden leveled off and belly-whumped the craft over the waves.

Whoops of excitement, applause, and whistles rang through their headphones and Mason joyfully pounded Holden's back. The Petty Officer shouted at Axton and Tregaskis, "Did you see that? Was that beautiful?" The Flag Operator exulted, "Good damned show, Holden. You can fly me any day."

The sunlight bathed the copter as they left the shadow of the storm on the horizon and flew through honey-smooth air down the radio path to the *McClusky*, a flat board in the distance, serrated with the folded wings of planes. Holden buzzed the carrier's island and saw the crew lined up to wave at them. The Landing Signal Officer guided him in. A swell raised the carrier's rear as the copter came down and the right gear crumpled up. Holden was reaching for the ignition to cut it off lest the spinning blades tilt against the steel when the engine coughed and died. The gas gauge was empty.

Axton and Tregaskis opened the cargo door and kicked out the broken bottles of sea water. Mason climbed out on his side, thankful to be on a deck again. Jeffrey Holden sat in the cockpit, hand gripping the pitch stick. They had to peel him out of the Long Ranger.

X PLUS 12 HOURS

THIS TIME the Fleet managed to get warnings out to air and sea transmitting stations from Singapore to Korea that atmospheric disturbances in the Central Pacific would knock radio systems off the air. When the storm tower touched the ionosphere that evening, the crews of the ships were out on deck to watch the fireworks.

As soon as the weather cleared around the *Adair*'s last position, planes circled the roiling waters. They found only an oil slick, some cork, bits of insulation, and a few bobbing chairs. The destroyer and crew had been swallowed up without a trace.

The remainder of the day Holden felt incoming lightning tickling his skin and saw spiders everywhere on the *McClusky* even though the sky was clear. When he became tired he became paranoid. He wondered if he had killed the men on the ship by letting Windowpane happen at all, then by running the laser a second time. He wandered through the lower decks of the *McClusky*, unable to eat or sleep, jumpy and short tempered, going over, again and again, every single step in Windowpane.

As the Windowpane planners had calculated, there were no widows, no orphans, or bereft mothers, no families to report to after the loss of the ship. Croft, Kilgallen, and the crew of the *Adair* would be buried in obscurity. Nonpersons.

Mason came up beside Holden to watch the storm tower in the distance which blotted out the scarlet setting sun. Over the *McClusky* stars appeared. Mason hiccupped rum fumes. "I owe you a keg of beer for being a good pilot."

Holden looked around the carrier, "Do you feel something?"

"Don't go doing that to me, Holden, just when I'm feeling nice and safe!"

"It's like eyes. Like being watched . . ." His voice was muffled by the earsplitting shriek of a Tomcat plane hooking to a stop on the cables.

"We're out of it, Holden. It won't reach as far as the Fleet."

"It's like being watched by something without eyes," Holden repeated stubbornly. Restlessly, he walked among the parked planes, Mason lurching along behind him, an amiable drunk. Axton and Tregaskis were sound asleep somewhere in the ship. The Captain had offered rum as congratulations to them all and Mason had overdone it a little.

"So you'll be seeing your girlfriend soon. What'll you tell her?"

"I don't think I'll be doing much talking, if you know what I mean. Mason, we've got subs, planes, and a satellite right here. The Navy ought to be investigating this storm."

Mason grimaced. "They're no good at this sort of thing. It's not their job. They'll stick it in some drawer in the Pentagon and forget it."

"At least they could leak something to a civilian team and see what they can come up with."

"Like you, maybe?"

Holden grinned, "Maybe."

"Civilians ain't any better at this crap than the Navy. I remember everybody landing on the Air Force over Project Bluebook and UFOs— then damned if some civilian outfit in Colorado doesn't tackle it and make fools of themselves. Some committee of scientists or something. They were going to release a report but even before it was out they were arguing with their own conclusions. Nobody is any good at this, Holden.''

Tiny legs rustled inside the intake of a plane next to Holden, causing him to jump backwards.

''Boy, you're a regular wreck, ain't you?'' Mason commented.

''Somebody is watching me,'' Holden said, grinding out his cigarette and striding for the bridge. ''It's probably one of the crew members.''

PROJECT
STORMFURY

X MINUS **120** HOURS

ADMIRAL CLAY turned to a wall map of Itrek. "What we have here is an atomic explosion that happened in the presence of peasants who never heard of atomic energy, who wouldn't know a nuclear bomb from a coconut, and are consequently forced to conclude that the gods became angry on Itrek."

They were in the conference room of the Naval Weapons Center in California. At the end of the table sat Matsuko Kayama, whose dark, smooth, bespectacled face wore a pleasant expression of bland dispassion. His self-possession was an oasis of calm in the presence of the Rear Admiral, a Project Director with ulcers, a hollow-eyed Jeffrey Holden, and CPO Samuel Mason, who stared out the window at the Mojave Desert, trying to sweat out his hangover.

Kayama cleared his throat. "The most substantial part of the phenomenon seems to have been this ball lightning. Yes?"

Holden nodded. "It was all over the place. Even before the storm began."

"If we could understand it, we might perhaps be enlightened as to the whole storm. The theories are simple. Was it two bolts of lightning intersecting each other?"

"Nope." Holden answered. "There was no lightning when we first saw it and none when it came into the CDA."

"Nor was it a junction between ground streamers and an incoming bolt."

"Like I said, there weren't any incoming bolts. Besides the balls wouldn't have held together as long as they did."

Kayama sipped tea from a ceramic cup, sat back, and beamed at Holden. "Ah. What was it, Mr. Holden?"

Holden doodled lightning bolts on a sheet of memo paper. "You're asking me?'' Being the center of attention made the blood of embarrassment sing in his ears.

"Mr. Holden is shy," Kayama said gently. "He feels he is about to be a clown."

"Out with it, Holden." Clay's hands were flat on the table. Except for a certain softness he showed toward Mason, the Admiral left Holden with the impression of cold intelligence scraped clean of emotion. He wondered if the Admiral was like that with all civilians and would have felt more comfortable with Mason alone. "This isn't a Board of Inquiry."

"I don't know what the lightning was," Holden said hesitantly. "But I can make a guess on where it came from. There was a constant electrical potential in the air before Windowpane happened. Mason swears all kinds of strange things happen in equatorial seas."

Mason's bloodshot eyes turned from the window to Clay. "Aye, sir. Stories. You've heard them, have you, sir?"

Clay nodded, eyes on Holden. "Go on."

"There's no iron on Itrek, none in the sea. I've never heard of air magnetized in my life. Ruling out the land, sea, and air *might* force us to look elsewhere."

Clay's eyes tightened to polished marbles. The Project Director leaned back in his chair and Kayama clasped his hands before him, listening with courteous but intense interest.

"We know the iron core of the earth has created an electromagnetic field around the whole planet. And the earth's charge is oriented between the equator and the poles. I've been thinking that since the Van Allen belts in space are parallel to the equator . . ."

"From space," Kayama gently interrupted him. "The storm is from outer space."

Holden tried to backtrack. "That depends on what you mean by space. Inner space might be a better word. The atmosphere goes out a long way, they've even picked up oxygen molecules on the moon. There's an inner Van Allen belt that touches the atmosphere at both poles. I don't think you'd have to look farther than that."

Mason looked at all of them. "What are the Van Allen belts? What's he talking about?"

"They're bands of solar particles trapped by the earth's magnetic field," answered Clay. "They didn't discover them until 1958."

"Thank you, sir," said Mason, subsiding with a mutter into his seat.

To Holden the Project Director said, "You're talking about some kind of invasion, aren't you?"

Holden said "Every time there are sunspots, the Van Allen belts increase in radioactivity, the ionosphere becomes more negative, and thunderstorm activity increases. Maybe this thing keeps the ionosphere's charge balanced like thunderstorms, only in the upper atmosphere."

Kayama held up one finger as if testing the wind. "A benevolent invasion, Admiral, sir."

"How so?"

"Perhaps if it were not for this thing, life on earth could not have evolved. You see, lightning is believed to have catalyzed life from lifeless molecular compounds." He turned to Holden. "Only Mr. Holden did not take his theory far enough. It did not merely repair the wound caused by Windowpane, Mr. Holden. It went after you."

Holden played with his pencil. "Yes, it did."

"An analogy would be a white corpuscle of the blood, no? Some antibodies repair wounded skin by forming scabs while others seek out the source of infection. This storm repaired the wound in the ozone layer. Then its nonthinking way of thinking directed it to destroy all the possible causes of that wound which could have been anything from a gnat to a shark to a Navy destroyer, anything with electricity in it. Anything and everything to make certain the infection was removed. The storm can retain within its substance the shapes of millions of different fields as ink retains fingerprints. And it can make ball lightning. I wonder, Mr. Holden, if ball lightning does not suggest what the thing really is."

"Not to me."

"It is a plasma. Perhaps?"

The fourth state of matter, many physicists thought. A dreamy phantom comprised of electrons and positive particles packed into a magnetic field as air packs into thin latex to form a balloon. A plasma would look like ball lightning. A fluorescent light was a plasma, a mixture of these packed particles in a state of agitation.

"You need about fifteen-thousand degrees of heat to make a plasma," the Project Director scoffed.

"Well, it was warm," Kayama pointed out. "About two degrees lower inside the pressure center. So. A cold plasma."

"And you have to feed energy into it to keep it intact. Like radio waves or . . . ."

"Infrared waves," Holden said. "And cosmic radiation, too, in fact any kind of radiation, any kind of energy."

"Yes," Kayama agreed delightedly. "Perhaps you were right all

83

along, Mr. Holden. It is a gremlin. Now, gentlemen, let me show you something. A postscript.''

From a manila envelope, Kayama withdrew several black and white photographs, which he passed among them. They depicted something that looked to Holden like clusters of marbles mixed with some kind of debris. By the fuzzy, uncertain focus, he knew they had been taken through a microscope.

"I asked one of the crews on *McClusky* to recover some rainwater from your evaporation tub and bring it here in a sealed bottle.''

"I should have thought of that myself,'' Holden admitted.

"Yesterday I put some under a microscope and found these small things in it. Do they look familiar to any of you gentlemen?''

Mason shook his head and put the prints back on the table. Clay and the Project Director looked noncommittally at Kayama. Holden said, "Yes and no. I don't know. It jogs the memory.''

"When I saw them I assumed they were dust particles, since we have recently discovered a layer of sulphate dust at an altitude of twenty miles or so. And, of course, the water lay exposed to the sky for some time. Then I looked more carefully. I pondered. Kayama, I said, you have seen these before. You see how well formed they are? Too well formed for dust.''

"Where?''

Kayama withdrew a thick book with a marked page which he passed to Holden. It was a medical textbook complete with illustrations, including one depicting spheres markedly similar to the ones in the photograph. Holden read the caption and felt Itrek come back to him. Croft had suggested it, he had thought it, but here in this quiet air-conditioned building the realization opened a ragged wound of sheer terror in his soul. It was a delayed reaction. He would have been happy to have had it delayed forever.

Clay snatched the book from him and looked at the picture, then glared at Kayama with a gentle suggestion of contempt in his expression.

"Amino acids,'' Kayama explained. "Which would tend to indicate the presence of life.''

"Coincidence,'' Clay answered. "I don't believe it.''

"Bull.'' The Project Director slid the book back to Kayama.

Kayama mopped his forehead with a white handkerchief. "As you know, amino acids are the building blocks of protein and have been created synthetically in laboratories. With the use of artificial lightning.''

"But not out of plain water," Holden replied.

"Life itself is constructed around combinations of only a few elements which exist freely in the atmosphere, Mr. Holden. Nitrogen, oxygen, hydrogen, which combined with oxygen forms water in the form of vapor. And innumerable compounds like carbon dioxide mixed with free elements. It is suggestive, no? There is life on the lithosphere, in the hydrosphere, why not the atmosphere? I am, however, disinclined to put this in any official report."

"I should damned well hope so." Clay rose to his feet signifying that the meeting was ended. The Project Director followed suit. Mason jumped up, gripped the table for support, and covered the movement by sliding a photo back to Kayama. Holden pushed his chair back and stood, feeling his cramped muscles unwind.

"Thank you, gentlemen. May I remind you that Project Windowpane is still under the highest level of classification? Is there anything else?"

"Yes," said Kayama, remaining in his seat to replace the book and photos into the envelope. "One fact is clear. We do not know whether the storm was a gremlin, a ghost, an invader, or merely an electrical phenomenon, or all of these things. But we do know that a certain part of the electricity comprising its body exists in a state of imbalance. This imbalance can only be corrected by four particular discharge points, which are Mr. Holden, Mr. Mason, Mr. Axton, and Mr. Tregaskis. The whole phenomenon may have dissipated by now. Or it may have returned to its domain in the Van Allen belts or wherever it is from. But it would be wise if none of the four of you ever visit Itrek or that part of the world again. And now having said that, I wonder if I may obtain a final cup of tea from the Navy before I leave?" He picked up his cup and favored the Admiral with a cheerful smile.

X MINUS **100** HOURS

THE PENSACOLA airport speaker announcing the arrival of the Los Angeles flight was a garbled jumble lost in the echoing voices and footsteps of travelers milling around the arrival gate. As Gina Lambert leafed through a magazine, Dennis helped himself to a pair of candy bars. She had to pay for them and throw them into a trash can. Dennis lost his temper, ducked from her hand, and began an angry march, a move consisting of walking in ever-widening circles around his mother until he disappeared into the legs of the crowd.

The child had an excellent sense of direction and Gina knew he never brought the drama to its logical end, which would be to walk until he disappeared. She waited patiently, glancing through a newspaper in which a story mentioned the loss with all hands of a ship called the *Adair* somewhere in the Pacific. That was where Jeff had been. She decided to save the article for him.

Gina pointed down the corridor to the gate. "See you down there, Dennis," she called and began walking. Sure enough, Dennis followed just close enough to keep her in sight and far enough to remind her he was still angry. Presently, the strangers unnerved him and he ran up to take her hand.

She watched the people file off the plane and through the doors. Old people, young people, fat and thin people. Why, she mused, do old men dress in overcoats in warm weather, for God's sake, especially if they just came from southern California?

What was Jeff wearing? Christ, suppose she did not recognize him? Maybe that would send him into a resentful funk lasting for weeks, building up to an explosion of bile that would wreck the relationship . . . She realized that lately she was oriented to disaster. She had to stop thinking like this.

It *was* remotely possible that she would not recognize him immediately. Even in school Holden had merged into the crowd, become part of the scenery—the result, she believed, of being raised in a family where behavior was so regulated.

Suppose he did not exist? James's death had split her personality in two, one of which had invented a fantasy lover, given him an apartment in Pensacola, populated him with invented ancestors, and no one would get off the plane. The other personality was locked away in a state institution somewhere.

"Gina?"

Too late to tuck in Dennis's shirt. Holden was carrying a flight bag, wearing the same clothes in which he had left. His face was brown from the sun, merging into pink on his neck. He kissed her hard on the mouth and looked her over admiringly.

She was dressed in a burnt orange blouse and darker rust pants, all clinging and diaphanous and appropriate for the heat of a Florida spring. She said to Dennis, "Remember this man, Dennis? He went away looking like a glass of milk, now he's Tarzan of the Apes."

Holden tried to shake hands with Dennis but the boy buried his face in his mother's pants leg.

As they climbed into the car, Gina handed him the newspaper article.

Holden read avidly as the automobile maneuvered past gas stations, hot dog stands, noon traffic, and potted palm trees thriving on carbon monoxide. "Investigators believe an ASROC torpedo tube was triggered by a bolt of lightning," he read out loud. The casualty figures were officially put at one hundred and nine.

Names were withheld pending notification of next of kin. Security had been right, Holden thought. There was no next of kin. No one would inquire about Jameson, Farnsworth, the Captain, or any of the others.

"Was that anywhere near you?" Gina asked. The wind lifted her hair, streaming it over her shoulders. Holden thought she drove entirely too fast.

"Not far," he replied. He folded the paper and stuffed it into the trash receptacle under the dash, and watched the heavy traffic hemming them into their lane. "I'm having a reality problem at the moment."

"Jet lag."

"Jet lag and a return to civilization." Holden realized he was finding it too easy to let information slip out to her. He would have to watch his words.

"Well, we spent the week in Miami with Don and Janette, James's parents. They absolutely adore Dennis, they fell all over him. They want him on weekends. We got back yesterday morning and I started doing over the apartment."

"Did you tell them about us?"

"I kind of hinted at it. I told them we'd be staying with an old friend in Pensacola for a while. You know something weird, Jeff? You and I have no parents, no family. James is the only one whose parents are still alive and he's dead. Is that an omen or something?"

"I think it's just one of the things we have in common."

She wanted to pursue the subject, then thought better of it. She was absolutely determined to think good thoughts. "Say hello to Dennis. He's scared of you."

Holden turned in his seat. "Hi, Dennis."

Holden's cramped apartment had been converted into a bright, comfortable home. He dropped his bag and stepped back to regard the yellow curtains hung over the picture window and the hanging plants on the plywood walls. His desk had been cleaned, papers stacked in place, and a space cleared for a vase of flowers. Dumbstruck, Holden wandered into the kitchenette where unfamiliar plates and silverware had been tucked into drawers. Unremovable stains from baked bean and canned chili dinners had been scrubbed from the stove. In the bedroom, the white sheets had been removed and replaced with blue flowered ones. Dennis's bedding was stashed against the wall, partially blocking the entrance to the bathroom, and surrounded by a music box and colored balls. The place even smelled different—the plants gave off a fresh earthy smell tainted with perfume.

On the wall he noticed a painting of a river winding through a forest with the initials JL. James Lambert.

He sat on the sofa which had been covered with a patterned counterpane and watched her.

"I'm just getting warmed up," she told him. "I only got back from Miami yesterday morning."

"I sure didn't know you could do this."

A scratching sound on the wall by his ear sent him charging from the sofa to the middle of the floor. Dennis was running the wheels of a model airplane over the wood. Holden's movement sent the boy scurrying behind his mother. Holden was about to sit in his chair when he became convinced that spiders were nestled in the cushion. He sat down on the sofa again.

Gina had been as startled as her son. "I didn't know you could jump like a kangaroo. Does Dennis bother you?"

"No, no. You'll have to bear with me because I'm about to say something that's going to sound really stupid."

"All right. What?"

"You didn't run across any spiders while you were cleaning up in here, did you?"

Gina blinked. "I found a century's supply of cobwebs on the ceiling but no live inhabitants. If there were any, Dennis would have caught them. He loves little beasties. Is that part of your reality problem, Jeff?"

"Yes, as a matter of fact, it is. I'm seeing them everywhere. What about the plants? Are there any in the plants?"

She looked at the plants. Then she looked back at him. "No. Since when are you bothered by spiders?"

"Gina, on a scale I'd rank them somewhere below athlete's foot and above the black plague." He opened his flight bag and rooted around for his toilet kit. The neatness of the room made him conscious of his beard stubble and the foul taste in his mouth from the airplane lunch.

"You look like you've been through a wringer. Were there spiders where you were?"

"A few. Do we have any plans for dinner?"

"I thought I'd fix a welcome home meal. It'll take a couple of hours.

Why don't you play with Dennis for awhile and I'll get started.'' She moved into the kitchenette.

Dennis and Holden gazed at each other, each sizing the other up. Holden had had little experience with children and realized he would have to figure out how to break the ice. He opened a drawer, withdrew a sheet of paper and folded it into a paper airplane. ''Dennis?''

Dennis's eyes grew enormous as the airplane skittered up to the ceiling, looped across the wall then swooped to the floor. Each time Holden threw the plane the little boy tirelessly caught it, holding it out to him for another toss.

That evening Dennis slept on the cushions, clutching the paper airplane, while Gina and Holden sat on the sofa holding hands. Through the window there was a faint glow from the lights of the city. Holden took her head in both hands and kissed her on the lips.

''That helps,'' she whispered.

Holden was full of good wine which had blended in some mysterious way with a veal stew she had placed on handsome white plates. Salad had been served to him in a clear glass bowl. At home, he and his mother had eaten beef stew from a can and left the dishes all weekend. Gina, it seemed to Holden, ornamented her life, while the Holdens merely lived theirs.

''Can I ask a favor?'' Holden asked finally.

''Of course.''

''There's just one thing wrong with the apartment. That painting over there. Can you put it somewhere else?''

''All right, Jeff.''

''I don't want you to forget Lambert or anything like that. But it's between us. You don't need it to remember him and I want you to think about me as much as you can.''

''You're very possessive aren't you?'' She really was quite beautiful, he decided, all nicely melded lines. Her back pinched in to her hips, which flared out, then in again, describing strong thighs that petered out into delicate knees and then, after the small burst of calf, even tinier ankles.

Holden gathered her up and sat her on his lap. ''Yes. I'd like to own your past as well as your present.'' He did not use the word future. Instead he buried his face in her hair.

''Do you like him?'' she asked.

''Who? Lambert?''

''Dennis. Dennis is the key to all this, Jeff. If things don't work out between us, it'll be extra hard on him because in a month or so he'll start thinking of you as his father.''

"He's a good kid. Kids are tougher than grownups. He'll get over Lambert before you do." Holden did not want to think about Lambert. When he got drunk, he grew maudlin.

"James liked the idea of children. Freedom, spontaneity, direct reactions, emotions. But he always got mad at Dennis. I think he preferred children in the abstract. It's important to me that Dennis be liked by whoever likes me."

"I'll try," Holden promised, which would be a hard promise to keep. Dennis was James Lambert's child, and he would always be there as long as they were together. It was a prospect more threatening than a simple picture on the wall.

Gina climbed off his lap and kissed his forehead. "Give me half an hour, then you can throw me a line—or whatever it is they do in the Navy."

When she entered the bedroom half an hour later, the light was dim and Holden, his face pale under his tan, was straightening his clothes in the closet. He sat on the bed, hands clenched, shoulders stiff, his body taut and compressed as though he were about to enter a hospital. Gina adjusted the light, slipped out of her nightgown and sat beside him. She kissed his cheek. "Something wrong with the closet?"

"I could have sworn I saw a spider in it."

From a haven of warm gentle breasts and rising rhythmic softness shaped like the planes of Gina's body, a continent of secrets and beauties, Holden found himself on the hard, white sands of Itrek. A freezing east wind blew and Kilgallen was screaming. A great black cloak spread over the island and Holden groaned aloud as spider legs delicately stripped the clothes from the struggling ensign and lifted him to the sky which was a great mouth lined with crackling lightning teeth.

He had kicked off the covers and was sweating and shivering when the light came on. Gina touched his shoulder and he jerked away from her.

"Jeff, stop it! Wake up!"

There were no spiders in the bedroom in Pensacola, Florida, at four-fifteen in the morning. He was safe at home. He sat up.

"Jeff, where in *hell* were you!"

"You don't want to know. I really mean that, you don't even want to think about it."

In the living room, Dennis had awakened and was crying. Gina stayed with him until he fell asleep again.

"This place is too small," Holden said as she slipped back under the covers and laid her head on his shoulder. "Got to get a bigger apartment."

"You know, Don and Janette have a beach house around Hudson. They said I could stay there anytime."

Another beach, he thought sourly, but the more he thought about it, the more he liked the idea. With Gina there, it would not be like Itrek, he would not associate Windowpane with every palm tree and length of sand. "Okay," he said.

"When do you want to go?"

"Tomorrow. As soon as possible."

"Can't you tell me anything?" she pleaded.

"No, I signed a goddamned contract."

X MINUS 96 HOURS

STEPHEN AXTON sat at his coffee table eating cereal and watching the colorful mollies, guppies, and Siamese fighting fish zoom about in his aquarium. Even though water was his career, he took little notice of the rain dribbling down the apartment window. It always rained in Seattle.

Sometimes Axton could contemplate waves on beaches and fish in tanks with such unbroken attention, his colleagues worried about him. He was unable to spend much time away from water, even though he had been raised in the Midwest. Its slow, sensual rhythms, the seductive beauty of underwater plants, mesmerized him.

Only once had he been frightened by water, the day in Beaufort, South Carolina, when he had been caught with too little air and surfaced fast, barely avoiding the bends. The memory had returned with exceptional force that day on Itrek.

Itrek. Axton could almost convince himself that Itrek had never happened. To him, the most unpleasant part of that whole business had not been the storm—or the laser—or the heat—but the people with whom he had been forced to spend time. Axton had a highly, morbidly honed sense of privacy. To Axton it was inconceivable that two people could spend more than an hour in the same room with each other. Marriage was beyond his conception and sex barbaric, an unsanitary

91

degradation which he had successfully avoided for most of his life.

Which reminded him that he had to call the State Environmental Protection Agency to find out if he was supposed to go out on Puget Sound today. He would be taking water samples of the sound to learn the effects of the constant passage of oil tankers through its waters. The ecologist he worked for was a woman named Esther Cook. The two of them had taken an immediate dislike to each other.

"Good morning, Mrs. Cook."

"Axton! When did you get back?"

"Night before last. I'm afraid I took an extra day off."

"That's all right. Mr. Carruthers continued your salinity samples. He told me to tell you your data is very thorough."

"Tell him thanks. I thought I would get some samples for oxygen analysis today. I have a program pretty well made out. I'll show it to you this afternoon, if you wish."

"This afternoon is out," she said quickly. "Why don't you leave it on my desk. I'm sure it will be approved with no trouble."

On the pier Axton checked the air tanks for the third time, convinced that the pressure was low. It was a cold, gusty day, and he could not decide whether it would rain or not.

"Mr. Axton, the tanks have been checked and rechecked," the exasperated man told him. "If I put any more air in them, they'll blow up on you."

Axton turned a valve and listened to a squirt of air. "Hear that? It should be higher in tone. I know the tank is low."

The man exhaled loudly and looked at the compressor. "Maybe the gauge is off, I don't know. But that's all that's wrong with it."

"I do have a feeling about these things."

"So do I. Take it somewhere else if you don't trust me."

Axton was accustomed to such rebuffs. His misanthropy summoned forth similar responses from other people. With a sigh, he checked the gauge again, then lowered his gear into the bobbing boat. In minutes he was making his way over the choppy waves of Puget Sound in the small boat.

Fog wafted in from the sea, enfolding him in yellowish mist until he could not even see the bow of his boat. He cut the engine and put on his air tank. Clearing the mouthpiece, he reached for his mask.

His hand stopped. He did not want to dive. The thought of going underwater today caused a peculiar, precise fear of rapture of the deeps, that delusion of ecstasy caused by the brain starved of air. Rapture of the deeps impelled a diver to swim downward into dark, quiet depths until the air ran out completely.

Axton puzzled over this feeling. It was the reverse of what he had felt earlier when he could not wait to get underwater. He decided to take temperature measurements instead. Lowering a thermometer over the side, he let the line string out to a hundred feet.

The fog was oppressively heavy, so thick and so tight around the boat it seemed he could not breathe properly. He pulled the thermometer up and listened for a sound of other boats. There was nothing. He was alone.

He reached for the throttle and a pleasurable tingle, an almost sexual *frisson* enervated his body. His hair stood out and a tic pulled at the corner of his eye. Axton felt himself in Beaufort again, the air running out of his tank. Disoriented by his weightlessness, he was not sure how to get to the surface.

Axton clawed for the air hose but it was not in his mouth, it was hanging around his chest. He pressed his temples, trying to chase away the feeling of being underwater. The delusion was strong enough to surge out of his memory and drive away both the fog and the realization that he was only on a boat in Puget Sound. He never even felt the lightning bolt that hit him.

X MINUS **84** HOURS

IN HIS Colorado office, Matsuko Kayama watched the computers digest the noon weather data pouring in over the Global Telecommunications Systems. The data was a tidal wave of information from ships, planes, local stations, airports—twice daily weather measurements sent out to the trunk lines of the World Weather Watch.

Normally it took around forty minutes for the computer to make a three-day forecast, but Kayama had pulled in one of his best students to help him with a twenty-four hour one. He was particularly perturbed about the alarming deterioration of weather in the Pacific Northwest.

The chart they examined was a map with hundreds of Xs on it. For Washington and Oregon, the forecast presaged disaster. Kayama tapped his finger on Puget Sound. "Now then, young man. It is interesting, is it not?"

The student nodded dutifully. "If it came in over the stormy latitudes, it should still be going north to the Gulf of Alaska."

"The graveyard of north Pacific cyclones. Yes. Most excellent. However, it is going south, is it not?"

The student adjusted his glasses, then peered at the tiny numbers. "It's too early to tell."

"When you are experienced, you can tell. This storm is definitely moving south. What else does it remind you of?"

The student struggled. "It's growing."

"Yes. Yes." Kayama's equanimity sometimes gave way to legendary bursts of samurai temper when confronted with unjustified stupidity.

The student said slowly, "You'll laugh at me but . . ."

"Yes, yes?"

"It almost looks like a tropical cloud cluster."

Kayama exhaled in exquisite joy. As if he were about to confer a medal on him, he solemnly grasped the embarrassed student's shoulders in both hands. "Very good, young man. It looks precisely like one of the cloud cluster systems that ring the earth at the equator. We must ask ourselves what it is doing up here. Do you see anything else?"

The student wiped his face and studied the chart. His courage up, he said firmly, "It almost looks like there are two systems to this storm. There's some cumulus out at sea and a wind connecting it to the coastal storm. I don't get it."

"And observe this also." Kayama's finger indicated a huge blob of cold, arctic air seeping southward over the hump of the Earth from Canada toward the west coast of the United States.

"I don't get that, either," the student admitted. "It's going to snow in the northwest."

"So it appears."

"Why's that air coming down? Do you think it's connected with the storm system?"

Slowly Kayama sat down and clasped his hands, regarding the student with a thoughtful expression. This time he was not going to commit himself fully. "It would seem impossible, no? This storm and that Canadian air, hundreds of miles apart. What possible relationship could they have with each other?"

"Absolutely none, so far as I can see," the student said dubiously.

Kayama held up one finger. "There is one, young man. It might have happened before."

"When? Where?"

Still thinking, Kayama looked out the window, "Once two hundred years ago and several times thousands of years ago. You see, it depends on whether there is electromagnetic activity somewhere.''

"Huh?''

"You realize that ice ages seem to be connected with intense sunspot activity. Solar radiation caused electrical activity in the atmosphere and by measuring the amount of radiocarbon in tree rings climatologists have matched it with glacial periods. When the sun changes magnetism, cold air results. And a similar event seems to happen with magnetic changes on the Earth.''

"I don't recall hearing about sunspots these days.''

"No, but there might be some electromagnetic activity somewhere. If so, it would be on one of this week's weather charts. Young man . . . ?''

The student flinched, realizing his day was gone and probably most of the night too. Kayama was known to be a slave driver.

"Will you kindly go through the weather reports of the past three days and see if there are reports of any unusual electrical activity along here?'' His finger traced out the stormy latitudes of the Pacific between sixty and thirty degrees north where warm tropical air and cold polar air even out the temperature of the northern hemisphere. "It would be from a ship or plane. Just the smallest comment or detail.''

"What kind of electrical activity? Thunderstorm?''

"Perhaps.'' Kayama pulled at his lips. "But I think St. Elmo's fire would be more likely. This will be your southernmost limit.'' He tapped a speck in the central Pacific.

"Itrek,'' the student murmured. "There's no traffic down there.''

"Kindly do it as fast as you can. You may be on the ground floor of something most interesting.''

X MINUS 72 HOURS

THE LAMBERT beach house was romantically dilapidated with a sagging porch, mildew streaks on the wood and a screened-in bay window looking over sand dunes to the Gulf Coast beach. It had been designed as a refuge from civilization. There was no radio or television; the water heater and pump worked uncertainly and Holden had to hook up propane gas tanks for the stove and switch on the electricity. The hypnotic pound of the waves lulled him to a peaceful sleep the first night in a bed full of sand particles. He awoke in the morning to the smell of bacon frying.

In the kitchen Gina passed a glass of orange juice to Dennis, who drank half of it, then stuck his hand into the glass and tried to grasp the liquid with his fingers. "Would you like eggs and sand or bacon and sand?" she asked him.

It was ten o'clock in the morning. Holden sat at the table and held out his hand palm downward. No shakes. No spiders. He was going to be all right. A good night's sleep was all he needed. "Throw a little seaweed into some eggs. Where'd the newspaper come from?"

"I went into town this morning and got it. I don't want to be cut off from the world completely."

Page one was devoted to a Pacific storm that had piled into Puget Sound, leaked over the barrier of the Cascade mountains and sent blizzards howling into the cherry, apple, and peach orchards of Washington's farmlands. Rather than dissipating, it had moved down the coast, crossing the Oregon-California border. A map diagrammed the system. It seemed to be two storms, one out at sea connected by a wind bridge to the one inland.

Holden lowered the newspaper and swallowed as Gina set a plate of scrambled eggs before him. He stabbed at them with his fork. The fork tines became jointed and hairy like spider legs. He cursed to himself, dug the fork into the eggs, raised it to his mouth but could not take a bite. No force on earth could bring that fork close to his mouth. It was as though the spider hallucination had scarred its shape so deeply into his brain, it would remain there like a permanent latent image. He set down the fork and began reading about the storm.

"This trip, Jeff. Is this going to be your career? Going off all the time for days on end?"

"I expect I'll go into teaching first. Most of the work will be done in Washington, planning and all that sort of thing."

It was a bizarre, mystifying storm. After stranding campers and burying cars in the passes of the Cascades with snow and hail, its departure resulted in temperatures of over eighty degrees that melted the snow by the following night. The warm spell would not last long. The Canadian air was no more than four to five days behind. In the last paragraph was a name that caused Holden to exclaim aloud and lay the newspaper flat on the table where he pored over every word of the article.

"What's up?" asked Gina.

"Did you read about this storm? It's really something. It'll be in California tonight. And there's a cold air mass coming down from Canada right after it. It says Matsuko Kayama is involved."

"Is that Japanese?"

"Japanese-American. I met him the other day. He's an expert on electrical properties of the weather. There are a lot of Japanese weathermen in the United States because of our computers. A quarter of Japan's fresh farmwater comes from typhoons which tear the hell out of the island. Its a kind of yin-yang thing, the weather that kills them also feeds them."

Gina poured coffee. "Where did you meet him?"

"At the Naval Weapons Center. He was . . ." Holden closed his mouth so hard he bit his tongue. "Gina? Name, rank, and serial number and that's it."

"Naval *Weapons* Center!" To Dennis she said, "He's not Tarzan, honey, he's the Manhattan Project." Her words belied the shock on her face.

Holden kept a diplomatic silence and tried to eat his cooling eggs again. No good. The fork tines writhed.

"That sounds terribly ominous. You have to admit that. I mean, what's a weatherman doing with a weapons center . . ."

"He's not working on any weapons, Gina. I can assure you of that. He's working on this storm. He says the reason the Canadian air is coming south is because the jet stream's moving south." It was a good chance to get her off the Naval Weapons Center and he grabbed it. "This is going to be my profession so I may as well bore you early."

She passed toast to Dennis who took a bite, then dropped it on the floor. "Go on."

"The jet stream is a six-mile-high river of air that runs around the earth. Its regular path is over Canada, northern Europe, Russia, the high latitudes. In the summer it moves north when the northern hemisphere heats up, in winter it moves south when everything cools down. You with me?"

"Yes."

"What the jet stream does is block arctic air from moving southward. It isn't a straight band like a belt or anything; it forms loops pointing southward. Some of these loops are caused by physical things. The Rocky Mountains, for instance, knock it southward and it doesn't get back on course until Newfoundland. It bends a little when it hits hard air pockets but it rarely makes more than five major south loops in the world. What's happening in the west is a big fat loop that just appeared one night and it's getting longer every day."

Her face was somber. "Why?"

"They don't know and believe me they'd like to find out. It's bringing cold weather down with it."

"Is this permanent?"

"They don't know."

"Will it snow in Hollywood?" She meant it as a joke.

"They don't know." Holden fiddled with the paper, then looked out the window at Dennis's sand pails and shovels scattered in the dunes. "What's really peculiar is the loop is aimed right at the storm like a gun barrel following a target. Like the storm is sucking it down somehow . . ." Holden lowered the paper, and although it seemed to Gina he was looking at Dennis, she realized he was looking at nothing at all. "There's one possibility. But it . . . No. It's not possible, not remotely." He was obviously trying to convince himself.

"Tell me. If it sounds good you get an A plus."

"There may be another reason why the jet stream is going south. They don't know why but it has something to do with moving magnetic fields."

"Speak louder, Jeff."

"Magnetic fields. Areas of magnetism. In the seventeenth century the magnetic north pole was just north of London and that was one of the coldest centuries on record. You could walk across ice from Manhattan to Staten Island. Nobody knows what the connection is but if that storm's got some kind of unusual magnetic or electrical field, it might be pulling the jet stream down somehow." Holden remembered the ball lightning soaring straight for his Harrier. Ball lightning would be a most unusual electromagnetic field . . . He was getting paranoid. They had left the storm back in the Pacific thousands of miles away. . . .

"You get an A, Jeff. We can always ask Dennis."

Holden said, "Kid, why's the jet stream moving south?"

Delighted at being addressed, Dennis flew a piece of toast at Holden. It landed squarely on his forehead, butter side in.

X MINUS 65 HOURS

CPO Samuel Mason was also absorbed in the storm as he sat in an office at the San Diego Naval Station. Outdoors recruits were marching around the grounds in ragged squares suffering the snarling abuse of Instructors. Join up for four years, then get out, unless there's an economic recession and you can't find a job. Mason did so after the Korean war, and another tour of duty somehow became his life's work.

Today an item in the *San Francisco Chronicle* on the storm was causing mental havoc for him.

By the time it hit San Francisco, the twin storms had swollen to such size and fury that flash floods struck the wine country inland and power had been killed in large parts of the city.

Supposedly it was a pair of thunderstorms. Yet the only lightning in the city had been reported at the University of California in Berkeley and it had been fatal to three white mice, six guinea pigs, a handful of earthworms in dirt-packed boxes, and two rhesus monkeys. Near Sacramento a farmer had suffered the loss of a litter of hogs, two goats, and a cow to lightning.

To get to the animals in the Berkeley Biology Lab the lightning had snaked through a window. There had been a number of animals in the lab, yet only a few had been hit. A lab assistant, who was cut by flying glass, had witnessed the phenomenon.

On board the *Knoxville* had been one goat, one hog, and one cow— obtained, Croft had said, from a farmer. The Berkeley Biology Lab was where Croft had worked. He had lived near the campus.

Mason could easily envision the lightning going through the window without the lab assistant's breathless description. He had easily envisioned it on the fishing boat in Loa.

Mason was not accustomed to launching grand-scale alarms over odd facts in newspapers, yet he remembered that Axton lived in Seattle, where the storm had first appeared, and Tregaskis in Santa Barbara, where the southern edge of the storm was now approaching. He was just down the coast in San Diego. Holden's address was Pensacola, Florida. And there was Matsuko Kayama's name mentioned in the newspaper story making some remark about electromagnetic fields and the jet streams. Mason could just see that smug little Jap in his white shirt.

Samuel Mason was not brilliant but he was tenacious. After mulling over the consequences of calling the Naval Weapons Center, he realized that all he had to do was call Steve Axton in Seattle and see if he was all right. He dialed the number listed in the Red Book.

There was no answer.

Let it alone! No sense in making a fool of yourself over your own imagination. Besides, the damned thing could not have found them across half the earth.

Mason's felt-tipped pen hovered around the phone number of Doug Tregaskis in Santa Barbara. Did he really want to talk to that flower? Not much talk would be required, just ask what the storm looked like, if

99

he was okay, then hang up and forget about it. Gritting his teeth, Mason dialed Santa Barbara.

The voice that answered the phone was soft and molasses smooth. Mason thought it belonged to a woman. "Yes, ma'am. My name is Samuel Mason. I'd like to talk to Mr. Tregaskis, please."

The voice called out Tregaskis's name and, in the background, Mason could hear him respond. "I'm coming, George." Scandalized, Mason took a deep breath. *George!* Security had really gone to the bow wows.

Tregaskis's voice was resentful. "What do you want, Mason?"

"I just want to know if it's raining where you are."

"Yes. Why?"

Come to think of it, Tregaskis was educated. Perverted but educated, which to Mason seemed to be what education was for these days. Educated people had answers. "You know that storm came down from San Francisco. Now it's probably nothing, but it says here in the paper that a bunch of animals in Croft's lab were killed by lightning in Berkeley."

It was the wrong approach. Tregaskis's voice gasped in panic. "No, it's . . . Wait a minute, wait a minute! That doesn't mean . . . Are you trying to scare me again?"

"No, I've just got a suspicious mind. Something funny's going on here."

"Holden said it went after everything at the test site. Why would it kill a bunch of monkeys in California, for God's sake? And how would it find them?"

"I'm not saying anything definite, Tregaskis, so calm down! It's just the coincidence. Croft's animals hit by lightning."

"Mason, the storm showed up in Seattle. It would have hit Axton up there."

"I just called Seattle and Axton wasn't home. It's probably nothing, but stay indoors and I'll get back to you if I find out anything."

Steve Axton had been attached to the State Environmental Protection Agency. What would he say? Hello, was Axton hit by lightning, by any chance? Wham, they'd hang up on him. That was not the kind of information State Agencies gave out over the telephone to strangers. Who did?

"Good afternoon, *Seattle Times.*"

Mason cleared his throat. "Could you put me through to your Obituary section? I wanted to ask about the storm."

The connection was broken before he finished his sentence. A woman's hurried voice announced, "Obituary."

"Yeah. I'm calling from San Diego. It's kind of crazy but I wanted to know if somebody named Stephen Yarmouth Axton died during the past . . ."

"Yup."

Mason was not certain he had heard right. Did that mean yes? "What did you say?"

"Stephen Yarmouth Axton," the woman repeated. "It was in yesterday's paper. It was in the news section rather than the Obit. We didn't have enough information on him for an obit."

"The oceanographer?" Mason creaked back in his swivel chair. "Are you sure?"

"The oceanographer," the woman confirmed. "He was with the Environmental Protection Agency. It was a news item because he was the only one that died in the storm. He was hit by lightning in Puget Sound. Do you want a copy of the paper?"

"No, thank you, ma'am, that's all I need to know."

Mason realized how he would be buried. The Petty Officer would be boxed up and shipped off to Illinois, which he had left years ago to run off to sea. No one would even send flowers.

He tried Holden's number in Pensacola, but to his irritated disgust no one answered there either. That left him back with Tregaskis.

"It's me again, Tregaskis. Listen carefully, now, and stay cool. Axton was hit by lightning from that storm around you. It's coming toward me, too."

Tregaskis dropped the phone with a cracked frightened cry. He would require exceptionally careful handling. Mason remembered the panic on Itrek. "Ma . . . Ma . . . Mason . . ."

"Listen to me, I said. You listening to me?"

"Oh, Christ Jesus, I thought it was all over, Mason."

"I'm bringing the Naval Weapons Center in on this. Clay is in Japan right now but I can still ring every alarm on the west coast. Is there any lightning near you?"

"Yes . . . No. No lightning, Mason, I haven't seen any. But then again it's down on the coast and we're in the hills."

"Do you have a car?"

"I have a station wagon."

"Get in it and come down here right away. Do it now before the storm gets worse. I'll be waiting for you at the main gate. And keep your car windows up. It can't get at you through sealed windows!"

"Can I bring George?" Tregaskis asked hesitantly. "I don't want to go alone, really, I don't."

"Not onto the goddamned base, you can't! Drop him off in L.A. somewhere and keep your mouth shut, you understand that?"

"I'm scared. Oh, Lord, Mason, I'm scared."

"Cheer up, digger, you didn't want to live forever did you?"

Before calling the Naval Weapons Center, Mason looked out the window at the north sky. It was not the sunniest of days but the gulls swooped around the ships and the breeze was warm, a peaceful world except for the recruits. Try as he might, Mason could not summon up a sense of emergency.

Samuel Mason was lonely. Even Tregaskis was not alone. Maybe he knew something Mason did not.

He dialed the Naval Weapons Center and in seconds was speaking tersely to the Project Director himself. Mason heard the sound of the ulcer tablet bottle being opened. "I'd better get hold of Clay. How long will it take Tregaskis to get to you?"

"It shouldn't be more than a couple hours, depending on traffic, sir."

"Bring him out here as soon as he arrives. About Jeffrey Holden."

"Sir?"

"We'll try to get him from here. He might be at school, he might just be out for a drive."

Mason blew out his cheeks and said, "Sir, there's another thing about him. He's living with a girl."

"It's not on his file. When did that happen?"

"Between the time he signed his contract and the time he went to Itrek. He asked me if it was illegal."

"It's not, technically, but I wish he'd told somebody. Do you know what her name is?"

Mason shut his eyes and put himself back on the beach behind Itrek's sea wall, just before they'd seen the lights out at sea. A mild breeze had blown in and he had been surprised at Holden's story. A couple of cute little lambs. *Lambs*. Lambert! "Her last name was Lambert. She's a widow and she has a kid. I'm sure it's Lambert."

"From Pensacola, right?"

"Right!"

The Project Director put him on hold for a few minutes and Mason looked over the newspaper article again. When he came back on the line, Mason asked, "Sir?"

"Yes."

"Why would lightning from this storm kill animals in Croft's lab?"
Mason told him about the newspaper item.

"I don't understand that. Did you bring any back from Itrek?"

"No, sir."

"I'll ask Kayama. Don't overstay your time there, Mason. That storm's moving fast."

"Yes, sir."

"This one's a bitch, Mason."

"That it is, sir. That it is."

Looking slightly exhausted, his favorite student stifled a yawn as Kayama read a two-day-old weather report. He lowered the paper to beam at the young man. "An airliner?"

"Yes. The plane went through St. Elmo's fire at ten-thousand feet, about a thousand miles east of Japan. They called it in and it went into the midnight data. They also reported cold air, but since they were so high up it didn't show up in the twenty-four hour forecast. I guess somebody figured it wasn't close enough to the surface to put into the computer data."

"Ah. So this is where it began."

"It's our storm, all right. Sir, it really is the damnedest thing I ever heard of. The whole system is almost four hundred miles long and it's pushing into Los Angeles right now as if the marine layer wasn't even there. What thunderstorms Los Angeles has, come up from the south."

"Yes," Kayama agreed. He pointed to the cluster of clouds outside of Catalina island. "This is the gas tank, as it were. This little storm here is evaporating water and the winds are carrying it to the coastal system. It can pump water vapor over ten miles into the stratosphere. Which is the mother storm, which is the child? Eh?"

"Mr. Kayama, I have never even heard of a double system like this where one actually feeds the other. It's not like a storm front or a cyclone or anything." The student lowered a satellite photo of the California coast.

Kayama looked the picture over and nodded with reluctant agreement. "Yes. So many important things are not made understandable with satellites."

"Sir?"

"Men of God. Tides of history. They cannot be seen; we can see only land, sea, and clouds. Surfaces, young man, not the underlying forms. The satellite sees everything and nothing."

Often the student had seen a pleasurable melancholy settle over Kayama. Sometimes he became wistful and full of weight as though carrying too much responsibility. Yet he seemed to enjoy this yin-yang, the confrontation of opposites. He was cross-grained, never content unless an equal amount of glumness were present to leaven his good nature.

Kayama roused himself. "Did I thank you? Good. Now you must inform the other students that I shall be gone for at least a week. Would you do that for me?"

"Where are you going?"

Kayama touched his finger to the side of his nose. "It is a secret. I am expecting a phone call momentarily. I should make the call myself, but I said, Kayama, let us see how long it takes brilliant men to guess the truth. Good day, young man."

When it rang, its blasphemous noise was an intrusion upon the temple of his thoughtfulness. He spilled his tea. He wiped up every last drop with a Kleenex, which he folded and dropped into a trash can, before answering. It was the Project Director with the news about Steve Axton.

"And where are the others?"

"Mason is waiting for Tregaskis in San Diego right now. We're trying to locate Holden. Kayama, can you give us a prognosis on this storm?"

"It will try to kill them all."

"Beyond that, I mean."

"Yes. I am worried about Holden because he lives in Florida. We really must find him and bring him west."

"Why?"

"There is a phrase, sir. Thunder on the right?"

Kayama's little flights of poetry were something the Project Director had become used to. "I beg your pardon, Kayama?"

"It is a Roman phrase. The Romans knew storms moved from west to east because of the spin of the earth. The Roman Senate faced south. Thunder on the left hand meant a storm was going away, thunder on the right meant one was approaching. Thunder, sir, is loudly approaching North America from the right."

"What's that got to do with Holden?"

"The storm will cross the Gulf of Mexico to get to him. It is spring, which means warm air from the Gulf will make its usual journey northward. And as is customary at this time of year it will meet cold air from Canada over the flat Midwest. The cold air comes downward from the Rockies and clamps over the warm as a lid seals a pressure cooker. At the points where this lid gives way, you have tornadoes.''

The Project Director's pencil snapped in two.

''It happens every year, sir. This year it will be far, far worse. This storm generates heat and it is also attracting the cold. If the Canadian air gets here when the storm is in the Gulf, then . . . it is truly incalculable, sir. The Midwest, the South, even the Mississippi valley will witness storms unlike any in memory. Hundreds of them, perhaps.''

''How much time have we got?'' The Project Director's voice was less firm than usual, almost shaky.

''The cold air is very slow moving. At this rate, it will take four to five days to work its way far enough south. It will give us time.''

''Time for what?''

''The Navy must revive Project Stormfury immediately.''

Had Kayama suggested evacuating the Midwest, the Project Director could not have been more astonished. Stormfury, the Navy's hurricane-seeding program discontinued in 1973, had been directed at the autumn storms sweeping into the Gulf each year. ''We can't touch it close to land, Kayama. Stormfury was in the Atlantic. We knocked a hurricane into Savannah, Georgia, just as it was leaving for the sea.''

''Sir,'' said Kayama. ''You must. When it gets into the Gulf, it will be far more dangerous than a hurricane or even many hurricanes. Can you not simply put Holden's name on the radio and television and ask him to call?''

''We will as a last resort. The FBI says it won't have any trouble locating him. I'm sending a plane for you. Can you leave immediately?''

''Naturally. I'm already packed.''

Kayama always kept a packed bag containing toilet articles, changes of socks and underwear, and three white shirts, all items devoted to personal cleanliness. He expected Stormfury would be generating a lot of sweat out of him in the next few days.

X MINUS 62 HOURS

THE STORM caught Doug Tregaskis south of Santa Barbara on U.S. 101 as George Dockman was changing radio stations. Following a thick gust of wind, rain splashed over the windshield, shutting off the world and muting all to a continual hollow hiss. Tregaskis moved closer to the road's edge, turning on both the headlights and the windshield wipers which carved feeble wedges of clarity through the running water. Oncoming headlights diffused into thousands of glares through the water droplets. The first lightning turned the highway into noonday brightness for a second. The lightning caused Tregaskis to trample the accelerator, cross the white line to pass a truck, then cut back in just before a startled oncoming car blared at him.

"The road's slippery," George Dockman said. "It's most dangerous when rain begins falling because it loosens the grease without washing it away."

Tregaskis's hands were bone white as they clutched the steering wheel, increasing rather than decreasing his speed. Lightning melded the silvers and grays of the storm into a single blaze accompanied by a crack from somewhere to their right.

"You're always overdoing things," Dockman observed. "You want to go to San Diego, we go in thirty seconds without even packing. You're very impetuous, you know that?"

"It's a bad storm, George."

"I know it is, it's dangerous because it makes people drive like maniacs. Slow down, for heaven's sake."

I will change my ways if I get out of this, Tregaskis swore to himself. I will be a better person. I will be nice to women and babies and I will start a garden club somewhere. I will get out into the world more and meet people, different kinds of people, instead of hiding in dark bars full of groping hands, among strangers who could be dangerous if you took them home. "George?"

"Yes?"

"You're all I have, you know that. You're my family. You're everything to me."

"Doug, please let me drive."

Tregaskis blew the horn, then swept past a tiny car forging wings of water from its wheels. Southern California was not designed to handle rain. The water was three inches deep on the badly drained road and there would be flash flood warnings out to the canyon residential areas. Tregaskis was ready to turn the wheel over to Dockman when the rain stopped and the wipers click-flapped over squeaky glass. Along the road, the houses were whitewashed by the storm, and past them, the sea was visible.

Tregaskis heaved a sigh of relief, then settled down behind a truck at a placid fifty miles an hour. They were leaving the storm behind them.

Dockman opened the window and lit a cigarette.

Tregaskis felt the cool air rebound from the back seat and stir the hair on the back of his head.

"Close it!" he cried, his voice breaking.

"I just wanted a smoke."

"No! Close it!"

The window crank had a plastic handle and it was this that saved Dockman's life. It was as if a bowl of pure light had been clamped over the station wagon, light that pumped in through all the windows simultaneously. A bone-deep ache vibrated from Dockman's finger. He pulled his hand away gasping in pain. The car slipped its two right wheels over the edge of a ditch. Tregaskis tried to wrench the machine back on the highway but the front end piled into a stone bridge spanning the ditch. Dockman hit the dashboard, Tregaskis piled into the steering wheel. The hood jackknifed, blocking their view, and the doors flew open.

Dockman remembered seeing Tregaskis's fingers reaching for the door handle when the world vanished behind a sheet of light. It was palpable light, so viciously bright he felt he could bite off and swallow some. He flung his hands over his face, hearing the car horns loudly honking on the road as two more attacks of light encased the car. He could sense them through his fingers.

Dockman heard brakes squeal as cars stopped before and behind them. A gush of rain drummed down on the roof of the car. Lowering his hand, he saw Tregaskis lying half in, half out of the driver's seat, his leg stretched out on the floor. The leg was totally stiff and straight and the shoe sole had melted into a puddle of reinforced rubber that congealed on the rug.

Two and a half hours elapsed in San Diego before Mason was forced to admit that Tregaskis was late. Except for a trip to the bathroom and a sandwich from the commissary, he had waited in the office, making half-hourly calls to Holden and watching apprehensively as clouds crept over the sky to the north.

That afternoon the fifty wind stations in Los Angeles reported that the city was about to get a rare visitation: a thunderstorm. The wind outdoors now whipped the waters into froth and Mason knew he was running out of time.

Where was Tregaskis? He couldn't have gotten lost. Even he was not that dumb, was he? Or was he! Flower punchers were capable of anything.

Usually Mason acted decisively. One phone call would confirm or deny the worst of his suspicions and he did not want to make it, but he forced himself to anyway.

Tregaskis was the first human casualty of the storm, according to the state police. He had been struck by three bolts that had passed power lines and trees to get him.

With a sense of battle fatigue, he called the Project Director. "Sir? Four down, two to go."

"Tregaskis is dead?"

"Yes, sir. And I am getting out of here before it happens to me. He left too late and I can see the storm from here."

"Stay put, I'll send a plane out."

"Begging your pardon, sir, no time. My car's just outside."

"Okay. All right." Everything was coming down on the Project Director's head, multiple disasters contained within one single catastrophe. The Director was a bureaucrat and felt himself unequipped to exert any control over these events. That was what Admirals were supposed to do, and Clay was thousands of miles away. "I'll tell you what, Mason. Hold off another half hour until Kayama gets here and we'll see what he thinks."

"No, sir, I can't do that. I can't stay here more than thirty seconds and I should have been gone an hour ago."

"Half an hour, Mason," the Project Director's bark was more like a chirp. "That's an or-order."

"Sir, I'm getting out of here, I ain't waiting for no professor to tell me what to do. I am taking care of myself, sir." Mason pounded his chest.

"Okay, okay, all right. Head straight for the Naval Weapons Center."

"No, sir," Mason stubbornly repeated. "That storm goes like a rocket and you're only a couple hours away. I am going south, sir. I am going straight into the Baja where there ain't no rainstorms, no Jap professors, no Navy, and no Admirals. I have damned well plumb had it with the U.S. Navy, sir, and you just might not ever see me again."

The Project Director reminded himself that he outranked the Petty Officer by a half dozen grades, yet he found himself fumbling. "I wish you'd look at this differently, Mason. Heck, I know you're scared—I don't blame you. But we need you . . ."

"Sir, thanks for everything, but I am off to join the Peruvian Navy because I ain't going to stop till I get there."

"Leave word with the Duty Officer where you're go . . ." Mason threw the phone down and listened for a few seconds to the terrible silence in the office. He had committed professional suicide for sure. He would be court martialed, tossed into whatever they used for a brig nowadays, and stripped of his pension.

Wind gusted against the window, rattling the panes. A line of black clouds split the sea from the sky in the distance. They weren't the dirty yellow hue he remembered from Itrek, but they were tightly together as solid as a thick stain of ink soiling the sky.

Mason decided he would head for the Baja and get a few hundred miles of desert between himself and the storm. Deserts were dry and arid, too dry for rain. Mason had never heard of a thunderstorm in a desert.

"How the hell did it find us?" he snarled as he ran downstairs to his car. "That's all I want to know."

X MINUS 58 HOURS

PAST THE drunken raucousness of the Tijuana border, Mason sped east toward Mexicali out beyond the Sierra de Juarez mountains. He kept the radio tuned to San Diego as long as possible and heard that the storm had smashed into that city an hour after he left it. By then he was over seventy miles away, driving like a lunatic through dry, warm sage, gnarled cactus, and empty hump-backed mountains. When San Diego faded, he dialed past pirate stations carrying rock, a handful of Mexican bands, and a late show from somewhere in California's Imperial Valley.

The road paralleled the Mexican border, and bars and motels were scattered along it. These faded as he crossed the mountains and reappeared as he descended the final slope into Mexicali.

He spotted the neon sombrero a mile ahead. The tubing was decorated with bubbly champagne glasses and women's smiling mouths. It was a fantastically elaborate sign designed to nail wandering gringos in the middle of the night. The motel was called "The Laughing Hat" and pickup trucks were parked outside.

The cantina was shaped like a stucco blockhouse. Behind was a modest-sized stone swimming pool and a gallery of rooms stretching back from the cantina. The pool was empty and cracked and only two room lights were on.

Mason examined the cantina, thinking about lice and typhoid fever. Amplified guitar music sounded through the door. By the trucks, Mason guessed most of the men inside were farm workers. A girl wearing silver pants and a scoop-necked nylon blouse peeked out the door at him.

There was not a breath of wind anywhere in the cool, desert night. Tumbleweed thrashed across the road. Between Mason and the storm lay two mountain ranges and a solid length of scrubby desert. He was surprised to see it was twelve-thirty by his watch. He was tired. It could be tension or, dreaded thought, it could be age. More than likely it was the driving. He got out of the car and walked into the cantina looking for the girl.

X MINUS 56 HOURS

KAYAMA LANDED in a military helicopter just outside the NWC's Echo Electronic Warfare Range in the Mojave desert. There the ground had been landscaped into the superstructure of a Russian ship, profiled with radar towers and nets and groups of equipment which when switched around could successfully duplicate the silhouette of a cruiser or a helicopter carrier.

The Project Director walked out to meet him, hand extended. Kayama paused. "Look at that," he said, pointing to the sky.

Fingers of cloud were sliding across the face of the moon, high clouds, wisps of altocirrus, shining with ice crystals that formed a ring around it. The Project Director said, "It must be part of the storm. It just started raining in San Diego."

"But what is it doing here? Quick now! Tell me!"

The Project Director controlled his temper. "Mr. Kayama, I am not a climatologist . . ."

"Is Mason around here? Quickly now."

"Mason cracked up or something. He drove down into the Baja!"

"The Baja!" Kayama's eyes narrowed as he turned his face back to the sky. "But that is following him. See? It is moving southeast. Why did you let him go!"

The Project Director had just been raked by a Petty Officer and was in no mood to be chewed out by a slant-eyed warlock. "Mr. Kayama, it's a desert! There aren't any thunderstorms in a desert!"

Kayama clapped his hand to his head and turned again to face the Project Director. "It is my fault. I did not make myself clear. Please accept my apologies . . ."

"Done."

". . . but I should have emphasized the extreme danger if the storm moves east. The Gulf of Mexico is east of us. Had you told me or had I spoken to Mason, I would have had him move *west* or south or north, any direction to keep him on this side of the continent."

"He may be heading south right now . . ."

"Sir. Please, sir. Those clouds are clearly and most definitely moving inland."

The Project Director examined the clouds. They made a spectral formation, a long arch across the stars, narrow and silently high, moving like a current. They had not been out five minutes before but now the moon was fading to a patch of haze.

Kayama turned to the helicopter pilot. "You must follow the storm."

Thunderstruck, the pilot looked from him to the Project Director. He laughed. "Mr. Kayama, you know that's ridiculous . . ."

"No, no, no, listen to me. The storm will descend when it finds Mason. You will be able to see clouds forming over him. A localized squall or storm will occur. Beneath it will be either a house or a motel or even Mason's car, perhaps. You must rescue him."

"Rain in the Baja?" the pilot asked incredulously.

"Lightning, sir. Lightning!"

The pilot looked at the Project Director, who said, "You heard the man. Get going."

The pilot walked backward to the helicopter, facing them both in case they came to their senses.

Kayama called out to him. "Do not worry, the storm will not bother you. Only Mason."

"Do I look worried?" the pilot asked sarcastically. In seconds he was airborne, a small, receding gnat buzzing down the sky, dwarfed by the line of clouds hurtling southeast.

All Mason had to do was put down his goddamned fifth margarita and walk to the telephone on the wall no more than twenty feet away. But he would have to go through a Mexican exchange, then an American one, probably having to translate everything, and even then the wires were probably lousy anyhow. He needed another drink before attempting that. He had been saying that for the past two hours.

The migrant workers had long since gone home. The gringo back-packers had pushed on. Mason wondered why educated boys and girls were walking a desert in shorts and hiking boots. Didn't you go to college to get those fool ideas out of your head?

111

The girl in the tight silver pants was the cantina singer. Standing by a Zapata-mustachioed guitarist on a raised dais surrounded by pink mood light bulbs, she trilled a medley of Mexican and American songs with a Mexican accent. Mason could not tell if her rendition of "Strangers in the Night" was worse than "Cielito Lindo." To him her metallic blonde fall looked stiff enough to bash dents in a steel bulkhead.

Mason tilted on the cracked plastic bar stool as the bartender poured out another margarita. "There's no water in the desert," he slurred to the bartender. "So you have to make do. Si?"

"Si, si!" The bartender was a round-cheeked man of infinite good humor and enormous white teeth. He beamed at the Petty Officer while drying glasses. *Señor Lonelyhearts*, the bartender decided sympathetically. "You would like a room and some company, Señor?"

The girl could be the bartender's sister, relative, lover, or even daughter, in which case Mason feared a knife in his ribs. "Si. Si, but first I must make a call."

"Perhaps some champagne for the lady." Half hidden in the bushy hair of the bartender's chest was a little gold crucifix on a chain. The shirt parted as the bartender indicated the singer sitting now beside Mason with an unlit cigarette.

Champagne? Mason had seventy dollars in his wallet. He slipped out a lighter and touched it to the girl's cigarette. She smiled and patted his thigh. Friendly child. To Mason's horror she was no more than sixteen. Even his sailor's conscience had trouble with that. "Excuse me," he mumbled. "Don't touch the drink."

He lurched off the stool and shambled into the parking area to sober up.

The girl picked up an enormous handbag, went into the ladies' room and emerged with fresh makeup and her Prussian helmet of a fall combed out. She stepped outdoors to find Mason swaying in front of his car, scratching his head.

It was cold with a wind coming out of the desert. A fine sheet of mist suffused the moonlight. "Buenas noches," she said to the Petty Officer. Mason rubbed his bristly jaw and tried to focus on the car as white heat lightning flickered far to the south. "Buenas noches," she repeated a little louder.

"Yeah. I can't figure out if this back window was open all the way from San Diego or if I opened it when I got here."

The girl felt cold and the gringo's interest seemed to be waning. She slipped an arm under his elbow. The other roamed elsewhere and Mason guffawed. "Listen, I really ought to make a phone call."

As he had suspected, the phone did not work properly. An operator promised to get the call through to San Diego, then the line went dead. The girl wrapped her arms around his waist and laid her head against his back.

"Hey," Mason said. "I got one great idea. Let's get married."

"Si, si," the girl agreed, smiling politely at his joke.

The bartender closed the rattling shutters and doors against the wind blowing sheets of sand into the cantina. The guitarist, who was his worthless, moon-eyed nephew, had already stacked the tables and swept at the dust blowing under the doors. Dust storms were common in the Baja, but each one made the bartender swear to move to Los Angeles where his brother lived.

Lightning strobed softly over the desert. Thunder skipped down the clear, sloping road to Mexicali and the scarred, parched land to the south. The girl returned without Mason, looking slightly frazzled, and the bartender poured her a beer. She had been gone nearly two hours.

"He's asleep," she said. She leaned to whisper out of earshot of the innocent ears of the nephew. "You know what he talked about?"

"No."

"Storms. Thunderstorms. Eh? Six times he asked when it rained here last time." She pointed her forefinger at her temple and made circles.

The bartender's loud guffaws of laughter rebounded around the empty cantina. "He likes to do it in the rain. It reminds him of the Navy."

The nephew leaned on his broom and cocked his head to the wind.

The bartender roared, "Get to work, you lazy . . ."

"Listen! Is that a helicopter?"

The rhythmic *whap whap* of the rotor blades came to them over the wind. It had to be a gringo, the bartender thought, only a gringo would fly in this kind of weather. He turned on the radio, hoping for some weather news.

Lightning struck the cantina, showering sparks from the radio, exploding fragments of light bulbs onto the scurrying nephew and clapping darkness over the interior.

The girl cried out a string of obscenities.

"Quiet!" shouted the bartender, turning on a flashlight. "It happens once every five years. It just blows the fuses . . ."

Two more bolts fired the windows. The telephone jangled once, then smoldered. The nephew dropped the broom and looked up at the cracking ceiling. The flashlight beam sectioned layers of dust in the air.

"So," said the bartender with a shrug. "After this it will not happen for fifteen years. Maybe I will stay after all."

Through the churning tumult of cloud, dust, and sage branches, the pilot could see the cantina by the sombrero sign. Lightning slashed enough details—the swimming pool, the single car in front—for the pilot to guide himself down through the murk but then a bolt flared, the sign vanished, and the power was killed.

The pilot switched on the landing lights and circled the cantina, hands struggling with the pitching stick. Land the damned thing, get Mason, then get out. The lights passed over the flat, fluted cantina roof with its air vent poking up, then spilled over a relatively flat piece of stony desert beside it.

It wasn't his helicopter; the Navy had thousands of them. The Project Director was a Commander and his instructions were explicit. A burst of wind hurled pebbles against the fuselage. The pilot feathered the rotors and bounced to the ground, rocking in the wind. He slid open the door and pebbles stung his face as he climbed out and ran toward the cantina.

The gringo crashed into the bar stuffing his shirt into his pants. Lightning slatted through the shutters across his white face. "Cellar! Where's the cellar! Come on, goddamnit."

"Señor," said the bartender, shotgun in hand. "A helicopter has just landed outside."

Mason grabbed the bartender's shirt, eyes bleary and red from tequila. "Cellar! *Comprende*? Cellar!"

The bartender knocked his hands away with the shotgun. "Señor, do *not* put your hands on me."

Someone was shouting above the wind, "Mason? Mason?"

A searing flash and a deafening, splitting crack pulverized a section of ceiling, sending stucco to the floor. The nephew collapsed, weeping, between tables as the bartender struggled to make sense of this devil's visitation.

Understanding burned slowly in Mason's boozy brain. Deliverance was at hand, the Navy was rescuing him, God bless the Navy, he was sorry for all those things he said to the Project Director. He shouted through the closed shutters, "I'm coming around front! Get back to the chopper!" The plan appeared in Mason's head as the next bolt came down. He could not expose himself long to the air, so he would dive straight into his car, roll up the windows, and drive the few feet to the

114

helicopter. All he needed was ten seconds to jump in and slide the door shut. *Less* than ten seconds—he would move like a barracuda.

The pilot did not answer, probably the last bolt stunned him. Mason prayed he was only stunned. He kicked aside chairs on his way to the door.

The bar exploded in flaming electrical snakes that splintered the roof and walls, producing lights so blinding the bartender fell to the floor and buried his head. The celestial fury erupted like firebombs, concentrated detonations of such awesome power, no vault could withstand it, much less his poor cantina.

Long after they ceased, the sounds clanged through the bartender's senses. Cautiously he raised his head to look at the ruined ceiling, the burst wine, beer, and liquor bottles scattered about, their pungent contents mixing with the plaster dust.

The lightning had stopped. The bartender threw open a shutter. In the dust blown night, he saw serpents marching upright across the desert, their sinuous bodies braiding into the sky. They were dust devils, the biggest he had ever seen, swirling ropes of sand-clogged winds, reaching to the heavens.

Ah, that gringo had carried a great tale within him. The girl was weeping, the nephew was clearing away some of the rubbish. The gringo was buried beneath it. The doorknob leading outside had been metal. The bartender crossed himself and said a brief prayer for the gringo's soul.

X MINUS 52 HOURS

THE PROJECT Director lowered the phone. He did not have to speak, his expression was enough.

Kayama said, "So. That leaves only Holden."

The Project Director turned to the wall-sized map of America hanging behind them. The Gulf of Mexico lay hundreds of miles away across arid southwestern lands. "The pilot said it was the only storm in the area. He had no trouble finding it."

"And he is all right?" Kayama asked with concern.

"Right as rain." The Project Director grimaced at his pun. "He says he couldn't have saved Mason anyway, the copter was ruined."

The telephone rang again. The Project Director spoke briefly, then hung up. "Clay's coming back from Japan. You're to set up Stormfury any way you wish. Seems to me we could find it before it gets to the Gulf."

"It will be too high for us." Kayama said. "We couldn't seed it even if we did find it. So! You must gather planes all along the Gulf coast loaded with silver iodide, ready to fly the exact instant it appears. We will have at most two days. I must warn you. When it strikes the Gulf, it will move and spread with tremendous speed, much faster than it has so far. The water is warm there."

"You'll have your own plane, Kayama. An EC-135 equipped with tracking radars. It's a flying command post."

"That is appropriate," Kayama nodded. "Storm warnings should be posted along the Gulf for the next several days."

"Done." The Project Director scribbled it out on a pad. "Do you have anything remotely encouraging?"

"Why, naturally! As soon as we find Holden, we will use him to draw the storm back to the Baja. If Stormfury goes well, we can tear it to pieces on the way down. He is the storm's leash. Holden must be kept alive, you understand. If anything happens to him first . . ." Kayama chose his words with care. "But of course, it will not."

"Go on."

"If Holden, God forbid, should die in a car wreck or something like that, the storm will continue searching for him even after he is buried. It will not know he is dead, it will sweep the earth searching, always searching for him, forever, if it must. That would be intolerable, would it not?"

"How did it find Mason and Axton and Tregaskis? We're thousands of miles from Itrek. How did it know where they were?"

"It did not know. Not exactly. This storm, you see, is quite stupid. It goes in the direction of its scent even after the scent is gone, which in this case led it northeast from Itrek. It is blind, deaf, dumb, and unthinking. It is mere electricity."

"Suppose Stormfury doesn't work, then? Where does that leave us?"

"But it will work. Try to look on the good side, sir. Pessimism is bad for the health." Kayama stood up. "May I take a rest?"

"Sure. Use one of the offices down the hall. Kayama? I almost forgot. Mason said lightning hit the Berkeley Bio Lab where Croft kept his samples. Why would it do that?"

Kayama pondered the question, looking from the map to the Project

116

Director. "Undoubtedly it is a simple answer. After I have rested I shall understand. Perhaps."

X MINUS 24 HOURS

HOLDEN WAS digging into a clam hole with Dennis when a rushing roar preceded the appearance of airplanes screaming like banshees into the Gulf. He grabbed the binoculars hanging around his neck and watched them disappear. "Something's up, kid. They've been flying ever since early morning."

In the distance, Holden picked up a second wing of planes flying out of the north. "Intruders. Bombers, Dennis, not fighters. They don't use intruders for much of anything any more except weather work."

Gina waded through the sand carrying a thermos full of coffee and sat on the dune beside him. Except for the sand seeping into their sandals, it was a perfect, cozy group. Until Dennis heaved his stick at his mother and ran down the beach a few yards.

The boy's temper had sharpened since Holden had joined them. He assumed that Dennis's single anchor in the world was the undivided attention of his mother and Holden threatened that. "I guess I'll have to beat that kid," Gina said. She was not really being funny, not at bottom. She passed Holden a steaming cup of coffee. "Those airplanes woke me at five in the morning."

"I don't know what's going on. Some kind of maneuvers, but I don't know why they're using intruders."

"Seen any good spiders this morning?"

Holden imagined a bushel of grasping legs bursting from the clam hole he had been worrying. He threw away the stick and clasped his hands around his knees. "It's not so bad today. I don't see them unless I think about them. Then again I try too hard not to think about them." Holden did not state the obvious; that his nervousness was ruining their vacation. He had not had enough sleep since the day they arrived and he threw up on an average of once a day. It was a crisis which he mulled over every hour and the only possible resolution was to tell her everything. So far he had not been able to do that. He kept thinking of his contract, extrapolating all the multitudes of disasters, security leaks, blackballings from government assignments if Gina let slip so much as a hint. It was an emotional block, not a rational one, yet he could not bring himself to do it.

117

Gina unwrapped a sandwich and took a small bite. She was not very hungry. "I've been thinking. The problem is you have to talk to somebody but you can't because of the contract, right?"

"That's about it, love."

"But it's like a bad infection. Strong silent people think the weight of silence will squash the problem with time but the reverse is true. The problem grows with time."

Holden blew steam from the surface of his coffee. "I've got this ridiculous feeling that something is following me, wanting to kill me. It's always behind me and every time I relax it comes closer. Yet I can't see it. I can't find it and even if I could, it's too big for me."

"Would paranoia be too strong a word?"

"No, that's about right, I'd say."

"What is this something, exactly?"

The skies. The heavens. The clouds. A thing with a nervous system extending possibly hundreds of miles. Better yet a huge web such as the one they had seen on the infrared that night on Itrek. "I don't know. A big spider, maybe."

"My idea is a shrink. You see you've got to talk to *somebody*. Shrinks are professionally bound to keep secrets, even government ones. James and I knew a guy in Pensacola. I could put you in touch with him."

"I've thought about it. I'm not sure what good it would do."

"It's not like being crazy, I hope you don't think that. You just talk and calm down and everything. I was thinking of calling on him myself."

Some affair, Holden thought ruefully. Two lovers needing a middleman to get through to each other. He felt a small twinge of self-loathing to add to his nerves. He was not much help to Gina. He ought to be a strong arm to lean on, a sympathetic ear, a reassuring presence, a masculine aid to bring her out of her grief. Instead he was adding to it. "I don't know what to tell you except don't worry. It's not a permanent thing, it's just a reaction to the . . . the . . . project. Lots of people freak out at spiders, you could make a club out of them."

Gina tucked her legs under her and hunched her shoulders against the sea breeze. Her shoulders were wide and narrow, almost like wings. *She's too thin*, Holden decided. *Thin and angular, she folds up when she sits down*. Gina said, "This psychiatrist once told me that there's a theory that a fear of spiders is a fear of your own mother. The web that holds you, the legs that embrace you while they're killing you."

That was a startling thought. Holden's mother had had visits from weekend "cousins" whenever his father had been away at sea after three weeks. Yet she had solemnly instilled in him an exaggerated respect for women, warning him to stick with "simple" girls. Holden had been raised in a world where women were either frustrated navy wives or soldier groupies—aging ladies with rhinestone glasses hanging around bases awaiting the marine of their dreams. Not to mention the simpering high school majorettes toting up a man's earning power behind glittering shark smiles. His mother had been truly shocked when he opted for the Air Force instead of the Navy. He was certain that his decision had sent her to an early grave. It was hard to translate memories of maternal resentment into the kind of buried, neurotic hatred Gina was suggesting, but nothing surprised him anymore. "I never thought about that," he admitted to her. "My trouble is I never analyzed myself much."

Gina continued, "You see, you could draw it out eventually to a hatred of all women. Webs and legs and everything. I've met a lot of men who thought women were vampires. Spiders are vampires. They tie you down and bleed you to death."

"Good Lord, is that what you're thinking?"

She peered into the clam hole. "Let's just say it crossed my mind."

He tried to touch her shoulder but she hunched defensively away from his fingers. "Gina that's . . . Never!"

"It's quite a coincidence, isn't it? I show up again and suddenly you're a nervous wreck."

"But this has nothing to do with you!"

"Not now, maybe, but it could be just a matter of time. We're just trying this affair out, remember, to see if it works. Maybe this is a warning that it won't."

Down the beach Dennis glanced back at the sound of their voices, then threw a stone in the water.

"It's not you," he said grimly. "I swear it isn't you."

"Talk to me then, Jeff. I can keep a secret."

He believed her, yet something stopped him—a loss of words, a lack of conviction, a fear that by breaking his word he would lose part of himself. Now he was afraid that he would lose her if he did not talk about it and that was an equally lethal prospect.

His quandary was underscored by another wing of intruders roaring overhead so low he clutched his ears. "Where the hell are they *going*! I've got this feeling I'm missing something. Like there's a party going on somewhere and I wasn't invited."

119

"Oh, I sure know that feeling. What kind of party did you have in mind?"

"All those planes running around. It's like skimming over eastern Europe. Every other day they scrambled planes after us and sometimes they chased us."

"Is that where you were? Chasing Russians?"

"No, nothing like that." And very simply Holden, beginning with a hesitant voice that grew stronger as he talked, lanced the boil inside him and let the poison out. He broke his contract, betrayed his ancestors, and told Gina everything about Project Windowpane. Everything. Vivid images of the storm, the lightning, Kilgallen's flying body, the laser, the exploding destroyer, the recurring spiders, all tumbled out of him and landed on her, like brightly colored, inflammable debris. It was a catalog of horrors to Holden but Gina listened with complete equanimity. She did not even seem particularly impressed, but heard him out with intense curiosity.

"Wow," she said, finally, passing a thermos mug full of hot coffee to him. "They picked you out of how many?"

"Oh, one or two. Me and Kayama."

"Ten thousand I bet. Fifteen thousand. They went for the best."

Holden very nearly found himself crying. "It was luck and good ancestors. That storm was the major discovery. I had this idea that it was from space but I don't really know that, none of us really know what it was. I don't know if this spider business is psychological or if the electricity did something permanent to my head. You can see it doesn't have anything to do with you. I sure hope you weren't counting on any trips to the south seas."

She slipped back up the dune, wrapped his arm around her chest as though to warm herself, and kissed his hand. "You know something? In a million years I never thought I'd fall in love with a soldier."

"I'm not a soldier anymore, I'm a weatherman. Besides, I wouldn't have told you anything if I was a good soldier."

"Sure, you're a soldier. You've just got combat fatigue. There's worse professions, I think. You're not a pimp, you don't make poisoned baby food, you're not a crooked lawyer. You're an officer and a gentleman. It's a privilege to know you."

"I'm a lunatic," he replied. "Soldiers don't run away from spiders. They run away from other soldiers if they have any brains."

She wrapped his other arm around her. By the small movements of her head, Holden knew she was watching Dennis. "Would they really use a weapon like that in a war?"

120

Holden thought of MIGs sailing in over Europe, tales of blood, atrocity, and hate going back to the Civil War told to him by his mother and, in the distant past, his father. He answered reluctantly. "Probably. In a war you start out like gentlemen and wind up using everything you've got. From what they said at the Naval Weapons Center, the laser will be mounted in satellites rather than ships. There's less light distortion in space." He kissed her to change the subject. "I thought it would be a burden to you, too. It's a nasty business. I didn't want *you* to see spiders."

She watched Dennis as he tried to make a seashell fly into the surf like one of the planes screaming overhead. "I have a couple of secrets myself."

ZERO HOUR

KAYAMA SPENT every waking hour airborne in a huge EC-135 cargo plane trying to track the storm that had killed Samuel Mason. In the emptiness of the Southwest, the skies were clear except for paint swatches of altocirrus clouds around sixty thousand feet. Like sheerest cotton, the delicate streaks moved eastward and began turning into fat cumulonimbus as they approached the coast of Texas. So gradual, so unspectacular was the descent from the upper atmosphere that only occasional bursts of static from the circling planes indicated anything unusual.

And then everything happened at once. Kayama's seat was at the back of the plane where his own radar was hooked into the giant radar weather fence running from Mexico to Florida to monitor Gulf storms. A NIMBUS satellite revealed spotty blanks of infrared being absorbed over an area of two hundred miles. Ships plied the Gulf from New Orleans, Port Arthur, Texas, and other seacoast cities to measure swells and temperature. Kayama was drinking tea and talking to the radarman at his console when the circling planes reported violent winds and clouds appearing along the Texas coast.

The storms literally exploded into life. Local weathermen thought them freak summer storms until the Weather Network reported they had appeared simultaneously everywhere. The rains gushed down into Houston, Texas, catching everyone without an umbrella, soaking into the parched grassland and grazing grounds of the ranches. For two hours it rained continuously with such violence, fishing boats were driven back to ports, then instead of slackening off, the rains increased to near hurricane intensity and one by one Kayama saw the storms spread, touch, and link together. Only then did the weather begin to clear over land as the storm formed a gigantic front that slashed into the Gulf with the prevailing easterly winds. By noon Kayama was watching it split in two like a dividing microbe, the western cluster forming a massive, sweating hot convection system that attached itself to the sea like a huge cruising fungoid, the eastern section becoming a brutal mass of gales and stinging rain. Connecting the two was a cloud deck of winds that pumped moisture from the western to the eastern section.

"It's like a cobra," Kayama said in wonderment to the radarman. "The head is the eastern cluster, the body is the wind bridge, the tail remains anchored to the sea. See how the eastern section forms squalls, how it moves around, here a thunderhead, there it's clear skies . . ." Kayama's voice trailed off as he contemplated the changing eastern cluster. It darted, sniffed, and circled, its eyes, ears and tongue, brief localized cloudbursts that popped up over the Gulf. Kayama said softly. "So. That will be our target: to cut off the head and watch it die. We must map this out in detail . . ."

"Which ought to take two hours," the radarman commented.

". . . before we seed it. You have observed that something is missing from both clusters."

"No. What?"

Kayama held up a sheaf of wind and humidity data which poured in over the weather network. "No lightning, no thunder. If there is no thunder, it is not a thunderstorm—so what is it?" Kayama's cackle attracted a few irritated looks from the rest of the crew at their consoles lining the aisle.

The radarman said, "You wish to seed the rain cells in the eastern storm."

"Yes. Before we do, may I ask if any American planes have ever flown directly into a thunderstorm cell?"

"Yes indeed sir, many times. Unfortunately none have ever flown out again."

"Most amusing. Remind the pilots, would you, that the core of a thunderstorm is vertical winds. The innermost core of wind goes straight up and spills out the top of the cloud, the outermost rush downward over the land. It is not like a hurricane's circular force, so delivering the silver iodide is likely to be tricky. The alectoes must be delivered through these winds into the rain cells." The alectoes were seven-pound, finned, aluminum cylinders which released cloud-seeding chemicals at preset altitudes. "In a normal storm they would plummet straight through with no problem but normal storms do not have wind shear like this creature. In this turbulence, an alecto could be blown right back into the plane."

"They're all trained bomber pilots, Mr. Kayama."

"Now, sir."

"Yes?" The radarman was impatient with Kayama's little dramatic pauses.

"Warn the air crews that this particular cobra might get mad. It has fangs. I should like to know how it uses them."

Kayama examined the storm charts. The rain cells looked like bacteria scattered over the Gulf. No one had ever flown into a thunderstorm and actually seen what went on inside. Now that Kayama thought of it, thunderstorms were like scavengers that threw excess ions back to the ground. In another way of thinking the storm cloud was the home of Zeus. The ancients had given the winds and lightning a personality ever since the first branch was burst from a tree. Was there a god inside them? Or many gods who lurked within the sheaths of wind, unapproachable by aircraft?

Alas, Kayama was not in the solitude of his office. He would like to pursue this thinking at some quiet time in the future. For now he felt the EC-135 bank toward the eastern cluster of storms. He put away his restless thoughts of electrical divinities and concentrated on the spinning computer reels and the diamond-shaped rain cells speckling the green screens of the target radars.

The Stormfury planes lifted off from airbases scattered along the crescent coast of the Gulf of Mexico, dozens of Grumman intruders, sweptwinged, crablike bombers that could jackhammer into the strongest headwinds. Kayama's silver EC-135 was their fire control and from it came the pilots' target information.

The intruders attacked the rain cells as though they were actual targets. They roared in from as high as forty thousand feet, the pilots and navigators rigid with concentration against the turbulence, then yanked the planes upward at the rain cells. From the bomb bays showers of alectoes spun at an angle that slingshot them into the radar blips. The alectoes released silver iodide at preset altitudes, an incredibly fine, smoky powder whose atomic structure resembled the lattice arrangement of ice. A cloud unable to tell the difference between a grain of silver iodide and a minute droplet of ice caused the particles to collect additional layers of water until the weight became so heavy, they rained out to the ground.

It was over an hour before the results became visible. The clouds ballooned upwards like giant cauliflowers. Onto the waters beneath the storms it began to rain in incredible amounts. The wind bridge from the western storm blew the water droplets ever higher, churning them around with unimaginable fury until hailstones the size of marbles pounded down on a shrimp boat straggling back to its New Orleans port.

The alectoes purged the waters from the clouds while other intruders dropped cannisters of dry ice over the rippled surfaces of cloud decks and carved great steaming canyons in them. The planes attacked the storm like wasps stinging a bull elephant. In his plane, Kayama pieced together the results.

They were not very encouraging. Despite the seeding, the storm continued growing in size and power until by nightfall it had crossed the Gulf and was approaching the Gulf coast of Florida. Every time a squall was extinguished a new one appeared. The storm swells washed saltwater floods over the farmlands along the Mississippi valley. At eight o'clock that night Chicago recorded temperatures of thirty-five degrees, a record cold for that time of year, while south of them St. Louis, Missouri, perspired under an eighty-degree night. Hot air from the Gulf and cold air from Canada were closing across the country like a pair of pincers.

Because of the ripsawing storms, the Federal Aviation Administration issued an aircraft weather advisory of Sigmet Active for the entire Gulf. Sigmet Active stood for Significant Meteorological Activity. This warning diverted all commercial and private planes away from the Gulf, leaving the storm wide open for Project Stormfury.

X PLUS 6 HOURS

To THE NIMBUS satellite the storm that night was a mass of white fuzz obscuring half of the Gulf. Kayama sketched arrows slanting from south Texas northeast toward Massachusetts. "Tornado alley," he said to the Project Director seated in the pilot debriefing room in Pensacola. "This is the path most of the twisters take. They travel like thunderstorms from southwest to northeast, their movement determined by the earth's rotation."

"Is Stormfury doing any good or do we hire raindancers?"

Kayama had not realized until then that the Project Director had a sense of humor. "Most amusing, sir. Today we hit it when it was still growing, so even if Stormfury's working it's not doing what we wish it to do, which is to shrink the storm's size. As for inland storms . . ." Kayama shrugged. "Stormfury may very well be helping with that. We are keeping the really hot cells at bay down in the Gulf but we are specks blowing around a mountain. We cannot halt the laws of thermodynamics."

"Then tornadoes can be expected by tomorrow night." To the Project Director the twin clusters resembled the figure 8 laid on its side. "You did not touch the western storm."

"We did late this afternoon with a dozen planes. We shall again tomorrow." Kayama had been eating a chicken drumstick. He had consumed it to the bone. He dropped the bone in the trash can, scooped up every crumb of crust, and dried his fingers. "Tomorrow we shall also try something more daring."

"What's that?"

Kayama tapped the narrow part of the figure 8. "The winds, sir. We shall pour silver iodide directly into the winds and let the cobra carry the poison through its own bloodstream. Our shot to the head was not so effective, perhaps poison in its winds will be ultimately more damaging. It will require several times the amount of silver iodide we used today."

The Project Director read off the wind speeds. "They've clocked those winds at seventy miles per hour, Kayama."

"I am assured by the pilots themselves that it will be, as you say, a piece of cake. Now if Holden were with us . . ." He left the thought unfinished. He had repeated that same sentence to himself all day.

"He hasn't shown up at his apartment. The FBI and the Florida police are trying to find him, but I'm beginning to think the FBI couldn't find a battleship in a vegetable garden."

"Yet that is why he was chosen for Windowpane, was it not? A man who would leave no trace if he disappeared. Your security staff did their work well."

"You recall we almost chose you. Would you leave a trace if you disappeared, Kayama?"

He would be a memory in the minds of students and a notation in publications dealing with weather sciences. He had always been too busy for women or friends. Yet Kayama was not bothered by his aloneness. He had always been alone but not lonely. "I would leave circular rings on tables from my teacups and much unfinished work. And I would not care. Isn't that terrible of me?"

* * *

That afternoon the FBI Regional Office in Pensacola began a serious effort to locate Jeffrey Holden. He had not returned to his apartment for several days, nor had he registered for classes at school, nor had his neighbors seen him. His car was gone and mail clogged his lobby box. The superintendent did not know a woman had been living with him, but the neighbors did. Nice girl with a cute little boy named Dennis.

The bank informed them that Holden had withdrawn three hundred dollars in cash. That evening a bag team with a court order entered Holden's apartment and searched it.

They found heavy winter clothes for a child, clean curtains, hanging plants, and textbooks. Dresses and skirts hung in a tiny closet and a few oil paintings by a J. Lambert were tucked behind them. To their amazement Gina Lambert had no bankbook, medical bills, job paychecks, or tax receipts. The reason was soon obvious. A red address book listed several numbers in the state of Oregon. Holden had no personal correspondence of any kind.

Bulletins with Holden's license plate number went out to police offices in Florida and Oregon and agents went to a small town in the foothills of the Cascades to interview the people in Gina's address book. They were painters, writers, a pair of actors, and several photographers all drawn to the area by its isolation. All had known James and Gina Lambert, none had ever heard of Jeffrey Holden. They said Gina had left after her husband died and assumed she was returning to Pensacola where they had lived before.

One of the agents figured, "She'd go back to her in-laws, right? She hasn't any family, she's got a kid, she wouldn't just show up at an old boyfriend's. She's got to have in-laws. If she's there, maybe Holden is, too."

How many Lamberts were there in Florida? Hundreds. How many with recently deceased sons who were painters? The Regional Office informed Washington that James Lambert was their only lead and that if he had parents in Florida they'd find them in twenty-four hours.

"Which we haven't got," Washington retorted. "We need Holden by evening and Lambert's a pretty tenuous lead."

"What's the rush?"

"You'll have to ask the Defense Department. They insist Holden be found by tonight. Didn't this guy have any friends?"

"Plenty. They're all in the Air Force. He doesn't know anybody in school, he's older than the other students. He's out of the service so he doesn't have to check in anywhere."

By noon they were certain that none of the Lamberts in Pensacola had anything to do with Gina or Holden. It would take hours to run down Lamberts in the other cities, the Regional Office explained to Washington.

Washington decided to go public. Holden's picture and name would be leaked to the wire services and television stations that afternoon, and a cover story was prepared asking people to report him to the nearest police station. The Regional Office was left with the distinct impression that a hefty percentage of the Defense Department was quaking in its boots about Jeffrey Holden. It must, they figured, be the biggest espionage case since the Rosenbergs.

X PLUS 24 HOURS

In the morning wave after wave of intruders with silver iodide smoke generators beneath their wings drilled into the hurricane winds between the storm clusters and sent hundreds of alectoes tumbling into the layers of clouds. Kayama could not count how many bomber wings participated in the attack. He knew they had flown in squadrons from all over the country and that it was the largest single assault ever mounted against a storm by aircraft.

The waters of the Gulf of Mexico were spattered by the empty alectoes, some of them blown miles away by the furies. There was no possible way of telling where the silver iodide went. Kayama had stressed that the only possible strategy was to fill the air so full of the powder, both storms would become saturated. After the first wave of planes a hailstorm sent one wing limp and dented back to its Eglin base in Texas. After that, Kayama could not tell if there was any effect at all.

Although he never gave the slightest hint of his feelings, the storm was getting to Kayama in a psychological way. It seemed his whole existence had been spent in a pressurized aircraft thousands of feet above ground squinting at digital readouts and blinking radar blips. The entire world was a groundless limbo in which humans in aircraft crept across vacuum screens trying to grapple with sullen clouds and furious sweeps of wind and rain. Kayama thought there was a metaphor for human existence in there somewhere. The satellite photos that came regularly into the plane seemed to confirm this. To NIMBUS's olympian glass eye, all of the thunder and the supreme human effort were but a faint discoloration of cloud in the Gulf of Mexico.

The radarman was talking insistently to him, leaning against the table as the EC-135 clattered over turbulence. "Something is happening, Mr. Kayama."

Kayama scanned the computer data. The winds in the eastern storm were slowing down. In seconds Kayama was talking to Admiral Clay at the Naval Weapons Center. "I am delighted to report that the storm has slowed its eastward move toward Florida."

Clay sounded relieved. "That's encouraging. This whole business is getting expensive. Is the storm getting smaller?"

"We will know that in a few minutes. I expect something dramatic is about to happen."

"Such as what, Kayama?"

"The storm is juggling its thermals around, sir. In response to the silver iodide?" The last statement was delicately toned in a rising suggestive voice. When Clay did not take the bait, Kayama said bluntly, "The phrase is that the storm will not take this lying down."

For a moment, Kayama happily thought Clay would respond with a derisive oath but the Admiral apparently thought a muttered curse of disgust sufficient. Kayama was overcome by a feeling of guilt. It was unfair to bait the Admiral just because he did not view Stormfury in the metaphysical way that Kayama did.

It was the intruder's fourth bombing run in five hours and the crew was exhausted. The pilot had lifted off in drizzling rain and near-zero visibility and the sheer concentration needed to keep the plane level had made his muscles knot up.

Below them the cloud deck was a white rumpled mattress, spanning the mountainous storms. From the intruder's vantage point it looked placid and soft, yet the crew was acutely aware that the winds encasing it could rend the plane into splinters.

The intruder carried two smoke generators that burned silver iodide smoke in a thin trail. Similar equipment was carried by the remainder of the wing flying behind them. The pilot examined the clouds, picked a section, and dove down.

They released their alectoes and were climbing back up to altitude when an enormous hole opened beneath them in the cloud deck. Through this hole there blew a volcano of wind which caught the intruder as it was standing on its tail and hurled it in a twisting, cartwheeling trajectory straight up as a chimney draft blows a cinder out the top.

The pilot flipped the intruder on its back, watching the altimeter climb to sixty-five thousand feet. Below him more craters popped open in the clouds and the winds mixed bits of tattered cloud with the intruders bouncing like ping-pong balls all over the skies. For a few moments, multiple disasters seemed inevitable as frantic pilots maneuvered their tumbling planes away from each other and tried to inch out of the columns of wind. The wing leader radioed Kayama's plane. "We hit some shear. Jesus, did we hit some shear! The whole cloud deck is breaking up!" To the pilot the punctured cloud deck looked like a cratered lunar landscape. The copilot managed to trigger the camera and photograph it, but such were the gyrations of the plane that he knew the film would be useless.

Before the eyes of Kayama and the radarman, the storm reformed itself, eliminating its twin clusters and becoming a single huge oval. The incoming planes smashed full tilt into headwinds that scattered their silver iodide all over the atmosphere.

Kayama's EC-135 had been flying through clear skies. Now it found itself caught in crosswinds with clouds forming above and beneath it. The plane reversed course so abruptly, Kayama's tea splashed over his white shirt. On the radars the neat, organized bomber formations became scattered confetti, and the air waves filled with pilots' shouted obscenities as they found planes roaring in front of them, down on top of them, and blowing up from beneath them. There were numerous wing-tip collisions but no deaths.

"The cobra has struck." Kayama mopped his forehead. "How interesting."

The radarman called out, "Mr. Kayama, we're picking up lightning activity."

"Where?"

"It's over near Florida." Kayama bent over his shoulder. "See? What's that cloud formation there?"

The storm was not a perfect ovoid after all. A finger of cloud was pushing insistently for the Florida coast. The lightning activity seethed within it. Kayama said, "There are no planes there and no seeding activity. Yet it's the only lightning in the whole system. How long has this been going on?"

"Just for the past five minutes. That cloud formation began forming about ten minutes ago. I wasn't sure if it was real or what. It's about ten miles from land."

A blast of wind thudded against the plane, almost knocking Kayama to the floor.

"There's no question that the storm is hurting," said the radarman. "It's almost as if it's tightening itself up."

"No," Kayama murmured. "It was not us. It was something else."

"Like what?"

Kayama made his way back to his own console and dialed the Naval Weapons Center.

"Clay here. Kayama? You really stung the thing this time. I've been getting all kinds of reports."

"It was not us, sir. I believe the storm has found Mr. Holden for us." Kayama circled a section of the Florida coast where the clouds were moving. "He is somewhere within three or four hundred square miles between Tampa and a place called Cedar Key."

Clay allowed himself one exclamation before putting Kayama on hold and calling the FBI. When he came back on, he was breathless. "That's great, Kayama. How do you know?"

"The storm itself has fingered him, as they say. He has about an hour, I would estimate."

"They won't find him that quick."

"He will find us, Admiral. He will realize what is happening any minute now. I hope he realizes it in time to save himself."

"Suppose he doesn't?" Clay said. "Suppose the storm gets him like it did the others. What would happen then?"

"Its charge will balance out. It will either disappear or return to its own domain, and the sun will shine again over the Gulf of Mexico." Kayama did not follow up with the obvious questions. Such thoughts were the business of Admirals.

"I must say it would solve a lot of problems. Goodbye, Kayama."

The finger of cloud lengthened, eager to get to land, and the rest of the storm closed in behind. Perhaps Holden already knew what was happening and had jumped in a car. He could very well be running for his life right now. Kayama found himself hoping the woman and boy were not with him. The description of Kilgallen's death on Itrek made Kayama think such things should not be witnessed by anyone.

Kayama finished the dregs of tea then went back to the washroom to put on a fresh white shirt.

The spiders were back.

Holden had been half asleep when the conviction that his bed was full of the creatures detonated him awake with a pounding, shocked heart. They were on the doorknobs leading to the living room, climbing the windows, plopping off tables in the living room.

Holden squeezed his eyes shut until tears of pain oozed out. Well, there was nothing wrong with mental illness, it happened to the best people. God knows he had undergone the necessary traumas for hallucinations. His mother had known sailors so shell-shocked, they passed their days in mental wards reliving Pearl Harbor.

Holden peered over the edge of the bed. Hundreds of spiders zipped under the mattress. "Hello, boys," he said out loud, his voice ringing through the house. Gina and Dennis had gone marketing that morning, leaving him to sleep as much as possible.

The floorboards were cold to his bare feet. Apparently the sun had decided not to come out today. He shook spiders from his shoes, walked into the kitchen, cleared spiders out of the refrigerator, and chased them out of the toaster slots. He buttered a piece of toast and raised it to his mouth, then decided he could not eat with a tarantula splayed on the butter.

"This is serious," he said out loud to the walls. "If you can't even eat, that's plenty serious, Jeff, old boy."

A faint rumble passed through the walls of the house. Holden thought the refrigerator had come on but there was no vibration, just the sounds of the surf. Furnace then? Water pump? Holden cocked his head listening.

Again the rumble, so low in scale it tickled his bones. *Now, what the hell!* It occurred to him the table looked like the one his mother had had in her study. He ran his fingers over the surface, touching the cracks, flicking away the spiders, suddenly recalling that his mother had had a calendar book with a dog-eared upper-right-hand corner and an ink stain on the first page. She had been angry at him because he drew airplanes on one of the pages, obscuring an entry about a dentist appointment. The dentist was a short man with bad breath who gave him some kind of yellow pills instead of novocaine . . .

What the hell!

Holden buried his head in his hands. He had not thought about such things since he was a child. No. *Not since Itrek!* The ring of the telephone propelled him from his chair and sent spiders scurrying everywhere, into curtain folds, under furniture, and down the sink drain.

"Tournedos with artichoke tops," Gina said gaily. "Vanilla ice cream. Potatoes au gratin, garlic bread, and rich red wine. Then eggs benedict tomorrow and, since you like slumming, some hot chili dogs just for you."

Holden imagined chasing imaginary spiders off Gina's gourmet meals as they cooled, and she wondered why he did not like her cooking. "If you don't bring potato chips, I won't touch the stuff."

"Okay, I'll eat it. Did you just wake up?"

"I'm not awake. I'm talking in my sleep."

"That's good, that's just terrific. Go back to bed, you won't miss another couple of hours."

"Sure." The bed covers rustled with gaily fornicating spiders. Holden snickered. At least he had not lost his sense of humor. How did spiders do it, anyway, with all those legs?

"How are you feeling?"

"Not bad."

"Oh, hell. What's wrong, Jeff?"

He switched the phone to the other ear. "My little friends are back. It's worse than it was yesterday. I'm seeing them everywhere."

She said, "It sounds like bad acid backing up on you."

"That's exactly it. I'm wondering if that storm didn't do something permanent. Seems to me if electricity shoots through your head, it might leave a few scars. It's happened to people who have had shock treatments."

"Flip a coin, Jeff. You can see a shrink or have an encephalogram. You were all right yesterday. Get out the bug spray and I'll be home in about an hour to hold your hand."

The house shook with the low sound, as if a heavy truck were passing. Holden looked at the refrigerator again, then with a flashlight tramped down the basement stairs. Fear of spiders prevented him from going all the way in. The basement was dark. He saw no water on the floor from a broken pipe and the furnace fan was not on.

Clinging to a light switch was a large furry spider. Holden clenched his teeth and touched it. Plain old plastic light switch.

As he got dressed, the wind blew and the sound came again. It was not in the house, it was outside. It was not from a passing truck. It was distant thunder so far away as to be barely audible.

He stepped outside with binoculars to see the woolen heaps of cloud on the horizon. The storm was pretty far out to sea, farther than it had been the day it hit Itrek, so it would not get here for another hour. Holden examined it with the binoculars.

The storm grumbled.

Holden slowly lowered the binoculars, smiling bleakly. He was neither surprised, shocked, nor terrified. If anything, he was relieved that he was not losing his mind or headed for a nervous breakdown. His enemy was out in the open. *Persistent bastard.* Life always formed little circles that kept returning to you. Itrek was coming for him as the Navy had come for all the men in his family. The island was in his soul and would not leave him alone. He rewrapped the binocular cord and returned to the house. He dialed the Naval Weapons Center and spoke to an officer for one minute. Then he packed and tried to think of what to say to Gina as helicopters came barreling into the beach and all but skidded to a stop on the sands.

Navy men swarmed over the house and beach as Gina drove down the dirt road leading to the house. Holden awaited her by the garage. He seemed relaxed to her but there was something disturbing behind his smile. He guided her to the side of the house. "This is wild. They've been looking for me for days. I have to fill out some reports in quintriplicate and swear allegiance to the flag and then I'll be back."

Gina had planned to let her weight go up for one more week before going back to cottage cheese and melon balls. Until now, it had been shaping up as an idyllic week. Now it looked as if war had been declared and Holden had been drafted. She looked at the helicopters. "All this for a few debriefings?"

"I'm sorry."

"They're overdoing it, aren't they? Did they really have to come in here and snatch you away like this?"

"The Navy never knocks on a door if they can break it down first." Holden tried to make it all seem bureaucratic nonsense but he was anxious and shifted weight from one foot to the other. He kept glancing at the storm behind the helicopters.

"Jeffrey, I must say you're beginning to get an air of mystery about you. Under any other circumstances it would be irresistible, but not like this. When will you be back?"

"I'm not sure. I'll have to call you tonight."

"What'll I do with the food? Mail it to California?"

"Eat as much as you can and save the rest for me."

"Should I go back to Pensacola?"

"No. Wait for my call and we'll take it from there." Abruptly he kissed her cheek and walked toward the copters, ruffling Dennis's hair as he passed. Dennis was gaping in joy at the helicopters.

"Looks like rain, Jeff," she called after him.

"Oh, yeah? Well, it's that time of year in Florida."

"Uh huh."

"Yeah, there'll be storms moving through central Florida all summer."

Gina waved listlessly as the copters churned into the air and headed out to sea. Dennis jumped up and down in excitement shouting at them as they faded to specks and disappeared into the haze.

It had been a guilt-ridden goodbye. Gina knew if she were a proper military girlfriend she'd wave away her noble lover with banked sorrow as he went off to war. But her confusion gave way to massive annoyance. She had bought enough food for a month and had been cultivating hunger all day. Angrily she loaded steaks into the refrigerator.

They had been inching toward a certain type of intimacy which she was going to use to explain something to him. Tonight she had planned to get him full of steak, nice and drunk and in a good mood, sufficiently cheerful to absorb certain revelations. In fact, she had planned the sojourn at the beach house around tonight.

Damn it.

Lightning blinked from the storm as it rode toward the shore. It was an ugly jumbled thing, all dirty yellowish mist and black mushroom-cloud domes. Rain foamed the sea beneath it.

X PLUS 26 HOURS

THEY EXCHANGED greetings in the EC-135 in Pensacola while awaiting a call from Admiral Clay. Holden sat at Kayama's radar desk and accepted a cup of tea. "Spiders," Kayama was musing. "That is what you feel as it approaches you."

"I put that in the report, Kayama."

"Forgive me. I only read the technicals. You are feeling well?" He asked with courteous concern.

"I've felt better. It's like being chased by a vampire. Is Stormfury working?"

"I think we are successful," he beamed. "Of course we will not know for sure until all the data is analyzed, but it's been crippled all day compared to its motion last night." He shook his head and looked into his tea, his basic calm forming a small island of peace on the plane. "It is remarkable. Remarkable. All of this for just four men."

Holden blew steam from the surface of his tea. "It was just a matter of time, I guess. I always thought it had found me when we were on *McClusky* that night. I guess it just goes in the same direction as its scent until it finds what it's looking for."

"Did you know it had killed animals in Croft's laboratory?"

Holden was startled. "No, I didn't."

They watched each other, hoping one would offer an obvious explanation, but none was forthcoming. Kayama said, "I have been pondering that and I must confess I don't understand. It is a small thing. I expect before this is over and we have vanquished it, we will find many, many other bafflements."

"Here's one that hits me," Holden ruminated. "How did it cross the Pacific without being seen?"

"It was seen by an airliner which flew through it. Remember?"

Holden shook his head. "It was just an electric field when that happened. On Itrek it was a beast of a storm. Here it's a beast of a storm. Why wasn't it a storm in the Pacific until it hit Seattle? The bigger it is, the faster and farther it can move, yet it shrank on its way to Seattle."

Kayama allowed a frown on his smooth face. He started to say something, then realized Holden's thought was far more complex than he realized. The telephone buzzed. Kayama handed it to Holden and picked up another one to listen in. Admiral Clay was on the line, his voice angry, as always. Holden thought it interesting that he sounded the same over a phone line as he did in person. "Holden? We went through bloody hell trying to find you."

"Before we go through more hell, Admiral, I'd better explain about Gina. She doesn't know anything. I was not with her at the time I signed the Windowpane contract . . ."

"Christ, Holden, nobody cares about that now."

"I don't want anything to happen to her. I am not in violation of my contract."

Clay's temper was squeezed between the press of time and Holden's delay. "I understand."

"Good. Kayama is my witness."

Kayama seemed to find the exchange hilarious. One small hand was pressed to his lips and he chortled soundlessly.

"Here's what we're going to do, Holden. We're going to pull a Mason on this thing. We're going to put you in Texas and hope the storm goes right back the way it came."

Aghast, Holden lowered the phone and looked at Kayama, who nodded. "What is the sense in that? We already know it can cross a desert."

Kayama said hastily, "At high altitude, yes, Mr. Holden. Above six thousand feet, its moisture is bound up as ice. But you will be on the ground, you understand, so the storm will stay on the ground to follow you. It cannot form ice then, so the aridity will dry it out. If we get it far inland, it will not be able to draw on the water of the Gulf of Mexico.''

"Oh." Holden was not enthusiastic.

Clay continued, "Kayama's worried about that Canadian air coming down, too. The Gulf is a hot box right now. Get it out of the Gulf and away from the Midwest and we might stop tornadoes from forming.''

"Okay," Holden perked up a bit at that piece of reason. "All you'll need is for me to run around in a car or something, isn't that right?''

"That's about it. If Mason had not stopped at that cantina, if he had gone a little farther north toward Texas, he might have stranded this thing in the desert himself. It's the longest, driest piece of land it's encountered, yet it stayed too high to lose its moisture.''

Something was wrong with that idea but Holden could not pin it down. The storm was as chained to him as he was to it—it would hug the dry, stony sands of New Mexico. If Holden could keep moving from grounded area to grounded area, he would force the storm to exhaust itself.

It sounded great. Holden wished he were more enthusiastic. "How long do you figure this will take?''

Clay and Kayama both spoke at once. Estimates ranged from two or three days to two or three months. Holden would keep moving, the Air Force would keep seeding, the storm would be unable to get to water. Rivers? They had them all mapped out. Any time it looked like it was going near water, Holden would move close to it and draw it away again before it could gain moisture.

"We're starting tonight," said Clay. "We'll set you down between Corpus Christi and Austin. It should start going after you around midnight tonight.'' Clay hung up without saying goodbye.

The EC-135's engines whined, the cabin pressurized, and the plane lifted off the runway of Pensacola heading west. Somebody brought Holden a ham and cheese sandwich. "Kayama? Do you think this will work?''

Kayama said carefully, "It is not so elegant, so clean-cut, no. But our virtue is patience. The storm will eventually weaken and one morning it will not be there anymore; there will be only some damp sand.''

"It's big.''

"You have noticed it gets smaller, more compact as it approaches its target.''

"You've got an answer for everything.''

Kayama sighed, revealing more uncertainty in the sound than he had in his words. "I do not know why it killed animals in Berkeley. That answer I do not have.''

136

"I wish I knew why nobody saw it in the Pacific. I'd feel better about this whole plan if I did," Holden chewed his sandwich moodily.

The storm closed over the west coast of Florida, socking it in with rain and fog. The EC-135 was headed in for its glide to Corpus Christi when the Stormfury pilots reported intense lightning activity in a small, concentrated part of the Florida beach.

They could see it happen on their own radars, the lightning erupting in such intensity, the static blotted out the beach. Holden felt his stomach rotate, the food, the tea, all congealed into an icy ball hardened by the purest horror. Lightning was striking the beach house. He stared at the screen, too shattered to think, to speak, to move, to do anything but mentally curse himself, the Navy, and the world.

Kayama ordered the pilot to head at full speed back to Pensacola. He called Clay and told him the timetable was changed. He did not speak to Holden, who sat before the radar screen, hands clasped before him, trying to fathom this event. The lightning strikes were a short, brutally intensive bombardment that lasted only seven minutes. When it ceased, there was no more electrical activity anywhere in the Gulf of Mexico.

Gina and Dennis had been sitting on a dune overlooking the tide, savoring the cool, fresh air coming in with the storm. Gina watched Dennis playing in the surf. He ran up to her with a stick and swatted her in the knee.

"Dennis, he'll be back."

The child was livid with rage, refusing to come into the house with her, preferring to watch the fat clouds piling heavily over them.

She tried to zip up his jacket but he pulled away and ran down the beach. She followed in a black mood, picked him up bodily, and carted him toward the house.

Fat drops of warm rain peppered the water and splattered the sand. This new phenomenon directed Dennis's attention from his anger. "Rain," he said, looking up.

The sunlight vanished as if God's eye had closed and they were plunged into an oceanic gloom which matched Gina's mood perfectly. Above them she saw a gigantic, yellowish sickle of cloud. Her eyes went to the rest of the storm and she was surprised to see how it was rushing toward them.

She dismissed the tremor of unease. She had not been to Itrek, this had nothing to do with her.

Dennis's gaze was fixed on the cloud sickle. There was something

137

strange about it, no question about that. It was not moving with the wind like the others. It hung in the sky as if nailed there, its color a lighter yellow than the others from the lightning glowing within it.

Lightning shot across the cloud with a grating concussion that knocked Gina to the sand. Rain hammered down, muddying the sand and soaking Dennis. The child sat on the ground, his eyes bulging, his hands hovering near his head as if trying to hear something. "Airplane," he said.

"Dennis, come on!" Gina grabbed his hand and dragged him toward the house. She felt her scalp tingle and the hair stand out from her body.

"Dennis!"

She flung him bodily away as the sand exploded in a white hot sunburst that seemed to scorch her flesh. Dennis landed on his back beside his tricycle as another bolt blew it to pieces. She grabbed his foot and ran up to the porch heedless of his body bouncing behind her. The door was, thank God, open. She slammed it behind her, easing the child to the floor.

With a fearsome, demonic crash, lightning struck the house, blowing sparks from the plugs, light fixtures, and kitchen appliances. James had once said the house was grounded with a lightning rod. However, he had electrocuted himself on a fusebox, so his advice on electrical things was not encouraging.

"Dennis, baby, are you all right?"

Her son had the most remarkable smile on his face, his eyes open in joyous wonder, hands lightly clapping to imaginary music.

"Airplane." He threw a piece of paper trying to simulate the paper plane Holden had made for him. Laughing delightedly, he looked at the rain slaking down the windows. Gina hoisted him up and carried him into the bathroom where she moistened his face with a wet rag.

His forehead was cool, pulse normal, and there were no burns or injuries on his body, but that mad smile would not leave his face.

"Oh, Dennis, my poor baby . . ."

The lightning hit the house like the fists of a delirious boxer, screeching loose the rain gutter which dangled before one of the windows, and sending shingles clattering down the roof.

"Dennis, please stop it. Please stop laughing!"

"Airplane, airplane, airplane . . ." Each concatenation seemed to overjoy him.

A gritty haze compounded of smoldering rubber and plaster filled the rooms. Despite the rain, the walls were heating up and turning the ramshackle building into a tinderbox.

What had Jeff said about the lightning on Itrek? It never got into the CDA but the walls there had been two feet thick and these would go within minutes. What had he said about lightning in general? Avoid metal radiators and overhead fixtures. Stay out of the bathroom, don't run water into a tub or sink because of the metal, do not touch water taps or pipes. The safest place to be was in a car.

The car. The garage was attached to the house by a kitchen doorway. "The car," she said to Dennis, who giggled in a mad undertone to the cacophony of rattling windows and thunderbolts. "Dennis, the *car!*"

"Bye bye," Dennis cried gaily, then coughed at the smoke.

Donning rubber gloves from the drainboard, she pushed open the garage door, then opened the door to the car. She knocked the metal seat belt buckles to the floor, pushed Dennis into the passenger seat, then sat beside him.

The ignition key was metal, the gear shift had a metal shaft, and metal spokes formed the steering wheel. The rim was plastic. Did plastic resist lightning?

She rolled the window shut, avoiding the metal lining, and started the car. From the house came the sound of crackling glass as the gutter pipe finally broke the window, then flashing detonations hurled the furniture about in the living room. Smoke poured in a greasy column into the garage.

The car faced the wall. She put the gear into reverse and accelerated backwards. The taillights crumpled on the door and Dennis banged against the seat back. With one hand she stuffed the child under the padded dash onto the floor and tried again.

It took three tire-screeching lurches to burst the door into boards. The car slewed out of the house onto the sand. By then smoke was pouring through the shingles, the broken windows, and the garage. The roof was holed by lightning and the wavering orange glare of fire cast dancing shadows of chairs on the walls.

Because there was smoke inside the car, she lowered the window while driving down to the highway. Lightning encased the car in a starry retina-burning burst of white energy. She screamed, Dennis screamed with her, and the car bumped into the gatepost. Some unconscious reflex or protective instinct desiring a barrier between themselves and the storm made her close the window again.

She rubbed spots from her eyes and looked at the blistered paint on the hood. She turned onto the road as the house began burning in dirty bellies of smoke, shredded by the wind.

Several miles away, after the lightning had stopped and the heat inside the car was intolerable, she cracked the window again. She was as prepared as she could ever be when it blew against the roof but Dennis shrieked and cringed on the floor, his cheerfulness replaced by terror. "Lesson number one, honey. Keep the window closed."

On Highway 19, trucks and cars swam through the rain with their headlights on. It was encouraging to see other people again, a thought that would never have occurred to her hours ago. In the rearview mirror, the storm remained close behind them so she steadily increased her speed until the car zoomed at sixty-five miles an hour over slick roads to Pensacola.

Dennis climbed onto the seat, eyes heavy-lidded and face pale. He muttered "airplane" again before dropping off into a shuddering sleep.

The rain let up, the skies broke to raggedy clouds, but she maintained her speed. She remembered Holden telling her about Windowpane. A sailor blown off the beach, people huddling in a cramped blockhouse listening to the skies burst. Jeffrey Holden had brought death and madness all the way back from the Pacific to her.

X PLUS 29 HOURS

BY THE time the copters swarmed over the beach, the storm was moving north, leaving drizzly rain that steamed in the smoldering wreck of the house. The men in slickers found no bodies in the debris and no car in the garage. Immediately they radioed this information to Kayama.

Holden's emotions had been held brutally in check. His relief was nearly as difficult to handle as the fear had been. "She got away. She's on the road to Pensacola and it's following her. It's a three-hour drive."

Kayama adjusted his tie over his third white shirt of the day. He smelled of deodorant and aftershave. Despite the close, warm interior of the plane, he looked cool, dry, and immaculate. "You wish to see her, don't you?" It was a statement, not a question.

"You bet I do."

"It will be very close, Mr. Holden. Once the storm has gathered its strength it will reach Pensacola in less than an hour. Perhaps we should have the police find her on the road."

"We can't! The storm will catch up with her. We can't let her get out of that car for even a second." Holden's feelings alternated waves of terror and relief. "Once she gets to the apartment, she'll be okay for a little while. You can't open the windows in there."

Kayama said, "You must get her to the Naval Air Station as soon as possible, Mr. Holden. We will fly her out to California and keep her safe."

"I will, I will. Have a car standing by at my apartment. I'll meet her there."

Half an hour later, the plane tilted down toward the lights of Pensacola crowding the Gulf. The crew spilled out the doors to breathe noncompressed air and stretch their legs. Then Holden jumped in a staff car and headed for his apartment.

The moon was high, the air was calm. But down on the Gulf, Kayama heard the pilots report the storm splitting in two again. This time the cobra's head was weaving north for Pensacola. The forecast was for rain in two hours.

Holden was in the car garage when she drove in, Dennis asleep on the seat beside her. Holden opened the passenger door and lifted out Dennis's bundled form.

"How was California?" she asked without humor. She was scared and exhausted.

"I didn't make it. Better not take your coat off, Gina, these men are taking you to the base."

"What for?"

"Kayama's going to fly you to California." He tried to maneuver her toward the car but she resisted.

"I have to get some things from the apartment. We left our clothes down there."

Holden carried Dennis into the elevator, then to the apartment door. Since Dennis was about to wake up, he laid him on the bed in the dark bedroom while Gina pulled sweaters, shoes, and underwear from a chest of drawers and stuffed them into a sack. Now Gina appeared more angry than frightened, and despite the time Holden knew he had better talk to her before letting her go in this state.

"Have we time for a drink, Jeff?"

"So long as it's a short one." He poured out three fingers of straight bourbon and handed it to her. She shrank onto the sofa and sipped as he told her about Stormfury and the deaths of Mason, Tregaskis, and Axton. "We've got to figure this out quick. The storm wants me, not you."

"Ha ha."

"It *does*! Tell me exactly what happened." He sat on his chair, trying to control his impatience as she described the bolts slamming into the garage and the drive back. She was succinct and thorough. "That's what happened in the CDA. That's what happened to me."

She seemed almost offended that his experience could in any way be as terrifying as hers. "You better tell the Navy to throw that fancy ray gun of theirs out." Her glass was empty. Holden took it from her to pour another drink.

"Do you want ice in this one?"

"No. It kills the taste."

Holden poured more warm bourbon and was handing the glass to her when a thought slipped into place in his mind, a thought upon which rested the weight of Stormfury. "Son of a bitch. No ice. That's why nobody saw it in the Pacific! Gina, you're a genius, you know that?"

She sipped the drink, wincing at its strength, then glowered at him. "What are you smiling at, for God's sake?"

He sat down and slapped his knees. "I mean it. You're really something, you downright inspire me."

"You're crazy. Besides, you're getting to be a good liar, Jeff. I really bought that debriefing business."

"So sue me. What did you want me to say—the storm's chased me from the Pacific and I might get killed? Then maybe I do get killed and you decide to blow Windowpane wide open . . ." Holden pulled his chair around so he could face her directly. "Look, this thing does not read minds, and it's not contagious like some kind of leprosy. There are two possible reasons for what happened to you, both of which hinge on one thing. Somehow, somewhere, it has imprinted you before. Do you understand?"

"More or less."

"Have you ever been nearly hit by lightning before? Any time in your life?"

"Once, when I was sixteen. On a tennis court. Lightning hit a tree just outside the fence."

He spread his hands as if to demonstrate how simple life could be if you only looked at it the right way. "There! Okay. Maybe that's it."

"But it didn't hurt me. It knocked me down and that was it."

"It's still a possibility. This thing could have been cruising around for years, it could be any of a hundred thunderstorms you've passed by. Lightning is absolutely capricious, remember that. Now, there's a second possibility. Have you ever been to the South seas or . . ."

"No."

". . . anywhere in that area. Bali, Malaysia, Singapore?"

"Never."

"How about the Baja or . . ."

"Nope." She was firm.

". . . anywhere on the equator. *On the equator!*"

"Jeff, I ski on my vacations. I go north."

Holden kept it up like a machine that would not wind down. "Mexico? Central America?"

"Will you cut it out? I've never been south of Tampa, Florida. Let's face it. It went after me because of you."

"Bull," he barked.

"Because we're lovers. We're beginning to think alike. You said it sniffs out electrical patterns in your head."

Holden shook his head. "We're not that close, Gina, we'd have to be Siamese twins or something. It's the tennis court. It's got to be."

"Fine," she said, draining the glass. "That and a dime will get you a ride on the Staten Island ferry."

He grabbed the glass before it could slip out of her hand. "We'd better get going. Kayama's waiting at the Air station. I'll carry Dennis, you bring the clothes."

"I have to go to the bathroom first." She climbed clumsily to her feet and tottered into the bathroom. Holden could hear her splashing water on her face. Sobering up three minutes after getting drunk, he mused, could be a hopeless undertaking.

In the bedroom, moonlight lanced through a crack in the curtains and spilled over Dennis's chest. The boy thrashed and swallowed loudly in his sleep as Holden tried to figure out how to pick him up without awakening him.

On the floor lay a wad of tattered paper, the remains of the paper airplane. Holden stooped down to pick it up, and as he did he glanced at Dennis's face.

The animals in Croft's lab!

From beneath the lustrous mass of Gina's hair and above the line of Gina's jaw, Holden saw the ghost of an old man whose bones were dust but whose face was locked on a tintype as surely as Holden's soul was locked in the storm. A face that stepped across a hundred years to confront him now in this room.

Oscar Holden of the *Hartford* and the Battle of Mobile, Alabama.

No!

Holden's mouth dried out and his heart seemed to collapse in his chest. For the third time that day, a revelation had struck him like a body blow, leaving him dazed on his feet. Another circle from the past had closed tight around the future. The bedroom was a time cage that assumed the outlines of the motel room he and Gina had shared three years before.

Three years. Holden's ability to calculate was reflexive. Dennis was a little over two years old, born nine months after Gina had returned to her husband in Oregon. She had said they were stuck with each other and, since her commitment to him was secure, they had had Dennis.

But Dennis James Lambert was the son of Jeffrey Holden, not James Lambert. Holden watched, fascinated when he stooped to a lower angle, as the boy's features rearranged themselves from those of his mother into the chimerical face and jaw of Oscar Holden.

As the lightning had killed the offspring of Croft's animals, so it had tried to murder Dennis. It was this child the thunders wanted, not Gina. Dennis's mind, his brain, his nervous system were Holden's.

Sleep, my son. Here stand I, your father and your executioner.

She had changed clothes and was putting on lipstick when he emerged from the bedroom. He sat in a chair and watched her impassively.

"I'm ready," she said. "I'm not sober, but I'm ready."

"There's been a little change in plans," he replied.

His tone indicated something momentous had happened. His expression confirmed it.

"What's wrong now?"

"Sit down. I'm calling Clay."

"I thought we were in a hurry."

"We are. But sit down."

She sat across from him, trying not to rub her palms on her dress. "What's the change in plans?" To Holden she appeared more sober than the amount of bourbon warranted. She must suspect what he was going to say.

"I won't be going with you."

She shifted position on the sofa as though trying to avoid him. "Whatever you say, Jeff."

"I have to talk to you about Dennis. I think I figured it all out. Yessirree. Got it all worked out. I think you know what I'm going to say, too."

She closed her eyes and covered them with her hands. "Yes, I think I do."

"Is it possible?"

"Yes. Possible. *Barely*. He was born three weeks early, but that happens all the time. I'm not *sure* though, Jeff, I won't be unless he starts to look like you. Children change, you know."

144

Gently he removed her hands from her face. He kissed them both. "Why didn't you tell me?"

"I was going to at the beach. You know how people always wait for the right moment, when everyone is relaxed and full of wine and everything. But there never is a right moment and, besides, you had your own problems."

He pressed one of her hands to his cheek. "Oh, Lord, Gina, that's why you came to me, isn't it?"

"I'd have come back anyway. And I'm still not sure, Jeff, it's just a feeling, the kind of suspicion you only get if you've been as close to Dennis as I have."

Holden nodded toward one of the tintypes on his desk. "He looks like that guy. From a certain angle, it jumps right out at you. Oh, Jesus, what a fix."

"Don't crack up on me, Jeff. I'm scared enough already."

"Oh shit, Gina I love you."

With her free hand, she stroked his cheek, tracing the beard stubble. "I'm not forcing anything on you, Jeff, I never intended to do that. I don't want you to think you're obligated to us."

"It's not that." He kissed her hand and released it. "I'll talk to the Admiral and you can listen in. I don't know how to break it to you otherwise."

She glanced at the bedroom door, then out the window where clouds were crawling across the stars. Understanding jolted the last trace of intoxication. "Dennis! It's Dennis!"

Holden was dialing the Naval Air Station.

Tears brimmed in her eyes. "It's *not* Dennis! No, forget it, we're not sure he's yours. We don't know!"

"Yes, we do, Gina. We're absolutely certain. I am, anyway."

X PLUS 29 HOURS 45 MINUTES

"HOLDEN!" CLAY sputtered after a stunned silence broken by the sound of Kayama sipping tea. "You are a prime, natural-born fuckup."

Holden counted slowly to ten. "Admiral, sir, I'd like to remind you I'm not in the service anymore . . ."

"Thank *God* for that!"

". . . so you take your goddamned opinions and stick them up your breech."

"That's the most ludicrous thing I ever heard! You're not even remotely like a child. You're bigger, taller, older. Your nervous system's about a thousand times more complex . . ."

Kayama cleared his throat. "Excuse me. Size is of no consequence to the perceptions of the bird family. A bird cannot tell a fifty-foot earthworm from a five-inch one."

"Kayama, shut up."

Holden held Gina's hand as she sobbed softly on the sofa. "Wake up, Admiral, it's the oldest thing in the world. Like father, like son. I'm no geneticist but I know certain mental traits recur in families—like schizophrenia, maybe alcoholism. At any rate, that's definitely it. The storm can't tell me from Dennis." Through the window Holden could see drops of rain slicken the streets of the city. "Kayama, what's the storm doing now?"

"The northernmost of its twin clusters is getting very close to Pensacola right now, Mr. Holden."

Clay said, "Wait a minute, wait a minute! It might be an advantage Kayama. With that kid and Holden we might have two hooks on this thing . . ."

"You asshole," Holden bellowed.

"What did you say!"

"You're not using my kid for bait, so you can forget that. You mention that again, Admiral, I'll sink the pack of you, Windowpane and all."

Kayama hastily cut in. "Certainly not, Mr. Holden, it is not even remotely under consideration. Mr. Holden, really, you must leave soon!"

Holden wiped sweat from his forehead. "Okay. Things are different now. I want Gina and Dennis in a safe place far away from here . . ."

"Yes, yes," Kayama said impatiently. "Bring them here."

"I'm not going with them. Kayama, remember I wondered why nobody saw the storm in the Pacific?"

"Yes. Yes, I do."

"Where did that airliner pass through it?"

"The plane reported it at latitude forty-five degrees north . . . Ah, Mr. Holden," Kayama's breath was like the wash of a soothing tide. "How marvelous. You are, of course, absolutely right. We should all return to school and educate ourselves again."

"Seattle is at forty-eight degrees north. The storm did not really get big until it moved south to California. By the time it hit the Baja it could go into a desert to pick out Mason."

"Of course, of course," Kayama agreed. Even Clay grunted in surprise as the implication struck him.

"It's home latitudes are tropical, equatorial ones. It needs the heat as well as the moisture. If we take it into the southwest where it's warm, it will hang on forever. So in order to pull its teeth we have to cool it off. We have to go north, not south."

"How far north, Holden?" Clay asked.

"The North Pole would be perfect, but Greenland will do. The air is dry and frigid."

Rain dappled the window and wavered the city lights. Kayama was right, it was time to get moving. He squeezed Gina's hand. It was cold and flaccid.

"You will have to draw it northward," Kayama mused.

"Yes. I'll lock it on me from the car and drive to Fort Jackson . . ."

"Hold your horses a minute," Clay said. "The point was to get it away from land, not march it through the south like Sherman's army."

"Fort Jackson isn't that far and, besides, the storm's already hit land. I'll need two planes, Admiral, one to get me to Greenland with a load of silver iodide and another in Greenland. I'd rather that be a fighter of some kind. And someone up there will have to know how to pack alectoes and smoke generators."

"You don't ask much, do you," Clay snorted. They heard a pen scratching. "There's an Air Force Base in Thule, so that's where you'll get your plane. And Greenland's a Danish territory, so we'll have to get them to agree to it. And I think the Canadians too."

"We're all in NATO," Holden pointed out. "And we're all at war, too, aren't we?"

Clay grunted. "Holden, take down another number." Holden jotted it on a corner of one of Dennis's coloring books. "I'll have a plane waiting for you at Fort Jackson but I better set up the rest of it with the Danes in Washington. If I leave now, I might get there by the time you reach Jackson. Before you leave, trace out your route in detail on some kind of road map and get it to Kayama. Kayama?"

"Yes."

"Get some of those planes to cover him as he drives north. You better move it, Holden. Keep that number in case you get in trouble, it'll reach me anywhere, including a plane."

"Gina?"

She looked up at him, her hair straggly, her eyes swollen. "What?"

"You'd better take Dennis."

Paralysis seemed to have overcome her. She played with her necklace.

"We've got to move. They're waiting for us now. The storm's coming."

She did not look at him as she spoke. "Do you love him, Jeff?"

"I've made up my mind to. You know me."

"He's James's son. What does biology mean, anyhow?" She became firm, willful about it, her mouth set, her body stiff as though trying to defy him. "He has grandparents, after all. He's all they have, now." She entwined her necklace around her fingers.

Now was no time to start an argument, but Holden felt he should say something. "He's a lucky kid, he's got two fathers."

"Yes. And Holdens die before they produce second children."

"Not this Holden. I told you, I'm different. I'm not in the service anymore. You know what's going to happen?"

"What?"

"In about one year, he's going to throw out all his toy airplanes and start messing around with paint cans and drawing pictures just like Lambert. And I'm going to feel like a damned fool. I thought we were pretty careful that weekend."

"We were," she said. "I sure was, anyway. Or I thought I was. Jeff, listen! Lightning always hits the tallest objects, doesn't it? That beach was flat as a pancake—the tallest things there were me and Dennis."

"Sure, sure!" He agreed, lying in his teeth. "Maybe we're just being overcareful. I'm sure he's safe." To Holden it was amazing how the two of them could juggle realities around until they found one they liked. The thought of lightning killing Dennis was so insupportable, Holden would gladly have convinced himself he was James Lambert's just to keep the horrendous vision away.

But he was still a rational man and part of him claimed Dennis for his own. Dennis was a Holden, he knew it in his soul. And for all his concern at Gina's unhappiness and his false aloofness from the subject of James Lambert, he was glad. It severed the unseen Lambert from her completely. Dennis had been the strongest bond linking them but now Gina was his. It was almost as though James Lambert had never touched her.

It was cold in the basement garage. Rain fell in a dull, pounding drizzle on the street as they bundled Dennis into the back of the staff car. Holden said to the driver, "Make sure neither one of them, especially the boy, gets into the open air for more than a second or so."

"Right."

"Give this to Kayama immediately." He slipped them a road map on which he had outlined in grease pencil the route he would take to Fort Jackson. He had kept to second-class roads as much as possible. "It'll keep me from towns even though it will take a bit longer. I'll try to call when I can. I hope to be there at midnight. You got that? He'll know what I mean."

The cadet rolled up the window. Holden held up seven fingers in front of Gina and shouted through the glass, "Seven days. I'll see you in seven or eight days."

She nodded, blew a kiss, and watched him as the car pulled out to the street. Just before they turned to the right, Dennis awoke and saw Holden through the window. They waved to each other.

Holden's gas tank was three-quarters full. As soon as he made some distance he would top it off. He climbed into the car, shut the windows, and pulled out into the streaming streets of Pensacola. He looked in the rearview mirror for some sign of the staff car but could only see the falling rain.

Holden drove out of the city across the East Bay anxiously looking for lightning but the storm was quiet and all he heard was the drumfire of steady rain falling in vertical lines, unmarred by a breath of wind.

Stolid and malevolent, the storm cruised over Pensacola, a blind titan searching for that tiny trigger of electricity in Holden that would correct the charge imbalance in its own body. Holden wondered if this imbalance were an itch, a pain that lured it restlessly over the world toward him. Did Holden torment it? Was he something to be possessed, to be captured? Or was he a drug to it, a kind of grail?

He stopped on the side of the road. After several deep breaths to calm himself, Holden opened the door and stepped out to the shoulder. In seconds he was soaked by sweet, clean rain that saturated his hair, stuck his clothes to his body, and collected in his shoes. He opened his mouth to drink some, thinking of primitive tribes who drank the blood of their enemies.

He felt something, too faint to analyze. Or did he? A faint tension so fleeting, he was not sure if it was fear, the chill of the rain, or even the subtle, bodiless touch of his nemesis.

A wind appeared over the bay that blew against the vertically falling raindrops, moving them like disturbed curtains of beads. His scalp tightened as lightning glowed inside a bulge of cloud and a fat globe of thunder belched across the bay. The wind turned squarely into his face, tasting of salt, and Holden felt invisible awesome forces gathering about him, coiling into a tight spring to enclose him.

You hungry bastard! I've got you. Come for me!

Jeffrey Holden, the rainmaker. A thirty-four-year-old, slightly heavy ex-pilot, who carried within him the forces shamans could only yearn for. Locked in the storm was power ten times greater than the biggest hydrogen bomb, hundreds of times greater than an atomic one. He wondered if any mortal had ever held such direct power in his grasp. Probably a chosen few had and they had become legends. It was a pleasurably masochistic thought. He would lure this hell demon to a frigid doom, rend its winds to feeble gasps and freeze its substance into lonely snowflakes.

The wind increased, sending leaves and branches scurrying against his car. A vault of cloud glowed, then a blade of light cleaved branches from a nearby tree. It had found him and thrown down its gauntlet.

Holden climbed into his car and shut the window. He checked his map, then sped east through the increasing rain, the angry impotent clouds growing in the rearview mirror.

The car carrying Gina and Dennis wheeled around Pensacola Bay toward the Naval Air Station and ran into a wall of rain charging in from the Gulf. The driver exlaimed, "Sumbitch," as he wiped fog from the windshield and turned on the defrosters.

The car interior rapidly heated up, fogging the windows and soaking Gina in perspiration. On her lap, Dennis's body was a hot box so she sat him on the seat. He was watching the planes when the car slowed so sharply, he slipped onto the floor and bumped his head. His lips quivered in humiliation as his mother bent to him before he could start crying.

The floodlights were on at the Base as the car pulled up to the main gate. A marine stepped out wearing a slicker. He held up his hand, stopping the car, and tapped on the window.

The driver shouted, "Come on rum dum. You know who we are."

The marine kept tapping, his bullfrog face settling into a scowl. A real hot dog, the driver thought, under strict orders because of Stormfury. You'd think this was a red alert. He cracked the window and said, "Coleman and Rose. We're headed for . . ."

Dennis smiled. "Airplane," he said.

"Shut the window," Gina screamed, frightening the driver and causing the guard to step back.

They felt the presence slip into the car, a ghost, an electrical phantom that filled the interior and infiltrated the air.

A light appeared in the clouds over the weather tower like a jet coming in low with its landing lights on. It was a light without wings or substance, a comet of fire, tail elongated by its speed. A second, then a third light popped out of the clouds to streak across the airstrip.

As Dennis giggled happily, Gina flung herself over him onto the floor and jammed herself between the seats. The fireball washed over the car, blistering the paint, killing the guard and driver. The other man reached for the window crank, then coughed as thousands of volts blew him against the roof.

The people walking outdoors stared at the balls of lightning cannonading over the tarmac past the planes in a steady relentless cadence. Some were blue, some white, some a sizzling green. Thunder pealed over the base burying the rising wail of sirens. Then mechanics, ground crews, the air crews resting between shifts, even the controllers in the tower scattered for cover as the balls hurtled past them.

The onslaught stopped as mysteriously as it had begun. The shining globes reversed course back into the folds of cloud and the thunder abated. On the airstrip, men looked up as a fire crew raced for the main gate, the lead truck carrying Kayama in a white shirt, which he had torn while running from his plane.

Clay got the call from Kayama in his plane. The pilot sensed by the Admiral's stiff demeanor that bad news had come in. "Okay, that's it, Kayama. You did your best."

Since Kayama seemed to exist in a perpetual state of sadness, his reaction did not seem so strong. "It is very sad, Admiral, sir."

"It's nobody's fault. Why did the lightning stop?"

"Holden must have drawn the storm to him at that exact moment. He would have lowered his window or even stepped out. How shall you tell him, Admiral, sir?"

"I won't," Clay answered. "He's going to need all his reflexes. Besides he . . ."

"He will what, Admiral?"

Clay had been about to say Holden would find out what had happened an instant after the storm killed him, as Clay assumed it would. The plan was hopeless. But saying such a thing implied that the Admiral contemplated an afterlife—heaven and all manner of metaphysical things. "Never mind. It could have been worse, Kayama."

"Oh, yes," Kayama agreed. "It could have been both of them. At least Holden still has a son."

X PLUS **32** HOURS

HOLDEN RACED through red dirt farmlands spotted with sentinel pines that shone under clear starlight. By now, the storm was a black maw in the rearview mirror.

Holden had easily outrun it over these winding, narrow, pitted country roads with their white lines faded by time and traffic. They meandered past tobacco and soybean farms with isolated houses in fields. The interminable zigzagging meant his trail was crooked and that was good.

Over a country music radio station, he heard thunderstorm warnings announced for Georgia and the Carolinas. The South Carolina border appeared at ten-thirty that night in the midst of a forest of pines. With any luck, Holden estimated, he would make Fort Jackson by midnight.

He pressed the accelerator. The embracing trees shut off the storm, leaving the skies pristine and innocent. Holden thought about Dennis James Lambert and considered the ways this event had deflected his life. He had planned to finish school and move to Washington, but so much had happened so fast. Dennis was a turning point in his life, not to mention Gina. Before she reappeared, he had vaguely envisioned slaving away in a school somewhere, coolly deciding to get married after a few pay raises. After being securely set up as a government consultant there came an even more ethereal image of a two-car garage, suburban house, and worry about the spread of his gut. Now his future was laid out for him and it weighed as heavily as his present.

Holden was growing tired. The woods thickened and he took curves with decreasing precision. He skidded dirt off shoulders and found the car wandering too close to the edge. Sometimes his speedometer touched seventy-five without his noticing it.

Now the country music was interrupted by bulletins describing the havoc caused by the storm. Power lines were washing away, floods had burst the banks of small streams. The storm thrashed steadily along behind him, no more than five miles away.

After the brief display outside Pensacola, he had seen no more lightning. Now a light appeared in the rearview mirror. It could be one of Kayama's planes or even one of those infernal lightning balls. When

Holden leaned closer to the mirror to examine it, he missed a curve.

The wheels hit slippery pine needles, the scaly bark of a pine tree filled his headlights, but his pilot's reflexes managed to shut off the ignition. He covered his chest and face as the car crashed.

His ribs were bruised, blood dripped from a cut on his head, and his lower jaw did not quite close against his upper teeth. But there were no ominous deep pains, broken bones, or numbness. His arms were bruised where they had struck the wheel but that was all. Holden pushed open the bent, sprung door and stepped onto the road.

Mixed with the fragrant smell of pine needles was the acrid pungency of gasoline. The front wheel splayed out in pigeon-toed awkwardness. The axle was broken, which meant the car was totaled.

It was a disaster but not quite a catastrophe. He remembered passing a house with lights some two miles back but that was in the direction of the storm. The road was a narrow tunnel that bored through towering pines, but there could well be a farm a few hundred feet ahead on the other side of that bend.

He began walking, limping slightly. He noted barbed wire and a No Trespassing sign lost in the brush. That was encouraging, someone lived close by.

Cloud fingers stealthily lanced through the sky, cutting down the moonglow, and a wind spun needles and leaves into whirling coils. Large drops of rain splattered onto the woods. Holden increased his limping walk to a limping run.

Think of something. Gina and Dennis must have arrived in California by now. Would they take her and Dennis out to the Naval Weapons Center? Holden could imagine Dennis swinging a stick at the Project Director. Or maybe they would have taken them to some other secure area, like Edwards Air Force Base. Come to think of it, they might wind up living in California, anyway, that was where the defense contractors were.

For the first time in hours, lightning flickered over the trees. Holden counted off the seconds. It took twenty seconds for the thunder to ripple over head. Twenty divided by five meant the storm was approximately four miles behind him.

As the wind rose, he ran, looking for a shack, a ditch, a tobacco shed, anything to hide in. They were probably all full of spiders. Goddamn, why hadn't the storm imprinted something other than those crawly little bastards—why not sleeping with Gina, or breaking his arm when he was ten—some other equally outstanding memory. Croft would have explained it. Spiders are fear, Mr. Holden, and fear takes very definite shapes in the nervous makeup. His spider phobia must be a really fat neurological structure.

Triumphantly the sky ripped open, releasing cataracts of rain into the hot, dry woods. The storm had found him. Holden looked desperately for a ditch, a hole, bushes.

Headlights shone on the trees ahead, accompanied by the sound of a rattly truck motor. Holden ran around the curve almost head-on into an ancient pickup with a chicken fence around the bed and broken shocks which rocked the machine. The truck honked at him angrily.

Between a tattered straw hat and the muzzle of a shotgun poking out the window was a rawboned face of hard jaw, tiny eyes, and gully-deep wrinkles.

"Accident," Holden cried as lightning split the night asunder. "My wife, my kids . . ."

"Git." The word crawled out between yellowed teeth. The muzzle jabbed his chest.

"Didn't you hear me? I said, an accident."

The truck accelerated, nearly tearing his hand loose from the latch Blind rage detonated inside of Holden. This cracker would leave his own mother to die. He pulled himself up by the sill as a thundercrack of lightning pulverized the night into noon brightness, freezing the face just long enough for Holden's fist to ram into the junction of jaw and neck. Holden felt the man's jaw dislodge from his head, as he slumped over the wheel. Holden pulled the door open, tore the man out of the seat by the arm, shotgun and all, and let him tumble to the road. The ball of rage still quivered in him as he slammed the door, hit the brake, and rolled up the window. He honestly did not care at that point if he had killed him.

The clutch was slippery but at least the damned thing moved. Holden backed around through the hell flashes of light and headed down the road at a bumpy fifty miles an hour, all the machine would do.

He was in a really beautiful fix now. Half the people in the area, including the police chief, were probably relatives of that man. Holden pictured himself in a southern jail guarded by a pot-bellied deputy who threw cards into a hat.

Holden turned off the road and moved east, anything to throw the storm off. The forest seemed to last forever, but after half an hour the rain receded as he entered the outskirts of a small town. Warehouses lined railroad tracks between Grain and Feed stores and shiny new tractors were parked on the street. The streets were dark and empty.

Moonlight flooded over the metal roofs and cast a faint shadow of the truck. The buildings yielded to trees again and the moonlight shone off the metal frame of a phone booth tucked into a rest area.

The sky was clear. He parked, fished out a dime, and ran into the phone booth, leaving the truck door open and the motor running. He dialed the number Clay had given him and, after the musical tinkle of closing relays, heard the Admiral's voice. "Holden, where are you? How're you doing?"

"I wrecked my car and stole a truck. That's for beginners."

To Holden's surprise Clay did not blow his top. In fact he sounded amused. "You get a B for balls, Holden."

And an A for Angst. "I'm on Route 25 headed east, Admiral. I just passed a town called Modoc. Can you get somebody from Jackson to meet me before I'm nailed for grand larceny?"

"Okay, stay on the road. Everything's shaping up fine. We've got a C-130 full of alectoes and dry ice waiting for you and the Danes have cleared you to Godhab, Greenland. They've just put up a new weather station there. That's on the southwest coast, okay?"

"Fine."

"Are you qualified for F-5s?" The F-5 was a plane Holden admired, slender, light, fast.

"Sure. I must have done three hundred hours in F-5s."

"There'll be one waiting for you in Godhab. The storm is leaving the Gulf, Holden. The tornado warnings are down in the Midwest but they're still up where you are. Once we get you out to sea, things will be safe."

"How're Gina and Dennis doing?"

Clay hesitated. "Just fine from what I heard. They're out in California now. Kayama's going to meet you at Jackson, so you'd better . . ."

"Wait a minute, I thought Kayama flew them out."

"Oh. We shuffled that around a little, Holden. Kayama wanted to stay on top of you so we put them in another plane. He's been directing the planes following you. Have you seen any, by the way? He's been running them a little ahead of your route . . ."

Why was Clay going on like a gabby old man? Holden wondered. It was as if he were trying to divert Holden's attention. Seconds ago, he wanted to get Holden moving, now he was babbling like a maniac.

Spiders were all over the phone booth. Tiny legs dug in his socks, rustled under his clothes, and ticked across his scalp.

The moon had disappeared.

Holden swan-dived into the front seat of the truck as a single blast of lightning fragmented the booth into hot shards of glass and metal. Hooking his foot in the door handle, he pulled it shut, banging his kneecap on the rim of the steering wheel.

He waited, breath held, for oblivion, his body curled away from the metal parts of the truck, but there were no more bolts. *Ha ha.* "Tough titty!" he shouted at the sky.

X PLUS 33 HOURS

Six MILES past the phone booth where the woods dwindled into rich, grassy pasturage, Holden saw oncoming headlights. He found a hammer in the glove compartment and laid it on the seat in case it turned out to be a policeman, but the car had no beacon. It was the depressing olive green the army used for land transportation. They blinked their lights, pulled to a stop together, and Holden found himself looking at a boy with close-cropped hair and acne, scarcely out of his teens.

"Are you Holden?"

"Yes."

"Colonel Kreuger's compliments, Holden," he said sourly. "I'm to drive you to Fort Jackson on this beautiful night."

Holden scrawled "Thanks for nothing" on the truck registration and weighted it with the hammer, still angry that the cracker had made it so hard to steal his truck.

Fort Jackson slept under a soft southern night filled with frog and cricket sounds. The huge, silver cargo plane gleamed under floodlights as the staff car pulled up to a stop by the airstrip.

Kayama was down to his last white shirt and, although he had spent fourteen straight hours cramped in a pressurized fuselage, bent over radars and computer printouts, he was as immaculate as ever with trim, clean fingernails and a smooth, shaven face. He favored Holden with such a crinkly smile, the pilot almost believed everything would be all right.

"How wonderful, Mr. Holden," he said, clasping Holden's hand with both of his. "The phone call was so disturbing. We did not know if the lines were down or you were." Kayama laughed gaily at his little joke.

"Is everything ready?"

"Yes. The copilot is waiting and the plane is loaded. The storm will be here presently. The last step begins. Eh?"

"I hope so," Holden said fervently.

They strolled under the plane's wing to the grass lining the airstrip, awaiting the clouds. Behind Kayama's cheerful smile was another more complex emotion, one which took Holden a moment to pin down. It was awe. Kayama was bemused by the shaman rainmaker in Holden. Kayama said softly, "I should attach a galvanometer to you, no? We could actually measure the ions leaving your body as the storm approaches."

"No thanks. I'd feel like one of Croft's animals."

"I am sorry. I did not mean it disrespectfully."

Holden looked at the buildings at the end of the airstrip. "I ought to call Gina before I leave."

Kayama remembered Clay's warning. Gina's death would affect Holden's equilibrium when he needed it most. "You do not have much time and they will be asleep by now."

Holden decided Kayama was right. If Dennis were awakened after his experience with the storm, he would never get back to sleep. "You'll tell her everything is fine, won't you? I don't want her to worry any more than she is now."

"She is not worried, I assure you, sir."

Holden pulled at his lip trying to remember something that had dogged his memory ever since returning from Itrek. It had escaped him then. Now he remembered. "Got it! Kayama, maybe you can help me with something."

"Wonderful."

"That old man on the fishing boat. He said the word 'Ku' several times. I'm sure it has something to do with this business. The first time he said it, he looked like the hounds of hell were after him, and the second time was on the radio while he was busy getting killed. What does it mean? Lightning?"

Kayama tapped his finger against his teeth. "I am so sorry, Mr. Holden. I do not know."

"I'm sure it was Japanese. He was in the war in the south Pacific. The way he said it, you got the feeling he knew about this storm."

"Could it have been a part of a longer word?" In the peaceful night, Kayama's calm face was earnest and sympathetic.

"No. That was it."

"Then it is not a Japanese word I know."

The reached the edge of the airstrip and watched the sky above the line of trees. A ball of cloud was scooting ahead. The night would soon be alive with the elements.

Kayama continued talking. "It will follow the warmth of the Gulf Stream as far north as possible, which will be around Newfoundland. When it reaches the Davis Straits opposite Greenland the cold will have shrunk it. The Admiral is arranging flights by the Canadian Air Force to help you seed it. It appears that the world has a set number of admirals and generals and they all know each other, do they not, Mr. Holden?"

The straggler cloud was joined by others, inching past the tree line, blotting out the star field. To Holden they looked like fingers of a hand reaching over a coffin's edge. The clouds became thicker and darker and larger as wind rustled the leaves around the airstrip.

A tremor passed through Holden, a quick cold shiver. "Bull's eye," he said calmly. "It's found me, Kayama."

Kayama looked from the pilot to the gathering clouds and marveled. "You felt it? That easily? You could actually feel it?"

"It's the other way around."

A good headwind was building as they strode back to the airplane. At the base of the ladder, they shook hands once again. Kayama said, "In twenty minutes NIMBUS will make a pass, Mr. Holden. I am determined to photograph this beast of yours."

"Send me one in a frame if you get it."

"I shall. They tell me you will have good tail winds to Greenland."

"You can depend on that, Kayama. When I get back, I plan to register in one of your courses."

"Do, sir. You will teach me."

Holden stood on the ramp, reluctant to leave. He tapped his fingers nervously on the rail and looked at the clouds, the green forest, and the planes parked down the runway. For the first time, he realized he was saying goodbye again to go off to a distant land, only now there was only Kayama to see him off. It was an unpleasant leave-taking, something a bit too permanent about it.

X PLUS 34 HOURS

FORTY-FIVE minutes later the rain was pouring down the windows and roofs of Fort Jackson. It whispered through the forest and collected in puddles on the walkways. Kayama studied an infrared photo of the American southeast he had just received from the NIMBUS satellite.

The storm lay over three states—northern Florida, Georgia, and South Carolina—like an elongated slug. By daybreak it would be completely out in the Atlantic.

"So very close," Kayama said to a sergeant. "The Canadian air will just miss it so there will be no tornadoes. Is this how wars are won?"

The sergeant considered, then nodded. "Yes, sir. That's how they're lost, too."

Kayama examined the photo for the enigmatic, wheeled structure the men had glimpsed on the TV screen on Itrek. But the storm looked like any other thunderstorm. If the magnetic field were inside it, it was as invisible as Kayama's own soul. If he had one.

He called Pensacola and instructed the planes to return to base. Holden was on his way and Stormfury was formally over. The skies were clearing over the coast and in the morning the citizens would survey the wet streets. Some would remember the terrible speed with which the storm had traversed the waters and farmers could count the damage from saltwater-flooded fields. The morning would be hot and stuffy in the damp cities but by nightfall most people would not think about the storm at all. There would be stories planted in the newspapers about all the aircraft spotted seeding the clouds. The Naval Weapons Center would devise a story saying they were testing out a new type of alecto. It was a believable story, alectoes had been invented by the Naval Weapons Center in the first place.

"Congratulations, Kayama," said Admiral Clay, who was in good spirits. "Not a tornado reported anywhere."

"I think we are safe. The planning, the pilots, the crews all worked magnificently."

"Did Holden get off all right?"

"Yes. He will sleep on the flight up, I think. The storm is moving after him."

"It's his baby, now. Either it gets him or he gets it. Are you returning to Colorado?"

"No," Kayama replied. "I shall fly to ESSA headquarters in Maryland. I wish to observe the behavior of the jet stream. It should return to its normal path as the storm goes north. Besides, Holden may still need assistance." ESSA, the Environmental Sciences Services Administration, was the country's major center for satellite photo analysis.

"I'll join you there. Good night, Kayama, and thanks again. You'd get a medal if it weren't for security." Clay hung up with those words. Nothing about Holden, not even a speculation. He had, Kayama surmised, all but dismissed him as a war casualty, unfortunate but inevitable considering the greater good.

PROJECT
GREENLAND

X MINUS 4 DAYS

BY THE next afternoon, the storm had snaked out of the Carolinas into the Atlantic where it paused at the Gulf Stream for several hours like a horse at a drinking trough before it began its sail north.

Residents of Maryland and Virginia awoke to rain blowing in from the sea. By nightfall rain from the northern cloud cluster was falling on New York City. In the cold waters off the coast of Massachusetts the storm began to shrink and break up into scattered cloudbursts, one of which socked in Boston's Logan Airport for a few hours. By the next morning skies were clear all the way to Greenland.

In Suitland, Maryland, Kayama directed the staff to watch the jet stream. The kink was now turning inside out. Normally the air runs from the bottom of Hudson's Bay up across southern Greenland but now it had passed midway up Greenland and warm temperatures were being recorded in Canada. Ice from splitting icebergs was clogging the St. Lawrence Seaway. Kayama groaned, "It's hopeless again. Now it is pushing the jet stream too far north."

The staff member scanned satellite photos. "I can't see a sign of it, not even any infrared absorption. At the rate it's traveling . . ." His finger hovered around Newfoundland. "Do you know anything about the Labrador sea current?"

"I know nothing about arctic weather. Frankly, I did not know there was any."

"They don't have thunderstorms, that's for sure. It's too cold for convection clouds to form. The Labrador sea current goes like this."

His finger moved down from Baffin Island between the continents of Greenland and Canada then at Newfoundland swerved directly east toward Europe. "Head-on collision with the Gulf Stream, Mr. Kayama. Off Newfoundland the currents join so abruptly ships sometimes measure a difference in ten degrees between the bow and the stern. Your storm won't be able to evaporate much moisture from the Labrador current.''

"It uses heat very efficiently," Kayama replied. "If there is heat to be found anywhere in the arctic, it will find it. There is something else to consider. Where does the Gulf Stream go after Newfoundland?''

"Straight for Europe. Here it becomes the West Wind Drift and it circles England. Why?''

"We have assumed it will go north simply because Mr. Holden has gone north. We might be wrong. It may cling to the Gulf Stream and search for him in Europe. It is in no hurry, you see.''

The staff member said, "You're suggesting that Europe will experience what we just did.''

"And Asia. And Africa—wherever it chooses to go.'' There was an ink stain on Kayama's shirt and a hint of exhaustion was revealed by the set mouth and tiny lines around his eyes. "Well, we must worry about that when the time comes.''

X MINUS 7 HOURS

THE COLD, clean air of Greenland seemed to clear Holden's lungs of layers of tobacco smoke and exhaust fumes as he watched the Danes wheel out the F-5 from the hangar. On the airstrip before the brand new Godhab weather station, the interceptor looked like a shark beached among the minnows of Twin Beeches and sedate Piper Aztecs.

The Danish ground crew servicing the plane had not the faintest idea what they were doing here. The ground boss was an officer named Haarskold who perspired freely in the cold and often kept his sleeves rolled up. He tried to interest Holden in his favorite meal of smoked herring washed down with aquavit but the pilot tried only the aquavit. Haarskold had been told that Holden was testing out a cloud dispersal system in combination with the Canadians over the coastal areas. Haarskold did not believe it for a minute, but he did not press his curiosity.

Admiral Clay had arranged a liaison with the Nineteenth Canadian Weather Reconnaissance Squadron to base themselves in Goose Bay, Labrador, and make daily sorties over the Straits searching for clouds, snow, or any weather anomalies. It was nothing like the force that had confronted the storm in the Gulf but it was all Clay could get from the Canadians. Or was willing to get.

Holden's flight suit was fleece-lined and waterproof, the joints ringed with constrictive elastic bands that stilled the blood surges in his body whenever he made supersonic maneuvers. Survival gear included a radio beacon, inflatable raft, and pistol with tracer bullets. He was acutely aware of their inadequacy whenever he flew over the Davis Straits. Bailing out over arctic waters was not exactly a pleasant experience. By the third day he had memorized the bay-scalloped coastline above and below Godhab so he would not get hopelessly lost when trouble came.

On the morning of the fourth day in Greenland his feeling of safety had approached boredom and he was becoming certain that the storm had been destroyed by the cold waters of the arctic. Haarskold was sitting at a chart table musing over a satellite photo that had just come in. "We just received a call from the Ice Forecasting Office in Canada, Holden. They wanted me to show this to you."

It was a speck of white in the middle of the straits resembling a brand new island that had impudently sprouted during the night. "What is it?"

"A bank of fog. Three hours ago, it doubled its size. It's headed for Godhab." Haarskold turned to a dish of herring and separated the small bones from it with his knife and fork. "It's pretty big. It's about fifteen miles in diameter."

Holden glanced over the weather reports. The fog was unseasonably warm for this time of year. It was definitely an anomaly and that could mean only one thing.

Haarskold smiled up at him. "There's a lot of fog in these waters, Mr. Holden."

"I'd better take a look at it. Can you call the Canadians and have them meet me there? I might want to drop some silver iodide in it if it's what I think it is. I'll know by the winds."

"That's low-level flying, Mr. Holden. Have you done much of that?"

"Some. It won't be low-level for long. It just might be a storm by tonight."

Haarskold shook his head sadly. "Is that what they teach you in America? Fog doesn't have anything to do with storms up here. How could it possibly become a storm?"

Holden talked while zipping up his flight suit. "If it had winds, they'll be moving over the surface of the ocean sucking up salt crystals and water droplets. If it can get water, it can juggle it around, condensing and recondensing it until it has heat. Then it'll become a storm. Get up some friction to raise the electrical potential . . . Hell, Haarskold, where there's a will, there's a way."

Haarskold smiled at Holden, thinking that he was brain-damaged from exhaustion. Anyone who talked about electrical potential in arctic clouds was suffering from terminal jet lag. But Holden seemed to know what he was doing, so he put in a call to Goose Bay.

There was wind in the fog, all right, a slow circular breeze in its center that stirred the white layer gradually over the water. Holden thought of the wind bridges in Florida which clocked speeds of seventy knots. It was too low to the water for the alectoes to do much good.

He circled it slowly as the Canadian planes arrived, then raised the wing leader. "I think this is it. Those winds in the middle, that's what we've got to get."

"Fine. We might not even need the alectoes. Maybe the generators will do it."

Holden roared into the white mist at near-wavetop level and ignited the smoke generators. The plane bumped through the central winds and in seconds he was out again, climbing into the cobalt blue sky. The visual effect of his passage was spectacular. A steaming gash had been opened in the center of the fog bank and the tattered edges were trying to close again. One after the other the planes shrieked in, dropping dry ice as well as silver iodide. Within minutes the winds increased to a feeble six miles an hour in the center and the fog was breaking up, gossamer tendrils of it whisked by their passage. The planes circled around, making pass after pass at the fogbank like hyenas tearing apart a wounded elephant.

It was too easy, too simple. Holden thought of Kilgallen flying through the air, of Mason, Tregaskis, and Croft all dying on the other side of the world, of the *Adair* exploding in the rain and of his son, cowering in fright as clouds shut off the sun. A terrifying thought had been weighing on Holden's mind since arriving here. Even if the storm killed him, there was no absolute certainty that Dennis would not trigger off a bolt anyway. Perhaps the imprint was in it forever and even Holden's death would be useless.

The wing leader radioed him. "We're flying back to reload and will rendezvous again at 1650 or thereabouts."

"I'll be here. The stuff will probably be gone by then, but we might as well make sure."

He looked at the tattered bits of fluff thrashing around the sea as he headed back to Godhab. One more attack would finish it off for sure. In just a few hours he would be going back to Florida.

It took the crew forty-five minutes to mix the acetate with the silver iodide and reload the generators. In that length of time, the fog knit itself together again and appeared on the radar thicker and deeper than before.

"It's moving faster," Haarskold said. "That's a rather poor seeding system you chaps have, if I may say so. I'd say you're making it worse rather than better."

Again the planes went in, this time at a higher altitude, which enabled them to drop alectoes. The winds had jumped to twenty knots and rising, a respectable speed that knocked them dangerously close to the waves. Again rip after rip lacerated the fog, their hot gas exhausts scorching tunnels through it. They emptied everything they carried and headed back to base, leaving disconnected hunks of vapor clinging to the water. But the cold prong of fear was back in Holden's stomach.

It stabbed deeper after he landed at Godhab and Haarskold pointed wordlessly at the radar. The fog bank was not only intact again, but faint sparkles on the screen indicated water droplets were forming. "I watched from here," Haarskold reported. "At best the silver iodide dampens it down for a few minutes. Then it reappears everywhere."

Holden flung his helmet over the table, kicked a chair, and smashed his balled-up fist into the wall. He stood back from the wall, then hit it three more times, breathing hard and babbling obscenities. Finally he said, "I don't suppose you happen to have any hydrogen bombs sort of lying around, do you, Haarskold?"

"No. However, I have an automatic pistol and a fishing pole."

"How much more daylight have we got, anyway?"

"At this time of year, the sun goes down around ten o'clock."

Holden paced the shack, hands jammed in his pockets. "Long hours of sunlight, that's it. No, that's not it, it's the same size at night as in the day." He leaned against the frosted window, looking out at the glaciered mountains. It was spectacularly beautiful in a crystalline, austere way, with deep blue skies and air so sharp, the smallest rocks could be seen on the mountains. Holden tried to entrance himself with the diamond-hard beauty of Greenland. He had lost. Defeat permeated his very nerves. He remembered Kayama's kind, solemn face in the lights of Fort Jackson. "I guess that's it, Haarskold."

"What, Mr. Holden?"

"It. I guess I ought to send a letter of thanks to the Canadians. Everybody's been a big help. Even Clay."

167

To Haarskold the pilot seemed to have shrunk in size. He said, to cheer him up, "Sometimes it's easier to disperse a cloud than fog, you know. If the water condenses into snow, it won't be so spread out. Why not wait until it forms a bigger target?"

"The point was to weaken it, not to let it get bigger."

"My only point is, let the moisture concentrate into a decent target."

Still looking out the window, Holden said, "I ought to call Gina while I can."

"Is that someone in the states?"

"Yes. I ought to before I go up again." Then he thought about what he would say to her and changed his mind. "No. It'll only make things worse. I knew I wouldn't make it to forty."

"Really, Mr. Holden," Haarskold said with irritation. "You sound as if you're about to be hanged. I'll work out another schedule with the Canadians. Let's see what happens with it. You should get some sleep, too."

"I can't sleep, Haarskold."

"You can't fly very well either in your condition. I'll have them set up kerosene burners in Godhab in case it gets too close."

"I suggest you warn them to ground everything, too. Godhab really isn't ready for this."

In a subconscious way he had known he would lose ever since the helicopter had landed at the beach house and the officer with the certitude of a medieval monk pronouncing sentence informed him that Mason was dead. Yet death was still an abstract, unaccompanied by fear. In Europe he had flown with the cold, sickening fear of being killed by that one MIG that would decide to test the rules. There was no such fear today. The storm would get him and that was that.

He turned over on the small bunk and relaxed. As he thought about his death, he automatically mulled over his next step in case this one failed. He would lure it ever farther north, to Thule if he had to, to the North Pole. That was how his mind worked. He could hold two completely contradictory beliefs in his mind and still function. The gift of the Holden forefathers.

Kayama strode down the hall to find Clay seated in an office with aerial Stormfury photos pinned to the wall. Three other ESSA climatologists were with him.

"Good morning," Clay said. "I just heard."

Kayama was in one of his bad moods. Tension had finally cracked his placid calm and he had been snapping at resentful Stormfury pilots all day long. Although the bulk of the Stormfury analysis would occupy the next several months, one fact had become clear that day. Stormfury had not worked. ''Our hopes were that the seeding had slowed the storm's eastward movement and caused it to pull together into a single entity. But these tapes, these measurements, show the winds began to die when lightning appeared in the Florida front. A connection between the silver iodide and the slowdown of winds has not been established. I think there is none.''

''So the whole thing was a waste of time and money.''

Kayama sat heavily in a chair and exhaled. ''The reason the storm slowed is simple. The forward cluster had located Holden that morning and did not need all the energy delivered it by the second cluster.''

Clay pointed with his pipestem at the latest NIMBUS photo of the fog in the Davis Straits. It was a thunderstorm moving steadily for Godhab. ''All through this business, the storm has formed twin systems. There's only one in Greenland. Are we absolutely sure this is it?''

''Yes. Once it finds its quarry it doesn't need a second system. In the Gulf of Mexico it slowed down as it approached Florida. We had thought that was because of Stormfury, but . . .'' He flung papers across the desk and watched them waft around. ''As for Greenland, its growth has the simplest of explanations. The planes themselves made that happen. It gained heat from their exhaust—not enough to make a tropical cluster of it, but a little heat in the arctic goes a long way.''

''Can it make lightning?''

''With sufficient vertical winds, yes. It can do it by mere friction of ice crystals. It will not be as big a charge as we witnessed here, but it will be able to eliminate Holden.''

''But it is weakened as you planned,'' an ESSA man said. ''This time it will work. It can't get moisture as fast as it could down here, it's too cold. I don't see what the worry is.''

Kayama speared him with his dark, cold eyes and held up the NIMBUS photo with both hands. ''Please. Observe that the planes made it grow. The exhaust gave it heat and the silver iodide did no good whatsoever. The two canceled each other out. In fact the storm now is growing on its own and it is doubtful if the silver iodide will do any good. Each time, it outwits us. Each time we contemplate this storm, something small happens that renders us useless.''

''What does that mean as far as Holden is concerned?'' Clay asked.

''He will seed the storm. It will do no good. If he gives up, he will get away this time, but one day lightning will find him. Maybe not for years, but it will eventually.''

Clay made a performance out of stuffing his pipe. When he felt the atmosphere to be sufficiently somber, he said, ''We are coming to the point where we will have to decide if Mr. Holden is indispensable to the existence of mankind. Or that segment of it vulnerable to bad weather whenever he shows up. We're all thinking that. We cannot protect him forever.''

''That's kind of like pulling the plug on the respirator, isn't it?'' an ESSA man wanted to know.

''Respirators don't strike people dead or cause tornadoes or flooding in the Gulf of Mexico. Holden knows what the score is.'' He lit the pipe and pumped blue smoke into the office air.

Kayama turned to the other men. ''Besides Stormfury, gentlemen, what other weather experiments do we know about?''

They rummaged around in their memories. One of them said, ''There have been thousands, but they all use dry ice and silver iodide. I recall somebody coming up with one involving the spread of carbon over ice to make it absorb sunheat and melt, but that's about it . . .''

''Skyfire,'' another ESSA man contributed thoughtfully. ''There was one called Skyfire.'' He jolted and slapped himself on the cheek. ''Oh, my God. Lightning suppression, that's what Skyfire was.''

Clay turned back to face him. ''Do you remember what they did?''

''Jesus, I don't. If it was silver iodide, it won't help us much. I think the Army did it.''

Kayama cried, ''But that is perfect! It's a magnetic field, is it not? If someone ever managed to stop lightning, think, think of what it would do to a plasma in a magnetic field! The storm could be grounded. It's *made* out of static electricity!''

The ESSA man was already running down the hall.

Thoroughly unimpressed, Clay continued smoking his pipe. ''I hope it was something simple. We haven't time to ship a lot of complicated gear to Greenland.''

ZERO HOUR

THE RISING moan of the wind sent the dream of Itrek sputtering off into leaf blown fragments, and drained the warmth from the small room where he slept. Electric heaters clicked on automatically, fanning heat over the tile floors.

Holden had slept in his flight suit, the elastic bands constricting his joints. He looked at the luminous dial of his watch. Nineteen hundred thirty hours. Seven-thirty, in civilized parlance. The wind was rising outside, a perfect flow for a takeoff.

Blue lightning glowed through the windows, a lurid, cold lightning, slow and lazy, not like the stuff in the states which flashed and vanished. Hot lightning of low current but long duration, the kind that burned rather than exploded. For his degree dissertation, he would write a personal analysis of the effects of lightning which would be filed in the National Weather Service or a school library.

Time to move. Holden pulled on his boots and zipped up his suit, then pushed out toward the hangar. Fog lay everywhere, making cotton balls of the floodlights and filming mist over the runway surface. Landing in this stuff would be nice and slippery.

The Danes were in the radio shack gathered around the green radar. They all looked at him with the same baffled, awed look Kayama had given him in South Carolina. They knew that somehow Holden was responsible for what was happening.

"That's much better," Haarskold observed. " Four hours of sleep can work miracles."

There was only one narrow rain cell on the radar and it was hanging just outside of Godhab. The storm stuck close to the Davis Straits, needing the moisture, cold as it was. The underside of the rain cell shifted and blurred. Winds were circulating to keep it aloft.

Haarskold said, "A nice target, eh? It's about seven miles away. That cloud center is about forty-six hundred meters high."

Forty-six hundred meters translated into fifteen thousand feet. Haarskold was right, it was a nice, ground-hugging target. He would bomb it with alectoes from twenty thousand feet.

One of the Danes tamped a cigarette on his thumbnail. "This is history in the making. Everyone in Godhab is outside watching the lightning."

"Is the plane ready?"

Looks passed among the Danes, which Haarskold avoided. "Naturally. All we need are the Canadians and you'll be ready to go."

Holden thought, they should have arrived already. The screen should be swarming with aircraft, unless they were told to stand down. He remembered Clay's suggestion of using Dennis as bait. *Are you alone, Holden? Yes, sir, Admiral, sir, I am alone, that's how I ended up on*

Itrek. We all die alone. "Call Goose Bay and find out what's delaying them."

Rather than answer, Haarskold flipped on the radio. For the first time, Holden realized his stalker had a voice. Lightning whistlers filled the shack, clear and high, following each rip of static. They were squeaks and whines somewhat higher than a professional soprano's range, electrical disturbances that accompanied lightning as it caromed through the earth's magnetic field. It seemed to Holden as if the storm were calling his name. Haarskold switched the radio off. "Rather peculiar, Holden. Whistlers usually hang around sixteen hundred megacycles. Not this frequency. Well, I expect the Canadians will be here presently."

"Get the plane out. If the wind keeps rising I won't be able to take off."

"You realize visibility is zero."

"I know. I can wait for them up there. I don't want to be on the ground, Haarskold, I'd just be a sitting du . . . Never mind. I'm ready to go now."

"Why don't you have something to eat first."

"I'm ready to go," Holden repeated firmly.

A movement of Haarskold's hand dispatched the ground crew. He clasped his fingers over his stomach, spat into the trash can, wiped his nose, and regarded the pilot. "Very well. You know all your instruments. Besides the station signals, you have your IFF transmitter. We can handle that here." IFF was Identification Friend or Foe, a coded frequency used when patrolling hostile borders where ground controllers might be tempted to lure an enemy pilot.

"I know all that."

"Stay within a radius of one hundred kilometers, Holden, I don't want to lose sight of you. Mark down every single course change. If you have to bail out, head due east over the coastal range, it's flat as a bloody pancake that way. Your beacon will cut through this stuff and we'll pick you up within ten minutes. That I swear. And trust your instruments, Holden. Up here one piece of ice looks just like another."

"Okay. One of these days I'll tell you what this is all about."

Haarskold laughed uproariously, slapping his huge hand on the table. "What I don't know, won't hurt me. Being allies is like being lovers, Holden, some secrets you don't want to know."

"Can you take a message for me? It's for a man named Kayama."

"Certainly." Haarskold pulled a sheet of yellow lined paper from the desk.

172

"Tell Gina to move to Canada or someplace far north where it's cold. Alaska would be perfect, there's a lot of men up there and Dennis will be safe as he ever will be. And she's got some money coming to her, insurance and stuff . . ."

"Holden," Haarskold crumpled up the paper after writing three words. "Send your own love letter. You can deliver it after you've landed safely."

The storm resembled a newly formed peninsula jutting from the coast out into the Straits. The gnawed inlets of the shore were smoothed over by fog. Dead center sat a black tower similar to the one on Itrek which soared over fifteen thousand feet into the air. The storm was smaller but still formidable.

Holden circled the tower from twenty thousand feet and looked straight down. From this vantage he could see the thermals actually working, the flow and ebb of cloud billows spilling out of the top and rolling down the sides.

It looks like an avocado plant, Holden thought, *perched on a soft layer of cotton.*

On his radar the rain cell was long and sinuous, buried inside the tower like metal wire sheathed within rubber insulation. Holden swung around to the north and came in for his first run, the cell glowing on his target radar. Before reaching the tower he peeled off toward the Straits, hurling the silver alectoes into the tower.

Angry lightning ignited from deep within, a sputtering exclamation of annoyance. As the first spurt of wind struck Holden's wing, the storm awoke. His second pass was poor due to shear sending the alectoes spinning uselessly into the fog. But the first pass had definitely hurt. Could a storm feel threatened? Holden mused. Could it feel fear? Holden fervently hoped so.

His headphones squawked and Haarskold's voice came on. "That first pass was perfect, Holden. They've spotted snow out in the water."

The blood of the storm would be snow. Exultant, Holden wheeled in again, spearing alectoes into the syrupy mass, stabbing at the tower, playing with it as a matador executes a corrida with a bull. The winds increased, the lightning became heavier. Hail cracked over the fuselage and the F-5 blazed with St. Elmo's fire, merging its blue glow with the orange of the exhaust.

More lightning sprang from the storm with each attack. The clouds were as bright as moonlight. The rain cell squirmed on the radar as

173

alectoes lanced through it, freezing the rain to ice and draining it onto the ground.

Holden had lost count of the number of passes when ball lightning rose from a cloud chasm and raced for the plane. Raising his right wing above the comets, he headed into another swarm. He was too close and too fast. Covering his eyes to avoid being dazzled, he felt the plane kick as a ball splayed into the nose and sparked along the wingtips.

They came at him from all sides, colored circles showering out of the tower, swirling up from the flat cloud deck. He dumped the remainder of his alectoes and cruised around the tower, estimating the damage.

The tower, taller but thinner now, glowed with a dull green phosphorescence. Its column was bejeweled by lightning beads which swarmed like angry flies. Holden thought of the two silver iodide smoke generators under his wings. If ever the time was ripe for the Canadians, it was now.

He ignited the cannister on his left wing, felt the vibration and drag that meant it was flaming, and headed straight into the crest of the tower. A cataclysmic flash and jolt of shear hit him as he passed through, followed by successive jolts that lit up the cockpit. He turned around in his seat to look back.

A thin, U-shaped strand of silverized smoke pulsed like a hot wire in the night. Lightning rippled from the tower, flashed down the smoke to slap his wing. He had left a trail of electrical fire, a glowing thread attached to the smoke generator at one end and the cloud at the other.

Another burst rocked the plane. Damn and hell, forget the generators. Electricity ran down the silver particles toward him. It was like carrying a leash secured to a Doberman pinscher, Holden thought. He shut off the generator and circled back, watching the winds disperse the trail of smoke into twinkling fireflies.

Where in hell were the Canadians? The radar crawled with rain blips. Half of the Air Force could be flying around out there and he would not know it.

"Haarskold," Holden radioed, "tell the Canadians to kill their smoke generators. They attract lightning. Stick to dry ice and alectoes, okay?"

Haarskold was either chewing herring or sound asleep. Irritated, Holden tried again. "Acknowledge, Godhab, the suspense is killing me. No generators, do you hear me?"

His own voice echoed back in his headphones. Holden touched the controls. There was not even static. "Haarskold. Godhab. Come on, is anybody reading me?"

Green light poured into the cockpit, illuminating his instruments from a ball of lightning that had crept up alongside his wing, a ghostly, sparkling apparition. Holden now knew how Tregaskis had felt in the CDA. The damned thing was watching him. If he looked hard enough he could make out a stupid, reptilian grin. He pounded his instruments and checked his couplings, but it was hopeless. It could have been the ball that hit the nose or the stuff that had struck his wing. One of those lightning strikes had killed his radio.

In the Godhab station, they saw Holden's plane pierce the cloud, then static rippled out as sheets of lightning struck it. Haarskold, attempting to call him, heard only dead air.

On the lower right quadrant of the radar screen, seven blips crept into view and held steady at a distance of about seventy kilometers. The Canadians had arrived just in time to miss the excitement.

"Godhab, this is the Nineteenth, do you receive us?"

"Yes. Where have you been?"

"It's a long story. What's that blip we're picking up around the storm?"

"It's Holden. He's been up there two hours waiting for you."

"You're going to have to get him out of there, Godhab. We're carrying modified phoenix missiles and we don't want to knock him down."

"Missiles! I thought you were going to seed the storm!"

"We are. Sorry we're late, it can't be helped. How about landing him and giving us a clear shot?"

"I can't. His radio is kaput."

After an incredulous moment, the pilot said, "Say again, Godhab."

"I said his radio is knocked out. It happened just a minute ago. We can't pick up or send anything."

"Son of a bitch! Can you get up there and lead him down?"

"Not in this wind. It's rising. All that seeding just made it worse. How about one of you? Can you get to him?"

"How much fuel has he got?"

Haarskold looked up as one of the mechanics held up six fingers and shook his head.

"Six minutes."

"Forget it. We'd never get there in time. Our orders are to stand off from the storm no less than fifty kilometers, so I guess that's what we'll do."

"That's a pity," Haarskold said. "I think he's getting lonely. I hope his compass is working. I'd hate to pull him out of the water."

Haarskold tuned the radio to the most minute exactitude of Holden's frequency but heard only the chilling steady whine of whistlers. They were not the normal static sounds but the haunting keen of sirens.

Haarskold was glad to be on the ground tonight. Lightning in Greenland and singing storms. A bolt hit the station power lines, dimming the lights.

X PLUS 25 MINUTES

HOLDEN SCREAMED northward away from the storm and up the coast, ball lightning snapping at his wing. The rocky fjords carved by tides and icebergs were gone. Only fog was visible, overflowing the scarred coast of Greenland. When the fog cleared, he was miles from Godhab. He turned east into the mainland, looking for the lights of the town. Not a window, not a headlight was visible, only the squat, octopus storm, sitting on a ululating blanket of white. Godhab and the weather station were so socked in, he figured he might as well be on the moon.

Holden flipped through the cards on his knee, found the station's VHF signal, and dialed an omni compass reading. Stone dead. He punched the receiver trying to get the needle to move. The same cemetery silence. His last possibility was a receiver which read out the distance to the station transmitter, but even that was lifeless. The lightning had killed everything but the radar and that would be no help landing in this weather.

By now Godhab would know he was in trouble. Haarskold might be able to hear him without being received. "Godhab, I cannot receive, my radio is out. If you read me, send someone up to guide me in."

After three minutes of circling at near stall speed, Holden realized he would have to bail out. His fuel was gone, the weather had grounded Haarskold, and the Canadians were not coming. He was alone with his nemesis.

He headed east for exactly one and a half minutes, slowly climbing up to seventy-five hundred feet, then reversed course until he was pointed at the storm. He checked his airspeed and switched on the auto pilot. "Godhab. I'm bailing out. Over and out."

Beneath lay the great, open expanse of the Greenland icecap, free of fog. He was gambling that the lightning would be busy with the silver iodide until he hit the ground and could be rescued. He cut on both generators, then took a deep breath and blew the canopy's explosive bolts. Freezing wind crushed him into the cockpit, squashing his body in the seat. Holden clamped his teeth, then counted off seconds. The cockpit exploded, the plane vanished. The seat detached and he was soaring through freezing air.

Trailing twin tails of smoke from the wing generators, the F-5 flew straight and true into the cloud tower, lightning gnashing at it. After an oily, orange explosion of bursting fuel, the plane emerged again in a thousand pieces, each segment trailing coronas of lightning that snapped and chewed at the metal as it showered downward.

Holden spread-eagled his arms and legs and tried to sail further east. He was checking his height when a burst of shear hurled him higher into the air like a rubber ball. Lateral winds seized him and suddenly he was no longer falling but tumbling end over end toward the tower, aware he was living the nightmare of Kilgallen being ingested into the storm's body. Above him cirrus clouds shut off the moonlight, below him a creeping cloud deck moved in like a tide, barricading him from the ground.

He had to get out of the winds feeding into the storm. He thrashed at the air, clawing at it, trying to find slots in the vicious updrafts through which he could escape. The bruising updrafts propelled him up and down for hundreds of feet and his gorge rose with vertigo. He gasped into his oxygen mask, terrified that he would vomit and choke. He would, he decided, rather burn with a quick blue flame than let that happen.

The moonlight disappeared and he floated in complete darkness, uncomfortably aware that his flight suit was stuffed with wriggling spiders.

A flash of orange light burst deep within the cloud tower and fountained out blossoms of electrical coronas that swirled like embers. The explosions, he knew, were not lightning bolts. They were man-made, discharging thousands of isolated spots of flame that resembled the insects dying on Itrek. This time it was not the insects that were dying, but Holden's predator.

He watched clouds being torn to glittering shreds as missiles homed in from the Straits and detonated in the tower. The embers whirled by him and he saw they were actually pieces of metal foil with coronas clinging to them. The tower lit up like a shaft of fire, and from its top spilled white wet snowflakes mixed with hail that drummed against his helmet.

*　　*　　*

The roar trembled the ice of Greenland like a gathering earthquake, splintering ice from the station roof and towers, pounding into their ears and resonating through their bodies. The Danes clapped their hands over their ears, opening their mouths to relieve the sound, but nothing would shut it out. Through the window Haarskold saw lightning throb across the sky in vast waves, its passage slamming the air together with fearful rumbles. The sound was sustained thunder, separate claps melded together into a seamless assault of vibration. The lightning stained the ice fields, the mountains, and huddled roofs of Godhab with a shifting blue-green glow a thousand times more intense than the northern lights. It crackled around the airstrip's wind sock, slithered along the length of the radar and radio towers, played off the aerials of the parked planes. The wind that kicked the fog into retreating scurries was hot, sending rivulets of water from the ice across the airstrip.

From out of the clouds rained thousands of fading sparks that settled over the station and town, extinguishing themselves with a hiss as they touched the snow. Haarskold ran outdoors and grabbed a piece of the debris. It was plain metal chaff, six-inch-long strips of foil used by pilots to confuse radar.

Directly overhead, a hole opened in the sky, its edges smoldering with fire.

A burst of hot rain fell, steaming on the cold airstrip surface. Through the hole Haarskold could see stars, and as it widened to link up with another hole, moonlight became visible. The sky was tattered with burning gaps that sent torrents of rain down onto the icecap.

Haarskold tried to sort out all the wondrous sights and shattering sounds. From Godhab came a cacophony of automobile horns. The phones rang continuously in the weather station, terrified people who thought that the spectacle quite literally presaged the end of the world. The only sensible advice Haarskold could give the radio station was to warn everyone to watch out for lightning.

They had seen Holden's plane disintegrate, but after the missiles came in, the radar screen dissolved to fluttering static. Haarskold could not tell if Holden had got out in time. The Canadians still hovered fifty kilometers away.

"Godhab, what's happening?" the Wing Leader asked.

"Can't you see it? The storm's breaking up."

"We can't tell. It looks like a forest fire from here."

Haarskold looked out the window. By now the storm lay in isolated patches of cloud, sidewinding electricity bursting across the stars. "It's turning clear. The visibility's up. What on earth did you do?"

The Wing Leader chuckled. "We loaded the missiles with negatively charged chaff. That's why we're late."

Over the emergency frequency came a low continuous howl that filled the shack. It was Holden's beacon piercing the interference. "He's bailed out," Haarskold said. "At least his signal's coming through."

He tuned the radar as two of the Danes rushed out to the hangar to start the helicopter. He discovered the blip of the parachute opening dangerously close to the ground, then the blip faded. "Did you see that? He hit the ground just after the parachute opened."

"We saw it. We'll join you there." The lead plane detached from the formation and pounded toward Greenland.

At the door Haarskold noticed something else. Static lines trembled on the screen just over the eastern section of ground where the chute had collapsed. Lightning? A disturbance caused by the chute passing through the charged air? Haarskold could not even begin to guess. He grabbed his pistol belt from his locker while racing out to the helicopter.

As he tossed through the air, Holden fought to keep himself conscious enough to pull his ripcord. Numbing shocks from pieces of electrified chaff stunned him and the winds blew hot and cold, like malarial chills across his body. The snow turned to rain, then to hail again, as the cloud tower was sawed to icy pieces by the metal. Holden watched it being chiseled away to snow and scurrying lightning balls.

In his head, spider visions triggered by the electricity through which he tumbled merged with the swarms of lightning balls that struggled toward him. As the air lost its conductivity they either winked out or plummeted down. Slowly the light of the moon outshone the hellish flickers of his gremlin. Like death rattles the enraged thunder fragmented to despairing cracks. Holden knew Croft and Kayama had been right, the damned thing really was alive. Small globes of light climbed painfully through the winds to pop harmlessly against his fingers. He felt his stomach turn over in his body and a constant rush of air against his chest. He fell like a stone through a cavernous hole in the cloud shoals, as the glittering icecap rushed up toward him.

Holden yanked his cord and the chute opened with the sound of a board being struck by an axe. The straps jerked his body upright with a force that constricted his armpits, chest, and thighs. He was fumbling for the guide lines when his feet hit the ice of Greenland with a horrendous force. Completely unprepared for the impact, he had landed on the heels of both feet.

Some part of his dazed brain registered an extra-body sensation without pain. He lost consciousness lying on his back on the ice as the parachute collapsed around him and a final rush of snow dusted his chest.

He awoke still on his back, staring up through clear skies at the muted, graceful pattern of the aurora borealis, the northern lights. There was not so much as a wisp of cirrus cloud to mar the still, austere beauty of the arctic night.

Holden's face mask was dislodged and he could hear his breath whistling against the rubber seal. The chute lines lay scattered around him and pieces of chaff littered the glistening crust of the snowbound land.

The storm was vanquished. Holden smiled. *Ding, dong, the witch is dead.*

He had thought the spectacle of the storm's death had been bestowed on him as a final gift, but instead it was a trophy, a victory to be savored in his memory. It was not his victory, really, it belonged to the Nineteenth Canadian Weather Reconnaissance Group, so he hoped they had seen it, too.

His emergency gear lay at the end of the line. When he tried to sit up, he realized both of his legs were broken, the left one badly, with a piece of bone protruding from his flight suit below his knee. The Holdens never did anything halfway. It could have happened while he was being bashed about by the winds but more than likely it was the landing. The freezing cold dulled the pain. He realized it was quite possible he would never fly again.

Son of a bitch! He laughed out loud, the hooting sounds carrying over the crust of ice to the North Pole.

From behind a hummock of snow a ball of lightning rose, its orange glow forming a pool on the white ground. Sizzling softly, it forged through the cold air toward him.

Holden reached for the line securing his emergency gear, but it was out of reach and he could not move. Propping himself up on his elbows, he watched the approaching lightning.

It swayed from side to side, its movements quick where it encountered metal. Avoiding pieces of chaff, it sniffed over the parachute shroud lines, a cobra emerging from a holy man's basket, trying to strike the moving flute.

With a burst of flying snow a helicopter appeared out of the night and crunched down on flat ground a hundred yards away. Holden made out the figure of Haarskold running toward him, followed by three other men.

The lightning ball found the beacon lying by the emergency pack. The beacon, still emitting high frequency waves, seemed to have an effect on the ball. It rotated over the antenna in slow, seductive circles, the radio waves passing through its substance like nectar.

Holden slipped off his watch and threw it. The metal Rolex missed by a foot and plopped in the snow. "Haarskold!" he shouted at the men who had stopped to stare at him. "Shoot it! Kill it!"

Haarskold fumbled for his pistol. The sphere moved up to Holden's body as he balled up a piece of chaff and flipped it. Again he missed.

Blindingly bright and hot, the sphere's heat penetrated his fleece-lined suit. Holden raised an arm to cover his face. He heard a shot, felt the wind of a bullet pass across his chest, then a quick ripping sound, like a zipper being closed.

He lowered his arm cautiously. The ball was gone, grounded by a metal-jacketed bullet. He laid his head back on the ice and contemplated the aurora, not wanting to be rescued just yet, wishing to gaze forever on the color scheme surging in the sky.

Haarskold kneeled beside him to look at his legs, then at his face. He still carried the pistol in his hand. "Mr. Holden, if I didn't know better, I'd say you were alive."

X PLUS **48** HOURS

"Ah, Mr. Holden, you are a lucky man. Did I not tell you that before?"

"No, you didn't." Both of Holden's legs were encased in what felt like a ton of plaster, and after a pain-filled day in a surgical ward, he was numb with drugs. Through his window, the sky was clear, cold, and blue and the sunlight blasted off the white snow. He had just been served a small portion of fish by an Eskimo nurse. "You saved my life Kayama," he said into the phone. "It wasn't just luck."

"It was very close, Mr. Holden, yes. We found out that Project Skyfire had also used silver iodide and I was in despair."

"How did you end up with chaff?"

Kayama chuckled. "You may thank Admiral Clay. Such a strange man, every time he wished to abandon you, he came back to help. A false cynic. We learned that the Army had tried other lightning suppression tests but we had no details here. So the Admiral roused everyone he could find out of bed and sent them searching for other methods. And someone remembered an obscure experiment utilizing negatively charged metal foil. It was done in New Jersey, I believe. The point of the metal was to cause electrical coronas to form about it. For precipitating water or ice, silver iodide works because it is so small. But for precipitating electricity, the larger the metal the better. The Canadians were delayed because they had to charge the strips in such a way that one end was positive, the other negative, and then pack it all into missile warheads. So many things have been attempted with weather, Mr. Holden. Cannons, bullets, loud noises. Did you know someone in the Midwest wanted to suppress lightning by dragging a mile-long wire from an aircraft through a storm?''

"Basic physics,'' Holden said, with a touch of bitterness. "It's like Ben Franklin with his kite. I even did it myself on Itrek with the microphone. I should have thought of it myself.'' It was one of those mental slips that form a basic frustration in life, he decided, comparable to carefully setting a billfold on a table where it would be easiest to find, then forgetting where it was placed. "It's really and truly dead, isn't it, Kayama?'' Holden asked.

"It is, Mr. Holden. The jet stream has returned to its normal route. And now we have a heat wave down here. Holden? I believe we would have had climate disasters all over the world had not that creature been destroyed.''

"Creature,'' Holden repeated, looking at the snow. The weather determined human attitudes as well as human existence. As a child, Holden had played in frost-covered yards and found it impossible to imagine that same area in spring. It was equally impossible to imagine what had happened over Godhab yesterday by looking at these clear skies. "There are other creatures, aren't there, just floating around up there?''

"Well, we know little about life at the bottom of the sea, eh, Holden? Except for those creatures which sometimes get trapped on the surface.''

"Look, is Gina with you? I'd like . . .''

"Ah, Holden!'' Kayama cried. "How could I forget! Ku!''

Holden stirred in bed and the movement caused sudden pain. The Eskimo nurse entered, smiling, needle in hand. He was going to be sedated again.

"I found the word in a mythological text. The Pacific Islanders had a god called Ku, the god of the east wind. Could that have been it?"

Holden remembered Mason on the boat, pointing to the old man with gold teeth who had been in the war. Guadalcanal, he had said, probably Tonga, too, and the other islands overrun in the short-lived Japanese empire. He would have heard about it down there on the sea of typhoons, of strange lights in the sky and ships that vanish. The old man had known about the storm, after all, and so in his way had Mason. "The god of the east wind," Holden said. "That sounds exactly right."

The nurse bent over with the needle, swabbed his rear and slipped it in. Peace spread over Holden's body. He wanted to keep Kayama on the phone. "Kayama?"

Kayama sighed, a sad sound of resignation. "Yes, Mr. Holden?"

"For some reason I can't get ahold of Gina, I've been getting a runaround down there. She's taking a nap, she's out with Dennis, it's all bullshit. Is she avoiding me?"

"No, Mr. Holden. She is not avoiding you."

Holden caught the sorrow in Kayama's voice but the creeping sedative tended to dull the suspicion growing in his mind. "Have you seen her?"

"No, Mr. Holden, but listen carefully to me now as I tell you exactly what happened."

He heard the story in fits of sleepiness mixed with graphic images. Kayama was terse and direct. But there was really not that much to tell.

After the car had cooled down enough to get a door open, the fire crew found the cadets entangled in the front seat and Gina lying in back. Her death had been instantaneous. Holden did not want to know how she had looked.

It was Kayama who noticed her body move as they attached tow chains to the car. Dennis's hand had slipped from beneath her, his fingers wriggling at the smoked glass. They rushed the boy to the base hospital where he was treated for shock and heat exhaustion. Under Clay's orders he was flown out to the Naval Weapons Center in California to await either the death of the Greenland storm or Holden.

Gina Lambert had been buried in a grave in Oregon next to her husband.

The child's grandparents had been located in Miami, both of them distraught with fear since learning of the beach house fire. They were assured the child was safe in California but had not been told why he was out there, or under the protection of the Air Force.

Had he made her happy? Holden wondered. *Had she thought of him or Lambert when the lightning struck?*

"I am so sorry, Mr. Holden. There is no painless way to break such news."

And Dennis had almost become an orphan. Parentless like Gina and himself, like the men on Itrek and the *Adair*. Yet his emotions were not responding properly. Fury, despair, and guilt suppurated within him but the sedative would not allow them expression. His sleepy mind tried to encompass this gigantic event in all its personal ramifications, yet his next words had nothing to do with himself. "What'll I tell the grandparents? They've lost their son and now their grandson doesn't even belong to them anymore. Dennis is mine."

"It is complex, yes."

"What'll they think of Gina for moving in with me? They'll hate us both."

Kayama clucked sympathetically.

"I mean, it'll kill them. And they may try to take Dennis from me, Kayama." Holden concentrated on the Lamberts lest the building volcano of his own grief overwhelm him. He could not think about Gina now.

"Have you met them, Mr. Holden?"

"No. Gina liked them. They sounded nice."

"Meet them before you worry about this. Perhaps you will like each other. Explain. Bring good will to bear. It is a human problem, nothing like the one you just confronted."

Holden remembered Gina's words gratefully. "What does biology mean, anyway? Of course he's their grandson. That's the way it's always been with them."

"Of course. Perhaps, Mr. Holden, you yourself just inherited some new parents." Kayama went on mouthing soothing platitudes, ceremoniously trying to comfort him. Holden knew that eventually the pain would heal as his legs would heal, the memory of Gina strong but manageable.

He fought onrushing sleep as Kayama said Dennis was climbing all over the base airplanes in California. Holden would discourage the boy from the military, but he knew that was an imponderable now, too.

The sedative was flowing peacefully through his brain, and he almost misunderstood the name when they brought Dennis to the phone. He heard heavy breathing and not much else. Missiles, thunderstorms, and lightning apparently did not faze Dennis, but telephones did.

"Hello, Dennis," Holden said groggily. "This is your daddy."